Also by Dana Middleton:

The Infinity Year of Avalon James

Open If You Dare

NOT A UNICORN

DANA MIDDLETON

chronicle books
san francisco

Library of Congress Cataloging-in-Publication Data available.

ISBN 978-1-7972-0305-8

Manufactured in China.

Design by Mariam Quraishi.
Typeset in Garamond.

10 9 8 7 6 5 4 3 2 1

Chronicle Books LLC
680 Second Street
San Francisco, California 94107
Chronicle Books—we see things differently.
Become part of our community at www.chroniclekids.com.

For Pete.

Magical Creatures

It's the first day of eighth grade and I sit where I always sit. In the back. My homeroom teacher, Mr. Oliver, stands at the doorway talking with the assistant principal, Mrs. Whatley. I feel them looking at me. When you're like me, you get a sixth sense about this kind of thing.

I pretty much know what's about to happen next so I close the notebook I've been drawing in and slip it into my backpack. And then I'm surprised, because it isn't my name Mrs. Whatley calls out. It's Noah's.

All eyes shift to the front of the class where Noah Samuels sits. As he grabs his things, his dark wavy hair falls across his eyes. A pencil slides off his desk and scuttles across the floor.

I want to say something like, *Don't move, Noah. That's not fair*. But I don't. I slink down in my seat instead.

Noah doesn't pick up his pencil. He passes Carmen and gives me a quick anxious look on his way to the door.

"I don't know how this happened, Noah," Mrs. Whatley says quietly when he reaches her. Everyone knows what she means, except for maybe the couple of new kids.

"Bye, Noah," I whisper to myself as the door closes, revealing the poster of the Eiffel Tower on the back of it. My eyes meet Carmen's before I look away.

Through the classroom door, I hear Mrs. Whatley's thick heels clicking down the hallway and imagine Noah's front tooth chewing into his bottom lip as he keeps up beside her.

* * *

Later, from our lunch table, I sneak a glance over at Noah. He sits at the nerd table next to his friend Ethan, who's about a foot taller than Noah and looks like a high schooler already. Noah did Odyssey of the Mind in elementary, and I hear he's building his own actual robot now. Ethan's not particularly smart or nerd-like but he's been Noah's friend forever and the other nerds accept him because his size means he's a bully repellent for all of them.

"Quit staring at him," Nicholas says from beside me.

I lower my eyes. "I'm not staring."

"Freak. You are."

Don't call me a freak. I say it low and quiet inside.

"He's going to notice," Nicholas says, "and I really don't want his Neanderthal friend coming over here."

Mystic reaches out and grabs one of Nicholas's Doritos. Her short black nails match the dark liner around her eyes. She's looking at the nerd table, too. "It's okay with me if Ethan comes over," she says.

Nicholas drags his bag of chips away from her. "Why do you like trouble so much?"

"'Cause." Mystic sighs, twirling the stack of bracelets on her wrist, a classic Mystic habit. "It's so boring around here." Mystic makes her own jewelry from things she finds or buys cheap. Sometimes what she makes is weird. Sometimes what she makes is beautiful. The bracelets are a little of both.

As usual, it's the three of us at our lunch table. Nicholas's hair has a green streak down the side, and his anime T-shirt, jeans, and white Chuck Taylors look brand-new, like all his clothes. Mystic is tall, almost as tall as Ethan. She wears clunky black boots and thrifted black clothes. I'm a regular height for eighth grade and have regular long brown hair. I wear regular clothes in regular colors.

"Ethan likes Brooklyn," Nicholas tells Mystic, and I know he's stepping on a mountain of fire ants.

"Shut up!" Mystic says sharply. "You don't know that."

"Just stating the obvious. Neanderthal Boy likes Popular Girl."

Mystic's eyes shoot to the popular table, where Brooklyn Chambers reigns. Around her, the other popular girls with their just-so clothes and silky long hair look to Brooklyn almost worshipfully, ever sensitive to her moods and whims. Emma sits across from her.

"Sorry, Myst," Nicholas says. "Reality sucks."

"No, Nick," Mystic says, grabbing her book bag. "*You* suck." Her chair expels a long moan as she stands and pushes it away from the table.

I throw Nicholas a sideways glance. Nicholas is my friend, but he sometimes sounds like a jerk. "Where you going?" I call out to Mystic.

"Out of here," she says, storming from the cafeteria.

So much for a great start to the school year. "Why do you have to do that?" I ask. "Ethan likes somebody else. Why do you have to rub it in?"

"I didn't mean to hurt her feelings."

"But you *did* hurt her feelings," I tell him.

Nicholas shifts uncomfortably. "She's got to learn sometime."

"That Ethan likes Brooklyn?"

"Yeah. Everybody knows."

"So doesn't that tell you something?"

He shrugs.

"Way to be obtuse," I say. "It means she doesn't want to know!"

"Obtuse?" Nicholas tilts his head. "Good one," he says and goes back to his drawing.

Mystic probably ran to the bathroom, her hideaway when she gets upset. I should go and see if she's okay, but then everyone will look at me, and I'm not in the mood. I glance toward the door and see Carmen standing there, staring at me. Why does she have to do that?

Annoyed, I go back to my drawing. Most lunches that's what Nicholas and I do: We draw. I'm not as naturally talented as him but I practice more so I'm getting better.

Nicholas's bangs hang over his eyes as he concentrates. He's copying an illustration from this graphic novel series we're obsessed with called *Highwaymen*. It's about a sheriff, an outlaw, and a barmaid from the Old West who fight but mostly rescue magical creatures in 1880s Hot Springs, New Mexico.

Nicholas never copies anything exactly. He always adds his own Nicholas-esque touches. Like giving a Cerberus four heads instead of three. Or making a dragon spew pea soup instead of fire. Today, it's a griffin walking down the dusty main street of Hot Springs that gets the Nicholas treatment. His griffin has six legs and a snake for a tail.

I'm drawing a horse. A regular, four-legged one. I use a No. 2 yellow pencil. Nothing special about it except that it's Noah's, picked up from under his desk this morning.

"He must have texted his mom," I say. "That's why Mrs. Whatley came and got him."

Nicholas is sharpening one of the griffin's claws with his pen. "Who?"

"Who do you think?" I say, weirdly offended that he doesn't automatically know what's in my mind. "Noah."

"Oh, him." He looks briefly at the nerd table, then returns to his griffin. "Makes sense. His mom is kind of intense."

"Ah, yeah," I say. That's an understatement. "She hates me."

"She's an overreactor."

"Who can blame her, though," I say.

"Uh, you can. It was an accident." Nicholas keeps drawing. "He's in my homeroom now. Whatley tried to not make a deal about it but everybody knew."

"You mean everybody knew it was because of me!" I almost hit him with my lunch tray. "Why didn't you tell me that?!"

He raises his eyes to meet mine. "I didn't want to hurt

your feelings?" he says. And grins. So I really hit him now. Right in the arm.

"Ouch!"

"Deserved it."

"Did not."

A giant sigh escapes my lips as he goes back to working on the griffin's tail. I watch him draw, then say, "A griffin doesn't have a snake for a tail. A chimera does."

"I know," Nicholas says.

"Just saying."

"Dude, this is totally legit. Ever heard of poetic license? It can be whatever it wants. It's a magical creature." Nicholas doesn't like it when I question his creative choices.

"Dude." I flick my hand toward my forehead. "Who's the expert on magical creatures here?"

"Are you kidding?" He looks at me like he can't believe I just said that. "You suck all the magic out of that thing."

"Whatever." I pull a straw to my lips and suck the magic out of the Diet Coke I'm drinking.

As much as Nicholas and Mystic think they've earned the right to sit at the freak table, their freakiness pales beside mine. For I, Jewel Conrad, am the undisputed Freak Queen. Because I am the only girl here—or, let's face it, *anywhere*—with a unicorn horn growing out of her forehead.

Unicorn Girl Lives!

Let's get something straight. I am not a magical creature.

I come from an ordinary town, have an ordinary mom, and mostly have an ordinary life.

If it weren't for the unicorn horn.

In case you're confused, let me be clear: I don't mean I found a unicorn horn on some enchanted street and have it stashed in my bedside drawer. I mean I have an actual horn growing out of my actual forehead that makes me look like an actual human unicorn.

And trust me, when you're a thirteen-year-old girl with a unicorn horn on your head, your chances of an ordinary life drop to zero.

I wasn't born this way. I came out like most other kids.

I was even a normal baby, with the photos to prove it. But things started changing around my first birthday. My mom noticed a hard, pointy knot at the center of my forehead. And then it grew. It burst through my skin and I got a one-way ticket to Freaksville.

There's nobody else like me. At least that's what the doctors said. And with our crummy health insurance, it wasn't like we were seeing specialists. So for a long time, nobody knew what to do about me. And as they talked and prodded, my horn kept growing.

That was about the time my dad said *adios* and hit the road. Okay, who knows if he actually said *adios*. Whatever he said, it meant goodbye. And no, it doesn't hurt to think of him, because he's not a real person to me. He's just a blank space at the edge of my heart that will never fill in.

When I was five, my photo showed up on a tabloid website for the first time. The headline read *Unicorn Girl Lives!* It went viral. The link is still live, and sometimes I click on it to see me back then. I was a cute little kid, but of course that's not what anyone ever saw. In the photo, I'm walking on the sidewalk in town holding someone's hand. Mom says it was Grandma's, but in the picture you can't see her face. You can only see my face—and my horn.

It's one of the rare photos where I'm actually smiling into a camera, because it was before I realized that cameras were the enemy. It was before the man with the camera started following us and taking pictures. It was before Sheriff Satterfield escorted the man with the camera out of our town.

Doctors loved this picture. They came to us with promises that they could remove my horn and make me normal. One even showed up at our apartment door.

Some of the doctors thought my horn was a cartilage buildup. That happens sometimes and makes people think they have horns when they do not. They have weird cartilage thingies. Pictures of weird cartilage thingies are everywhere online.

No weird cartilage thingy for me. Mine was a real, live horn. Doctors slid me into MRI tubes. Took X-rays and ultrasounds. Even brought in veterinarians who specialized in the dehorning of animals—which, by the way, is a pretty horrible process anyway—but guess what? Turns out my horn is not even like an animal's horn. I've got so many blood vessels and nerves up there that it would be a surgical miracle to separate my horn from my skull—at least in a way that ensured my continued breathing.

Finally, the doctor hive mind concluded that removal was impossible. So, one by one, they went away. Leaving Mom and me to figure it all out by ourselves.

* * *

Even though it's the first day of school, I already know that fourth period will be my favorite. It's French with my homeroom teacher, Mr. Oliver. Right now I'm here early for the computer station and the free school-sanctioned internet. If I were most kids, I could have done this on my phone at lunch, but my phone is so old that emails don't load anymore.

But it's okay because I like being in this room. Posters in French are all over the walls. There are scenes from Paris: Notre Dame, the River Seine, and the Eiffel Tower; maps of cities and historical French places; and funny posters, like a piece of cheese that says, *"Qui a coupé le fromage?"* Over the computer is a poster that reads *"Il me court sur le haricot."* Underneath is the literal translation: "He's running on my bean." That's the French way of saying "He's getting on my nerves." Whenever Nicholas gets on my nerves, I imagine he's running on my bean, and it always makes me laugh inside.

As I wait for my email to open, I feel a little burst of butterflies in my chest. Maybe today's the day. Maybe it will be there—the email that changes my life.

My inbox is empty, though. Not one single email for conrad.angela32@gmail.com. Angela is disappointed. Angela gets disappointed a lot, but she never gives up.

"Hey."

I turn to see Mystic leaning over me and quickly close my email.

"You okay?" I ask. "Nicholas shouldn't always say everything he thinks."

"Yeah, he texted me and took it back twice. He said he was sorry for hurting my feelings."

I grin. Good on Nicholas.

"What you up to?" Mystic asks.

"Just research. Internet at home is worse than ever."

"What about your neighbor's?"

"Yeah, well. Kind of depends on which way the wind's blowing."

Mystic plops her backpack at her desk, which is at the back of the class next to mine. "Why am I doing this again?" she moans.

"'Cause you like me," I say, and go sit down beside her.

"I could be in drama right now," Mystic says.

"Oof."

"What's wrong with drama?" she asks.

"Acting in front of all those drama kids?"

"Uh . . . yeah. Sounds okay to me."

"Really?" I ask.

"Just remember I chose YOU over them," Mystic says and turns just as Tall Ethan walks through the door. I'd like to believe her, but more likely, she's here because Ethan is here.

Ethan doesn't register Mystic, though. He sits at his desk, several rows up from ours, and stares back at the open door, waiting like he always does. As the bell rings, Brooklyn breezes in and takes her seat up front while Ethan clocks her every move. I hate that Mystic has to see this. She may be in denial about Ethan liking Brooklyn, but she can't be blind.

As the rest of the class gets settled, Mr. Oliver walks in. In French class, we call him Monsieur Oliver, and we pronounce "Oliver" with the emphasis on the first and third syllables: AH-lee-VAIR.

"*Bonjour,* my little French fries," Monsieur Oliver says, using his pet name for us. I love it when he calls us that, but when I see the stack of papers in his hand, my stomach lurches.

"Most of you turned in an essay before our summer break, for which I say: *Merci, beaucoup!*" When he speaks to us in English, he always peppers in some French words. "I appreciated the summer reading," he says wryly. "But there's something you didn't know." He says this last part with a glee reserved for a pop quiz, and he's met with immediate groans.

"*Calmez-vous,*" Monsieur Oliver says, holding up his hands. He points to his ear. "*Écoutez, s'il vous plaît.*" But I'm not sure I want to listen. Something about his expression makes me feel like a bomb's about to go off.

"The Alliance Scolaire Américaine," he continues, "is the American organization that supports French education in schools. It holds a competitive essay competition each year. We've never sent a student from our school to compete before because . . . frankly, we weren't ready. Until now." Monsieur Oliver taps the top of his stack. "I asked for this essay to be personal and for the language to be *magnifique*. Although many of the essays were worthy, there was one that was . . . well, *complètement excellent.*" He looks at me. "Congratulations, Mademoiselle Jewel."

Everyone in the room turns to me, and my face goes hot. I must look confused because Monsieur Oliver says, "Yes, Jewel, you. We want you to represent us at the competition." He scans the room and adds, "Right, class?"

My eyes catch Josh Martin's. He's really good at French, too. But he nods at me like this is okay. He even looks happy for me. Monsieur Oliver begins clapping, and everyone else joins in. Some enthusiastically, like Mystic. Others less so, like Brooklyn.

And then it hits me. *My essay is going to the regional competition!* A deep smile burns inside. Monsieur Oliver liked my essay. He chose it!

The assignment was to make the essay personal, and I did. I wrote in French what I've never been able to express in English. What it's like to be me. What it's like to be a girl with a horn on her head—who underneath it all is just a girl.

Bubbles tingle in my chest. I clasp my hand over my smiling mouth.

As the clapping dies down, Mystic pokes my arm and whispers, "Way to go, Mademoiselle."

"Now, something else you didn't know," Monsieur Oliver says. "This isn't just an essay competition. Jewel will be representing our school by performing her essay in front of an audience and judges representing the Alliance. If she wins, she'll move on to the statewide competition."

The bubbles in my chest instantly pop. What does he mean, *performing* my essay? In front of people? In front of *judges*?

The class breaks out in whispers, giving voice to my fears. When I was in second grade, I had to stand in front of the class and recite something from *The Wizard of Oz*. But when I looked out at the other second-grade faces, I realized I wasn't Dorothy, I was the witch. Minus the green face paint, but plus an impossible-to-miss horn. I was so embarrassed, I peed my pants.

Monsieur Oliver smiles at me, the only one in the room not reading my mind. My mouth is completely dry as I picture the audience at the competition. All those faces. All those strangers.

When the bell rings almost an hour later, I'm startled back into my seat, realizing I haven't been listening for the rest of class.

As Mystic zips up her backpack, she asks, "What's wrong?"

"Nothing," I say flatly.

"It's amazing, Jewels! You should be excited."

She's right. I should be excited. I *would* be excited, if I looked like her. Okay, maybe not the clunky boots and the ultra-black eyeliner. But that forehead! What wouldn't be possible with a smooth, unmarred forehead like that?

As I follow Mystic toward the door, Monsieur Oliver calls out, "Jewel, could you wait for a moment?"

Mystic looks back at me. "You okay?" she mouths, and I nod and step aside to let the others pass.

As the room goes empty, Monsieur Oliver approaches. "Your essay is wonderful, Jewel."

"Really?" I say quietly. "My French was okay?"

"Way more than okay. You know that. But it's what you wrote that was so special. You could go to the state finals with this," he says and smiles. "I think people would be very interested to know what it's like to be you."

"I don't . . . I mean, I didn't know I'd have to read it in front of a lot of people."

"I thought that might make you nervous. Maybe I should have given you advance warning. But this is a great opportunity, Jewel, and honestly, I didn't want you to say no."

"I'm glad you liked it," I say, still processing. "But—"

"And you won't be alone. We'll come with you. You'll have your own cheering section."

My teeth bite into my bottom lip. "I don't know. Maybe you should send someone else."

Monsieur Oliver looks confused. "Like who?"

"Josh," I say, and then I can't believe what comes out of my mouth next. "Or Brooklyn."

"Brooklyn?" he asks.

Actually, she is pretty good at French. And maybe the judges would rather hear about what it's like to be the captain of the cheerleaders or the most popular girl in eighth grade— or maybe about her particular talent for stealing best friends.

"You know, teachers aren't supposed to say this, but"—he looks around the classroom like he's making sure no one's hiding under a desk and listening—"you're just better than everybody else."

This fills my heart and hurts it at the same time. I worked hard on my essay. I was proud of it. "Yeah, but nobody else has a . . ." I can't even bring myself to say the name of the thing that causes me more stress than all my life's homework combined.

"Exactly. Being uniquely you is what made your essay so great," Monsieur Oliver says warmly. "And anyway, so what?

Yours was the best essay. By far. I'm the class judge, and I chose yours."

That may be the nicest thing anyone has ever said to me. So the words catch in my throat when I say, "I just wish things were different."

"Listen," he says. "Let's take our time about it. The competition isn't until November. *Ça va?*"

"*Ça va,*" I say awkwardly, knowing it's not really okay at all. "I've got to get to science."

"Think about it. I know you can do it." He says this with confidence, like he's sure I'll change my mind.

He doesn't know me very well.

I nod and turn carefully so I don't hit the doorjamb with my horn. It's rare to talk about my horn with anyone out loud, and our conversation leaves me feeling strange.

As I step into the hall, I keep to the walls. It's safer that way—not just for me, for everyone. That doesn't stop a sixth-grade boy from bumping into me. And, yep, here it goes: When he looks up at me, he freezes.

I watch the thought bubbles explode above his head: *What is that thing?! Get me out of here! Where's my mommy?!* If he were just a little older, there'd be a pity bubble there, too. But he's only a sixth grader. No pity yet.

Slowly, he unfreezes and backs away into the middle-school tide. I stand by the wall and watch him go.

How could Monsieur Oliver have read my essay and still think I'd want to get up in front of a crowd? It's bad enough to have one sixth grader look at me that way. Imagine a whole audience.

Then it's my turn to freeze. Because there she is.

Emma.

I watch her approach, wearing her cheerleading camp T-shirt tucked into super-nice jeans. Her sandy hair is as long as I've ever seen it. Her smile is for Brooklyn though, who is waiting at her locker.

There's no acknowledgment of me, good or bad. I've become completely invisible to her. She passes by and I wonder. My features aren't bad. I have a good nose, deep brown eyes, long lashes. My lips are the right amount of full, and my teeth are pretty straight for someone who can't afford braces. But that's not what anyone ever sees.

* * *

I sit cross-legged on my bed in front of my laptop, a hand-me-down from Nicholas, doing homework. My room is small for two twin beds. Mine is the one nearest to the door.

A collage of pictures of faraway places hangs over my bed—the Eiffel Tower, the Statue of Liberty, the Venice canals, and other places I wish I could go. I made the collage myself from photos I cut out of travel magazines from the library's recycling pile.

I'm wrapping one of Mom's old scarves around my horn when headlights appear from the parking lot outside. Peeking through the blinds, I watch Emma's mom's car pull in. Emma gets out of the passenger side and doesn't look my way. She hasn't looked my way for a long time.

Carmen does though. She's on the sidewalk gazing up at me through the slats in the blinds. No matter what I do, Carmen always has a way of seeing me. I know she's hurting, but it's complicated.

Emma walks past Carmen as if she wasn't there, either. At least she's consistent.

I flick the blinds shut and sit back on my bed. Grabbing the small stuffed unicorn that hangs from a ring on my backpack, I rub it between my fingers.

Emma and I have lived in the same low-income, single-mother apartment complex our whole lives. Our rooms even face each other's across the parking lot. She used to say my horn made me special. When I didn't believe her, she bought two little stuffed unicorn key chains, one for me and one for her, which we hooked to our backpacks so everyone would know we were unicorn girls together. As long as Emma had her unicorn dangling from her backpack, I never felt alone.

Then came middle school and Brooklyn. Emma's stuffed unicorn went away. And so did Emma.

The door creaks open. "Can I come in?"

"Yeah," I say, and Grandma enters. There aren't many girls my age who share a bedroom with their grandmother, so I'm a lottery winner there, too. Ever since she went on disability from being injured at the ball-bearing plant, she moved in with Mom and me. Which means she moved in with me. Hence the second twin bed.

"Movie over?" I ask her.

"Uh-huh," Grandma says. "They sure don't make movie stars like Barbara Stanwyck anymore." I silently nod, even though I'm not exactly sure which one Barbara Stanwyck is. Grandma likes watching movies—mostly the kind that were made before she was even born. I still don't get why someone would watch a black-and-white movie when there are plenty of color ones available, but Grandma tells me if I'm lucky, I'll understand when I'm older.

"I like your scarf," Grandma says, and sits at the end of my bed.

Self-consciously, I wind it off my horn. "It's Mom's. I should give it back." Mom is at Walmart, like she always is this time of day. Working, not shopping.

"She won't mind," Grandma says. "How was your first day of school?"

I could tell her about how Noah was taken out of homeroom because of me. Or how Emma ignored me. Or how Angela's inbox was empty. But ever since French class, I've had only one thing on my mind. "Remember that essay I wrote for French class before the summer?"

It takes her a second, but then she says, "The one you read out loud to me and I didn't understand a word?"

"That one," I say. "Guess what? My teacher picked it for the regional competition."

Her face lights up. "That's wonderful, Jewel!"

"Monsieur Oliver told me how great he thought it was. He said it was the best essay in the class."

"I'm so proud of you." She pats my leg with her good arm. Her left arm hasn't healed well since the accident. "I could tell it was excellent."

I laugh. "But you didn't understand it!"

"Didn't have to. I just knew." She grins at me. "So, what does all this mean?"

"That's the bad news. I have to read it in front of people. Judges."

"So?"

"Grandma!" I point at my horn.

She swats at the air. "Pish. Do you want to do it?"

I hesitate, then say, "Yeah, I do."

"So, you'll do it," she says, like it's a fact.

But it's not. If things were different, of course I'd do it. There'd be nothing that could keep me from that stage. I want it so badly, but . . .

I look at Grandma and fight the sudden urge to tell her about the emails. How hearing back just got a hundred times more urgent. And how everything is so much closer to being possible now.

I smile at her instead. *Soon*, I tell myself. *I'll tell her soon.*

The Trouble with Noah

"Have you guys seen my bracelet?" Brooklyn calls up to us from the track below. Mystic and I are sitting on the bleachers waiting for PE to start. "It's real gold with a pink stone in the middle."

At first, I'm confused. Is Brooklyn really talking to us? "I don't think so," I call down to her. "I haven't seen any bracelets."

Brooklyn's perfect shoulders slump. "Everything gets gone in that locker room. I only left it on the bench for half a second."

Mystic leans forward. "We'll let you know if we see anything." She says it cheerfully, like she actually cares.

Brooklyn mutters a "thanks" and goes to join Emma and some other girls by the track. Carmen is down there, too, looking up at us.

Coach Tuck is late, so Mystic and I don't move from our place on the bleachers.

"Cheerleaders," she says under her breath. "Why do they have to have everything?"

Mystic's eyeliner is so thick, she looks like a painting of Cleopatra. "They don't have everything," I say.

"Really? They have nice houses and nice things and—"

"Emma doesn't have a house at all."

"Okay, so *one* of them lives *kind of* like us. But you'd never know it, the way she walks around like a queen." A part of me wants to defend Emma even though she probably doesn't deserve it. But before I can, Mystic asks, "So, are you going to do the French thing?"

"You mean am I going to read my essay in front of a bunch of total strangers?

"You really should."

"That's easy for you to say."

Mystic cocks her head. "Is this about your horn?"

"Uh . . . duh."

"I get it," she says. "Actually, real talk, I *don't* get it. But you're *good* at French. Like a natural talent or something. What if you went all the way to the state finals?"

"That'd be even worse!" I catch sight of the shadow my horn is casting against the bleachers and put my hand up to obscure the image. "Unless I didn't have it anymore."

Mystic eyes shift to my horn. Rarely does she look at it so directly. "What's that supposed to mean?"

"Um." Mystic was in Florida to visit her dad over the summer and I promised myself I wouldn't talk to her about it till she got home. Now it's time. "I've been emailing doctors."

She squints against the sun. "What kind of doctors?"

"Specialists. I've been researching them for a long time."

"Like, how long?"

I clear my throat and croak out, "Since . . . Noah."

"Since Noah?!" Her eyes go wide. "That was like two years ago."

"I know," I say. I know all too well. It was back when Emma and I were still best friends.

It was the beginning of middle school. Emma and I were sitting in the cafeteria together when Thomas Kelly, like the jerk he is, came up and started making fun of my horn. For no reason. In front of everybody.

Usually, I can take the jerk stuff. But on that day, I couldn't. Grandma had just had her accident at the plant, which was really scary in the first place, and that morning,

Mom had told me she was moving in with us. It was a lot to take in, and I was NOT in the mood to be teased.

Thomas wouldn't stop though. "Don't listen to him, J," Emma whispered, but I couldn't help myself.

"Shut up, Thomas!" I yelled. Of course, that made it worse. Yelling always makes everything worse.

"Aww, the unicorn wants me to shut up!" He mocked. "Come on, freak. Wanna make me?"

I'm not going to lie. A part of me wanted to run him through with my horn, just to call his bluff and actually shut him up. But I knew better. I'd never use my horn to hurt someone, even jerk-face Thomas Kelly. I knew I needed to get out of there, so I swung around and bolted from my chair, full of rage I couldn't express. Except I expressed it right into Noah.

It happened so fast that I tasted the milk from his lunch tray before I realized my horn was lodged in Noah's stomach. There was screaming. Not from him. But from others, including—I couldn't *not* hear her above everyone else—Emma. Noah and I fell to the floor, attached together. And when we came apart, there was blood everywhere. Blood on his white shirt. Blood on his face. Blood on my horn. He had just been passing by, an innocent bystander. And he could have died. I could have killed him.

"Why didn't you tell me?" Mystic says, startling me back to the present.

"That I was emailing doctors?" I shrug. "I don't know. I haven't told anyone. I've got a notebook full of names and I've read tons of research articles. It wasn't worth telling until now." I pause for effect, and say, "Because I think I've found him."

"Found who?"

"The doctor."

"Okay, I'm confused," she says.

"Who can take off my horn!"

"Oh," Mystic says, and pauses, taking it in.

"He's doing this trial, kind of an experimental thing," I tell her. "But he says I could be just what he's looking for."

"Who is this guy?"

"He's a vascular surgeon. He does veins and arteries. Really complicated ones."

"And Angela's cool with it?" Mystic asks.

Angela—the real Angela—is my mom. "Well . . ."

"What does that mean?"

I look away.

"Jewels?"

"Angela doesn't know about it."

"Dude!" Mystic exclaims. "You're doing this behind Angela's back?"

"What are my options?" I say, and stare back out at the track.

The doctor's name is Dr. Stein. I sent him every scan I've ever had—which wasn't easy for tons of reasons including my internet situation—and I've been emailing with him for almost four months. Except he doesn't know the emails are from me. I made up a fake email with my mom's name and have been emailing him like I'm Angela the whole time.

"You've got to let that Noah thing go," Mystic says, shaking her head. "I can't believe you're still thinking about that. You can't let it mess you up forever."

"I probably *started* looking for a doctor because of Noah. Who, allow me to remind you, I'm still barred from sharing classes with. But the reasons keep piling up."

"The French competition," she says knowingly.

"The French competition," I repeat.

"So where's this doctor, anyway?

"LA."

She grabs my arm excitedly. "Los Angeles! I'd love to go to LA."

I scan the mountains that rise beyond the bleachers. We're about as small-town as you can get, which has its advantages when you've got a horn on your head—fewer strangers, fewer eyes—but sucks when you're Mystic and want to be where things happen.

"Me too, but . . . you know." I force a grin. Mystic knows it's my dream to see all the faraway places on the collage in my bedroom. And that it's one of my greatest fears that it will never happen. Paris is full of strangers, after all.

Coach Tuck's whistle blows down by the track. "Conrad. Jenkins," he calls out, like we were the ones who were late. "Any time now."

"We're coming," Mystic says, and we start down the bleachers. The other students are already running, and Mystic hates running. As we step onto the track, Carmen moves toward us. Our eyes meet. So much for pretending she's not there.

"Hop to, ladies," Coach T. says, then blows his whistle in three short, sharp bursts.

Mystic and I start running, if you can call it that. Carmen follows behind, even though she could go so much faster if she wanted to.

Looking across the track, I catch sight of Emma running alongside Brooklyn. What would she think of me getting my horn taken off? Two years ago, she would have been the first one I told about Dr. Stein. She was the first one I told about everything.

As she runs, her sandy hair bounces on her shoulders, and when Brooklyn says something that makes her laugh, I feel a pang.

"So what happens next?" Mystic asks.

"I don't know," I say. Which is the total truth. I don't know what's next. I don't know if Dr. Stein can even do it. And then I've got my mom to deal with.

Mystic elbows me. "Don't worry so much. It'll be okay." She grins at me and I feel suddenly grateful to have landed on Team Mystic. She acts tough on the outside but she has a sweet and nougaty center.

I nod back and try to settle myself into the run. There are too many unknowns right now. I'm ready for some answers. I'm ready for an email. Come to think of it, I'm ready for everything.

Carmen

The next morning, I'm at my locker waiting for Nicholas. I texted him earlier, but he hasn't texted back, which means my phone is acting up (likely) or Nicholas overslept (equally likely). While I wait, I dig out a couple of old candy wrappers from the recesses of my locker while Carmen watches me from down the hall.

Lately this is nonstop! I'm not looking at her, but I can feel her looking at me. I'm trying my best to ignore her when I feel a tug on my backpack. Swinging around, I say, "Where've you been?"

But Nicholas isn't there.

A bunch of other people are though. Grinning. And not in a nice way.

Tall Ethan is standing by the lockers across from me. Our eyes meet as Thomas Kelly yells, "Unicorn!" And if evil grins are going around, you can bet money that Thomas is involved. He lobs something through the air, which is caught by another boy, then tossed again. *No, no, no, no!* My hands fly to the bottom of my backpack. My little stuffed unicorn is gone.

Horn first, I plow down the center of the hall. Thomas Kelly literally leaps out of the way, shouting, "Unicorn, coming through!" Others flee to the walls. As I pass Carmen, she falls in behind me.

I'm hating every horrible kid in this school when I turn the corner and almost collide with Noah. It's like a bad dream, a nightmare replaying my worst memory. I stop short, horrified. He's the last person I want to run into. He's the last person I want to make afraid. I'm about to apologize when . . . I see my unicorn squeezed into his hand.

What is he doing? Is this some kind of payback?

He backs away from me into a bank of lockers. I want to scream, *Give it back!* But I feel frozen. Kids, mostly boys, gather on both sides of us. "No-ah! No-ah!" I can't believe they're chanting for him.

Noah doesn't move. He seems frozen, too. His eyes are locked on mine—until they shift to something behind me.

Just then, Thomas Kelly reappears and grabs the unicorn

out of Noah's hand. He flings it into the air and my unicorn disappears among the flailing arms and legs of all those boys. It's as good as gone.

I look back at Noah for one long miserable moment. "Thanks a lot," I say, then walk away.

Pushing through the crowd, I hear Nicholas calling out, but I don't wait. Instead, I escape into an open hallway to find Mrs. Whatley heading toward me with a ready-to-accuse-me look on her face. So, horn down, I keep moving.

"Jewel!" she calls out, but I storm past her. I can feel her scalding eyes tracking me. *Focus, Jewel.* I focus on my feet. I focus on the space they create between us.

Air.

I've never left school like this before. With each step I take away from that door, I realize my chances of detention are rising to suspension and more. Mom will blow a fuse. She'll never understand.

And how could she? I mean, it's just a dumb little unicorn key chain, and I don't even want to be a unicorn. But Emma gave it to me. Holding on to it was no doubt my way of holding on to her. It seems so stupid now.

Tears burn my eyes, and I wipe my snotty nose with the back of my hand. I was starting to think that all my hopes were getting closer to possible. But now . . . how could things actually change when the list of what's wrong in my life gets longer every day?

- My precious stuffed unicorn was stolen.
- I just almost gored Noah. Again!
- My best friend is no longer my best friend and won't even talk to me anymore.
- My essay gets picked for this really big contest and of course I can't go.
- Dr. Stein still hasn't answered my last email.
- And all because of this STUPID horn.

It's so frustrating that I want to scream. But I don't because I'm not alone.

As I step off school property and onto the sidewalk that leads toward town, I realize Carmen is behind me. I would know that sound anywhere. Even as I hear her get closer, I don't look back. I don't encourage her. But she keeps coming.

It doesn't take long for her to be close enough to step on my heels. *Not today, Carmen, okay? Just leave me alone.* But Carmen doesn't listen. She never listens.

I've had it. I whip around. She jerks back and stops.

Carmen stares into my eyes. We haven't been this close in a while. "Go away, Carmen," I say. But she doesn't. So we just stand there, horn to horn, while she shakes her white mane, dirty and tangled with thorns. She stamps her massive gray hoof and lets out a defiant whinny.

Stubborn unicorn.

An old man wearing a beige hat with a brim approaches and notices me, with my horn and my teary cheeks and my snotty nose, and gives me a look that says he's concerned yet surprised at the same time.

"Are you all right, young lady?" he asks.

I'm tempted to say, *No, I'm not all right!* Instead, I mumble, "I'm fine."

He cocks his head and says, "It won't always be as bad as today. Things get better. They do. I've been around long enough to know."

It only takes a flick of Carmen's tail to knock the hat off the old man's head and send it skyward. As he grabs for the top of his bald dome, the hat floats like a glider down the sidewalk.

"Did you feel that breeze?" he asks, clearly confused by the windless sky.

I shake my head, knowing that he can't see Carmen.

"Remember what I said," he says, and hurries after his hat.

"Thanks," I say to him, fighting a smile. Carmen is mischievous like that. When I used to let her in the apartment, she was always knocking things over or hiding things for fun. Her favorite person to prank is Nicholas though, and I don't know why. She's hidden sweatshirts from him, knocked over his books, and even brushed her tail across his face to see how he'd react. That last one sort of freaked him out.

When I was little, I talked about Carmen all the time, but when I got older, I stopped. Everyone probably thought she was something I outgrew. But trust me, Carmen is not outgrowable.

Carmen's pawing at the sidewalk now, and I look into her eyes, feeling guilty. Everything changed between us after the Noah incident. Emma left me, and I left Carmen.

But Carmen and I are different. When Emma abandoned me, I gave up. What was the point of trying to hang around with her if she didn't want me there? Carmen, on the other hand, never gives up. She follows me almost everywhere, whether I want her there or not. I feel guilty whenever I see her, but I also feel angry and sad and regretful. *Why am I like this?* That's the question that always hovers between us.

"Go!" I say and point away from the sidewalk. Carmen shakes her big horse head and stares down at me fiercely. My eyes sting. I don't like being mean to her, but it's too much. She's too much. Carmen is a constant reminder of what's wrong with me. "Please," I whisper. "You've got to stop following me everywhere."

Carmen whinnies back softly, and I sigh. Her eyes are so sad. She leans toward me and nudges me with her nose. And when our horns touch, I can't help it—my eyes close. I feel it down to my toes. I feel like every cell of my body ignites. It feels like . . . like . . . *Stop it, Jewel. It does not feel like home.*

A car horn blasts from the road and I open my eyes. Carmen is still there. I clear my throat and gather myself. *I want to be normal, Carmen. Can't you get that?* I gaze into her huge eyes. If I were still a kid, I'd hug her neck now. But too much has happened. I can't be doing that anymore. So I turn and walk away.

Glancing back, I check to make sure she isn't following me. She's just staring, watching me go. Before, I never hid anything from Carmen. I told her all my secrets, all my fears . . . everything. I didn't even have to say things out loud because somehow, she always knew. Now I wonder if she knows what I'm planning.

What if Dr. Stein says yes? What happens to me and Carmen? Will she be mad? Will she still be my unicorn? So much I don't know. And so much I'm willing to risk now.

Leaving Carmen behind, I trudge toward the town square. Most people know me here, but I usually avoid the square when the leaves change in the fall, because that's tourist season. As I turn the corner at Sisk's Pharmacy, Mr. Sisk is sweeping the front steps of his store. "Hey there, Jewel!"

"Hi, Mr. Sisk," I mumble back, hoping he doesn't realize I'm supposed to be in school right now. I speed up past Wendy's Wine Shop, Antiques of the Mountains, and Caruso's Restaurant.

I'm almost to the square when I'm spotted. A little girl—it's always a little girl—is coming out of Fudge Factory. She looks up at the horn, of course. I know it's hard for a little kid not to point, and she promptly does. I mean, I'm the unexpected attraction.

"What's that?" she asks, innocent and inquisitive, like they always are. "Are you a unicorn?"

I feel the NO gather in my stomach and start making its way to my lips when a hand reaches out and grabs hers.

"Danielle, don't be rude." Danielle's mom's eyes shift from her daughter to me and . . . three, two, one . . . there it is. The look. Neither innocent nor inquisitive. It's the special expression reserved for parents of small children who see me for the first time. She pulls Danielle away in a manner that suggests whatever I have might be contagious. As they step into the pedestrian crossing that leads to the other side of the square, Danielle turns her little head back to look at me. *I wish I had an answer for you, kiddo.*

When I get to the gazebo, Nicholas is waiting for me. The gazebo is in the public garden on the far side of the square where no one ever seems to go but us. Nicholas lives down the street in one of the old white houses on Park Street. Usually when we hang out here after school, Nicholas's dad drives me home.

I stare at him with my hands on my slouching hips like a lazy Wonder Woman with a horn.

"I took the back way," he says, perched on the gazebo's white rail and looking down at me, breathing slightly harder than normal. My backpack is propped up on the bench next to his feet.

I thought I wanted to be alone, but I'm secretly pleased he cared enough to come after me.

"I closed your locker," he says. "And grabbed your backpack."

"Thanks," I say, meaning it more than what it sounds like. "Don't you have history?"

Nicholas shrugs. "I did have history. But now it's actual history. Get it?"

He's trying to make me smile, but I can't. I put my hand over my eyes. "Mom is going to kill me."

"Yeah, probably. What happened?"

"Stupid Thomas Kelly stole my unicorn! Then Noah ended up with it," I say, picturing Noah's face. "I think he thought I was going to hurt him again."

"You wouldn't hurt him again," Nicholas says. A breeze blows between us, and the leaves rattle in the trees.

There's a secret part of me that wonders what it would be like if the thing with Noah never happened. Mystic's type is clearly Ethan. If I had a type, I think it would be Noah. Or . . . I thought it would be Noah. Maybe not so much after today.

"There was a silver lining though," Nicholas says, snapping my thoughts back to the here and now. "After you left, Whatley looked like her head might explode."

"Please tell me it did."

"Nah. But also—Noah was different."

"What do you mean?" I ask.

"He wasn't his normal whiny self."

"Noah's not whiny."

"Noah *is* whiny," Nicholas says back. "But it was weird. When Whatley did her 'poor Noah' routine, 'poor Noah' yelled at her and pushed her away. All by himself. With his tiny whiny hands."

"No way!" I actually grin at that.

"Yes way!" Nicholas says, nodding and grinning himself. "Wanna go back?"

I shake my head. "Not really."

Nicholas's grades are almost as good as mine, but he's a friend before he's a valedictorian. "Come on then. Let's go."

As we walk down Park Street, Nicholas asks, "Hey, when were you going to tell me about winning the French thing?

I look over at him, surprised.

"What?" he says. "Did you think Mystic *wasn't* going to blab?"

It's been almost two years of our threesome, and I'm always amazed at how easily Mystic and Nicholas share things with each other, and with me. Sometimes it reminds me of how things used to be with Emma.

"I'm not going."

"Mystic says you're like by far the best in the class. We'll come with you."

"Aren't you forgetting something?" I say sarcastically.

"No. How could I forget that? It's right in the middle of your head."

I spin toward him. "Dude!"

"It's not a bad thing. It's just a thing. You're the one who makes such a big deal about it."

"You *would* think that."

"It's how I see it," he says, putting his hand on his hip. "When *you* look at *you*, your horn is like ninety percent of what you see. When *I* look at *you*, it's like ten percent. And an awesome ten."

"You big liar. You're the one who said you made friends with me because of my horn."

"Okay, guilty. But I didn't *stay* your friend because of your horn. How shallow do you think I am? To my complete shock and surprise, you turned out to have a whole lot more going on than just a horn."

"Really?" I say, fighting a grin.

"Yes, really. Now don't let it go to your horn . . . I mean head."

"Very funny," I say, as we step onto his driveway. Nicholas's house is like most of the houses on Park Street—white, wooden, and super old. It's two stories and completely beautiful.

His dad, Barry, works from home, and when he hears us walk in, he comes out of his office. Nicholas explains everything that happened at school, and I hang my head and play my part by basically looking exactly as miserable as I feel when I think about that stupid situation.

"Can we take a mental-health day, Dad?" Nicholas asks.

When Barry looks at you, you can just *feel* that he makes amazing oatmeal chocolate chip cookies. "Of course you can," he says. "That sounds horrible, Jewel. I'm so sorry kids can be like that."

Yes, Barry is an actual, real, live dad, who actually, really says things like that. Imagine! When he calls my mom to tell her, I'm way relieved when he gets her voice mail. I'll deal with the fallout later.

We go upstairs to Nicholas's room, with the double bed all to himself and the floor-to-ceiling bookshelves. Miniature planets dangle from the ceiling replicating the solar system, and a telescope spies through the window that faces onto Park Street. Through it, I know I would see Carmen. I can sense that she's in the front yard.

On the wall next to Nicholas's bed there's a huge framed map of North America with little red flags pinned on specific towns and cities. There are thirty-four of them so far, spreading from Bathurst, New Brunswick, to Manhattan, Kansas, to San Luis, Baja California.

"Ta-daa! Here's the new one," Nicholas says, holding up the latest issue of *Highwaymen*. Every month, Barry drives Nicholas the forty-five minutes it takes to pick up the new issue at the closest comic store. I can't imagine my mom having that kind of time—or gas money.

Nicholas grabs another red flag from his drawer.

"You waited for me?" I ask.

"It's more fun when we do it together. Where does it go?"

As he hands me the new issue, I arrange myself cross-legged on his bed, ignoring his question. Instead, I ask what I always ask him at the start of every issue. "Why is it called *Highwaymen* when the most kick-butt character in the whole thing is a woman?"

"How many times do I have to tell you, it's metaphorical," Nicholas says. "And highwaymen are the bad guys. Instead of robbing stagecoaches, they go after magical creatures."

"I know," I say. Because I *do* know. It's just annoying, and somewhat patriarchal, and if it weren't the coolest, most amazing graphic novel in the entire world, I might boycott it solely based on its name.

But then I open to page one and enter the world of Hot Springs, New Mexico, circa 1888, and like always, my breath literally catches in my throat.

The illustrations are so real, I feel like I could step onto Main Street and walk into the local watering hole (called the Watering Hole) and share a sarsaparilla with Esmeralda (the barmaid and most likely-to-kick-the-crap-out-of-you warrior woman of all time), Chet (the outlaw and most likely to show up late for a battle), and Beaumont (the sheriff and man of few words).

Esmeralda would tell me all about the magical creatures they fought. Chet would reminisce about the ones they saved (because even though Chet is the outlaw, he's much more soft-hearted than Esmeralda). And Beaumont would just tip the front of his charcoal cowboy hat, tap the silver star pinned to his vest, and say, "All in a day's work, young lady. All in a day's work."

Hot Springs is the ultimate faraway place.

It's also a real place, a town in New Mexico. Only it's not called Hot Springs anymore. In the 1950s, a radio show called *Truth or Consequences* held a contest: If your town renames itself after our program, we'll come host our show there. Hot Springs entered . . . and won. Their town has been called Truth or Consequences ever since. I don't know what Beaumont or Esmeralda would think about the townspeople's choice, but it's a true story. I looked it up.

Nicholas fake-clears his throat and taps the top of the issue to get my attention.

"Oh, sorry," I say.

"There's a drake," he says, clearly having read this one already. "Page eight. Find it."

I flip to page eight, and sure enough, a drake—or what most people would call a dragon. Below the drake there's a caption in small, light print that reads *46.12 N, 112.94 W.*

"Got it," I say, and tell him the numbers, which he

immediately records in a notebook. He pins a piece of yellow yarn to the side of the map right above 46 degrees latitude. Then he takes another piece of yarn and pins it at the top of the map, just west of 112 degrees longitude.

I go over and grab the longitude string and pull it to the bottom, while Nicholas guides his yarn across the latitude line. Where they cross, Nicholas stabs the red flag into the map.

"There," he says. "It's just west of Butte, Montana. What's there?"

This usually happens. The places where the coordinates meet are mostly in small towns, too tiny to be represented on Nicholas's map, even though it's gigantic. I enter the coordinates into his laptop. "It crosses at a place called Anaconda, Montana," I tell him. "Population nine thousand two hundred and ninety-eight."

Nicholas steps back and studies the position of the new flag. "Anaconda, huh? So that's where drakes come from."

"They also come from . . ." I lean in to get a closer look at the map. "Comfort, Texas, and Scotts Hill, Tennessee." This isn't the first drake to show up in *Highwaymen*.

Okay, I'll explain. Every time a new magical creature arrives in Hot Springs, they come with what we realized must be degrees of latitude and longitude written beneath them. The intersection of those lines is called a global address.

We think these captions tell us the original global address of each magical creature. In other words, where it came from before arriving in Hot Springs.

"I can't wait till we can finally drive and take a road trip to all these places," Nicholas says, gesturing grandly across the red-flag-studded map.

It's a good idea, one we talk about all the time. One that I'd be lose-my-mind excited about . . . if I didn't have a horn on my head. All those red flags represent lots of strangers. "It'll take a whole summer," I say, hiding my thoughts from him.

"Perfect summer." Nicholas grins.

I return to the *Highwaymen* in my hands and go back to page one. Every issue begins the same—during a calm and normal moment in Hot Springs. Sometimes a tumbleweed is literally bouncing down Main Street. It never ends that way, though. By the last page, the carnage will have been . . . let's just say *significant.*

Today, Esmeralda and Chet are riding out of town under the azure sky. Esmeralda's white horse is named Sheba. Esmeralda raised her from a foal after Sheba's mother was killed by one of Wesley's baddies.

Esmeralda looks over at Chet, and he grins back at her. Here's the deal: Esmeralda loves Chet. He's an outlaw, and some people think he's bad, but not Esmeralda. She sees the best in him, even though he's oblivious to her feelings.

Beaumont, the sheriff, loves Esmeralda, but she doesn't have a clue.

Usually, Esmeralda, Chet, and Beaumont rescue the magical creatures who have been captured or injured, mostly by Wesley and his baddies. Wesley collects magical creature trophies—a fang from a Mongolian death worm, a talon from a griffin—whatever can bring the highest bidder. It's a booming business, like elephant poaching in Africa. Wesley takes what he wants, leaving the dead and wounded behind. Whenever a new magical creature appears in Hot Springs, Wesley usually isn't far behind. Esmeralda, Beaumont, and Chet make it their business to stop him.

I turn the page.

* * *

Overhead, the phoenix lets out a loud cry, and Chet and Esmeralda whip their heads around. A drake is crossing the distant plain and lumbering toward town.

Drakes are one of the few magical creatures on their enemies list. That's because when drakes show up, they always try to burn everything down.

Esmeralda and Chet pivot their horses. They watch the drake trundle across the desert floor.

Chet says, "He's a big fella, ain't he?"

That's when the big fella lets out a bellowing eruption of fire.

Esmeralda reins Sheba toward town. "I'll warn Beaumont," she says. Dust flies up from under Sheba's hooves as she gallops away. Sheba gains speed and her great big beautiful wings spread wide. Sheba is a Chollima—a flying horse from actual mythology. As she and Esmeralda take flight, the phoenix follows, a purple tail to Sheba's dove-white kite.

Chet watches, awed. He can't help himself. He's always awed when Esmeralda flies away on Sheba's back. When the magical moment passes, Chet squeezes his legs into the sides of his distinctly nonmagical regular horse. "Gid-up," he clicks, and follows Esmeralda toward town.

* * *

"Look what I found!" Nicholas says, coming into the room with a bag of Flamin' Hot Cheetos. I didn't even realize he'd been gone.

I reach for the bag, but he pulls it back. "No orange fingers on *Highwaymen*."

Putting it aside temporarily, I get a handful of Cheetos, and Nicholas plops down on the floor.

"Do you think Esmeralda and the gang would think you were a unicorn if they met you?"

"Like in person?" I ask.

"Yeah, just hypothetically."

"They would probably think I was a freak."

"They'd think I was more of a freak than you," he says.

I look at him sideways. "You could be normal. Heck, you practically are."

"Are you kidding? You don't have to have a horn to be different."

Whatever, Nicholas. Ever since we met in sixth grade he's done his best to convince me that he's *so different.* Not buying it.

"Boys like me don't live in Hot Springs," he says.

"Yeah. Because boys like you don't know how to ride a horse."

"Or something like that."

It annoys me when he tries to be a freak like me. I mean, if he wants it so bad, he can have it. But until Nicholas has a horn on his head, there's no way he can understand what it's truly like to be different.

Fallout

"I can't believe you just left school," Mom yell-whispers. "You can't worry me like that!" Mom doesn't want to upset Grandma in the other room, so we're talking low. She's making mac and cheese from the box, still in her Walmart vest.

After Mom heard Nicholas's dad's message, and the one from Mrs. Whatley, she called me. She was so mad that she made me give the phone to Barry, who got an earful from her. Super embarrassing.

"It wasn't anything," I say, and Mom's eyes bug out.

"Wasn't anything?!" You're not like Nicholas. You don't have *parents* to *pay* for things like college and everything else. You've got to keep up your grades, work hard, get scholarships. NOT SKIP SCHOOL. And you just got picked for the French competition. You don't want to ruin that. What got into you?"

I told her about the essay competition after I told Grandma, and like Grandma, she was like, "Of course, you have to go!" I choose to ignore that subject for the moment.

"It's not my fault!" I yell-whisper back. "Some kid stole my . . . stuff." Now it sounds dumb even to me, but the feelings come rushing back.

"Some kids are going to always be mean." Mom sighs. "You can't let them bother you. You've got to keep focused on the big picture."

"Please don't big-picture me."

"I *will* big-picture you!" Mom says. "Every minute of every day if I have to."

"It's not just the other kids. It's everything." I say, standing my ground. "You don't get it."

"Well, then, we're even, because there is so much you don't get either. You have to trust me. If you just stick to the plan, it's going to be—"

"What? Just more of the same amount of bad?" I shake my head. My mom is fixated on my grades and getting a scholarship to college. "Maybe we need a new plan."

"What does that mean?" she asks.

"Maybe it's time to take a break."

Her hand goes to her hip. "A break from what?"

"School," I tell her. I'm making this up as I go, but it's sounding pretty all right.

"What do you mean, a break from school?"

"You girls okay in there?" Grandma calls from the couch in the adjoining room.

Mom grimaces at me. "We're fine, Mama." She's trying to sound like everything's okay, but her voice is never that high-pitched unless she's worried or lying. "We're going to eat in just a minute."

When she looks back at me, I whisper, "Yeah, a break from school." And why not take a break? Because just think, if Dr. Stein can remove my horn, I can always go back. And if he can't—well, what's changed, anyway?

"Oh, don't *even*." Mom glares at me. "You can't quit school." She takes a deep breath, then says, "You're so smart, Jewel. *And* so beautiful. You can't just throw away an education, sweetheart."

How come when she calls me sweetheart, it doesn't sound so sweet? "None of that matters if I can't go anywhere without people being distracted by this thing!" I say, pointing to my horn, in case she's forgotten.

"They're not so distracted that they don't reward you for good work. He chose you for the French thing."

"Because I wrote about this!" I gesture to my horn again. "But it's because of this that I don't want it."

Mom shakes her head. "Listen, I don't know a better way to make lemons into lemonade than that. You're the one who chose to write about your horn. And he wants *you* to do it. How you're so good at French, I will never know, but you are." She looks at me with exhausted eyes. "Can't we just go with it? Say an easy yes for once?"

I want to scream. What kind of logic is that? "I'm not up for everybody staring at me."

Mom shoves a bowl of leftover string beans into the microwave. "Not everybody stares at you."

"Yeah, right."

"Let me tell you something," she says, looking hard at me. "Your life may be tough. It may be unfair. But you are going to finish school. You are going to graduate from college. Got it? You're not going to end up like me."

That last bit makes me pause. "What's wrong with ending up like you?"

She rolls her eyes at me with a bitterness that makes me think she's forgetting I'm her daughter, not a friend. "Please. Really, Jewel?"

"You're a good mom," I say, meeting her gaze.

"Yeah, regular Mom of the Year," she says, and looks away. She punches the timer on the microwave and presses start. "Go on and set the table, okay?"

* * *

After dinner, I grab my laptop and head out our apartment door. Sam, the nine-year-old kid who lives downstairs, is kicking his soccer ball against the side of the building. He's completely unaware of the unicorn standing only a few feet away from him. Sam doesn't look up at me, but Carmen does.

Our apartment building is two stories, and we live on the second floor. Emma's bedroom window is directly across from mine, with a parking lot between us. So close, and yet so far.

Sitting on the steps outside our front door, I open my laptop and hope for an internet connection. Sometimes it's better out here. I finally get in, but "Angela's" inbox is still empty.

I look down at my green sneakers we got from the local thrift shop and my pink laces I snagged from the Dollar Store. Secondhand sneakers with a buck's worth of laces. If that doesn't say it all, I don't know what does.

The soccer ball gets away from Sam and rolls past Carmen. It bounces off the hood of my mom's brown Corolla, which is minding its own business in its regular parking space below. As he retrieves the ball, Sam looks up at me and gives me an up-nod. Nine years old and already too cool for an apology.

My eyes meet Carmen's. She stands so patiently at the bottom of the stairs. What is she waiting for me to do? Get on her back and ride away with her?

That almost happened once. A long time ago, I climbed onto Carmen's back from the hood of my mom's car.

I was six years old and saw Carmen from my window, nodding her head up and down at me like she did when she wanted my attention. It was late; Mom was asleep. I snuck out and ran down the stairs in bare feet and hugged my unicorn, which really meant I wrapped myself around her giant front leg that was taller than me. When I let go, she bowed low and I knew exactly what she wanted me to do. I climbed up onto the Corolla's hood and clambered onto Carmen's back.

I had never been on top of Carmen before. I was up so high that I should've been scared, but I wasn't. As she clomped across the parking lot, I tightened my fists around her white mane while the streetlamp threw her enormous shadow and my smaller one across the pavement. At the two-lane street, Carmen stopped and looked both ways before crossing and taking us into the woods.

I remember everything about that night so vividly. Carmen threaded through trees while I rocked gently back and forth on her back. Soon, I realized I didn't have to hold on at all. Carmen wasn't going to let me fall.

I couldn't tell how much time passed—it could have been an hour or a handful of minutes—before we reached a big boulder by a stream. Across from the boulder was a narrow descending trail covered by an awning of vines. I couldn't see where the trail led, but it was leading somewhere. I felt that with certainty.

When I slid off Carmen's back, the boulder was cold under my feet. I can still feel it when I think about that night. We stood there staring at each other, horn to horn. It was the first time we'd stood like that—I'd never been so high up before. I remember reaching out and placing my hand on her face. I don't know how I knew what Carmen was thinking, but I always did—I always do—and as I stood on that cold boulder half a lifetime ago, I knew she wanted me to come with her down the trail. But I had the feeling that going with her meant not coming back.

Eventually, Carmen lay down and I climbed off the boulder and curled up beside her. I wasn't afraid, because I knew Carmen would watch over me. I remember feeling as loved and secure as I ever had. When I fell asleep, I dreamt of her.

The next morning, I woke up on a pile of leaves and Carmen was gone. When I heard strange voices calling my name, I got up and wandered toward the sounds.

When they finally got me to Mom, she hugged me until I thought I might break. After that, she got a deadbolt for the front door and hid the key. So I could never scare her like that again.

* * *

"Mind if I join you?" I look up to see Grandma standing beside me at the top of the stairs.

"Sure," I say, and she sits down next to me, holding an old photo album.

"Did I ever tell you that my grandfather only got an eighth-grade education?"

"Really?" I turn to her, brightening, before I realize she must have overheard at least some of me and Mom's fight.

Grandma cocks an eyebrow. "You sound like you think that was a good thing. He was a smart man who would have loved an education. But back then, by the time you got to eighth grade, most kids had to give up the books to work on the family farm. That's how it was out in the country." She pauses, then adds, "But that's not how it is for you."

I tip my head back and groan. "We were trying to whisper."

"I may be old, darlin', but I'm not deaf. I hear a lot of things you and your mother don't want me to hear."

"So you're taking her side?"

"I'm not taking anybody's side. You know me better than that." She squeezes my hand. "I'm just presenting *another* side of the story." She opens the photo album with her right hand. "And here's another."

"How many sides does this story have?" I scoot toward her and look down at the pictures stuck behind cellophane. There's a girl holding a baton in a short sparkly outfit with her hair up in a bun, smiling into the camera. "Is that Mom?"

"That's my Angela," Grandma says. "I took this at the state finals in baton twirling. She was third place of all the twirlers in the entire state."

"The state finals?" I gaze at Mom more closely. I knew she twirled, but I didn't know she was this good.

"She was the star at football games." Grandma turns a page, and there are more pictures of Mom in front of the whole marching band on the high school football field.

"I've never seen these before," I say, staring at my teen-aged Mom, who looks so young and hopeful. So *not* how she looks now. "She was . . . amazing."

"She is amazing," Grandma says. "She was my miracle. You know that, right?"

I nod. Grandma likes to tell me this story.

"They thought your grandpa and me would never have a baby of our own. And then lo and behold, forty-year-old me gets pregnant." She claps her hand on her knee. "I don't think we really believed it for the longest time. Your grandpa would stare at my growing belly, afraid to touch it, bless his soul. And when your mama finally came," she says, her eyes sparkling, "she was everything we'd hoped for."

"I know, Grandma."

"It's easy to think your mom's being hard on you," she continues, her voice growing serious. "But you need to know she had dreams, too. She wanted things. To be a teacher. To have a nice home. To have a big family. To have a nice husband." She pauses. "And then life didn't work out like she . . . well, expected."

"Because of me," I say weakly.

"No! Oh, no, sweetie, not because of you!" She pulls my chin toward her, and I reluctantly look her in the eyes. "Not because of any one thing." She pauses. "Maybe because of your deadbeat father. But never because of you."

Mom got pregnant and married my father in college. She had a plan back then: to graduate and become an English teacher. Then I came and grew a horn, and we all know the rest.

"You're the one good thing in her life," Grandma says. "I know that to be true. So just . . . don't be so hard on her. That's all."

I know Mom and Grandma mean well, but all their great life advice is for someone who doesn't have a horn. The way I see it, I'll only get what I want in this life—the things *they* want for me—when I'm without it.

"And," she says slyly, "maybe going to the state finals would be good for you, just like it was for your mom."

I sigh. "How do you know I'll go to the state finals?"

"Didn't I tell you? I had a word with my crystal ball."

"Funny, Grandma," I say, but we smile at each other.

"It would be good for your mom, too," Grandma says. "To see you up there doing what you love."

I flip back to the photo of Mom at her state finals. She looks so confident and sure of herself. Don't they know that all I want is to feel like that?

Other People's Property

Mystic sits at the desk next to mine in the middle of Coach Tuck's class. Coach T., who teaches PE, history, and detention, gave Mystic detention as soon as we showed up late for PE. I guess you could call that the circle of life.

That was yesterday, after I spent forever in Mrs. Whatley's office trying to convince her that I did have a good reason for leaving school on my own. She, however, saw it differently. *There's never an excuse to leave school without permission! Something could have happened to you and the school would've been responsible! Don't you know you could have come to me to deal with the problem instead!* Blah. Blah. And blah.

No dice. She may be the *WORLD'S GREATEST MOM* according to the coffee mug on her desk, but her only gift to me was a weeklong detention slip and a hall pass to the gym.

Outside Whatley's door, Mystic was leaning against the wall, waiting for me. A nice surprise, but a dumb one. We'd both be late for PE now, which would mean detention for both of us.

Nicholas, on the other hand, does not have detention. Barry emailed Mrs. Whatley with some flimsy reason about why he left school early, and she bought it. Such is the circle life on Park Street with a stay-at-home dad.

Detention is almost empty. Behind us are a couple of seventh graders I don't know, and a solo sixth-grade hooligan wearing a hoodie near the door. Carmen is waiting outside in the hall. Not even she wants to be in the detention room.

We're supposed to do homework, but instead I'm drawing a distinctly nonmagical creature, a fox, on the back of an algebra handout.

"What's he doing here?" Mystic whispers. I look up: Noah is walking through the door.

"You're late, Mr. Samuels," Coach T. says from behind his desk.

"Sorry, Coach," Noah answers. "I've never had detention before."

I can tell from the look on Coach T.'s face that he thinks that's a dumb excuse. "Well, take a seat, rookie." Noah's eyes meet mine before he scoots into a desk a few rows ahead of us.

Could he be in detention because of my stuffed unicorn? Nicholas said Noah yelled at Mrs. Whatley. Would she have thrown him in detention for that?

I glance over at Mystic, who's contentedly catching up on her math homework. Her pencil flits through problem after problem with the precision and speed of a hummingbird. "What do you think he got detention for?" I whisper.

Coach T. lets out a "Shhhh!" before going back to grading the stack of papers on his desk, so Mystic just shrugs.

I stare at the back of Noah's head and wonder where my little unicorn is now. Probably at the bottom of a trash can, frightened and alone. Thanks again, Noah.

Coach T. stands all of a sudden. "I'll be back in a sec," he says. "No talking, unless you want to add to your sentence."

As soon as he closes the door behind him, the seventh graders start whispering. I turn to Mystic, but she's still engrossed in her math. There's her usual stack of homemade bracelets on her arm. But there's something else, too, tucked between her creations. Another bracelet. A really nice one. Gold with a pink stone in the middle.

Her eyes dart from her homework to me, and her sleeve comes down fast.

It takes two seconds for me to put it together. "Is that Brooklyn's bracelet?" I whisper.

She ignores me as Noah looks our way. I wait for him to turn back around, then I whisper harder, "Mystic!"

"No," she answers quietly. "It's nothing."

"No, it's not!" I say, low but urgent. "That *is* her bracelet!"

Her eyes fire back at me. "Don't worry about it, okay?"

Slowly, I turn back to my fox drawing. What does she mean, don't worry about it? Did Mystic steal Brooklyn's bracelet?

Mystic has an invisible moat around her that keeps most people away. For a long time, her moat made me think she didn't like me. She was friends with Nicholas, and I was becoming friends with him, too. But at that point, Mystic and I hadn't gelled yet.

Then one day, a few months after the Noah incident, we were walking down the hall when Robert Davis pretended my horn was a basketball net and his empty cup was a basketball. He shot and scored, landing the paper cup on the tip of my horn. I was embarrassed, but Mystic almost clobbered him. That was the day her moat disappeared, at least for me, and I was granted access to Castle Mystic.

Anyway, it's been a long time since I've felt her invisible moat, but I feel it rolling toward me now. The image of her plucking Brooklyn's bracelet from a locker-room bench and secreting it away pings around in my head and can't find a place to land. Mystic is stealing. I force Mystic's gaze to mine. "Don't lie to me."

Just then the door opens and quiet snaps over the room like a whip. Coach T. is back. He scans the room as if sensing words have been spoken here. "Twenty-five more minutes, people."

✳ ✳ ✳

"Well, at least he got detention, too," Nicholas says. We're in Nicholas's room doing homework on the floor next to his bed, and by "doing homework," I mean Nicholas is rereading a back issue of *Highwaymen* while Mystic is helping me with algebra.

Nicholas waited for us outside detention with Carmen. He didn't know she was there, of course, and when we walked out, I caught Carmen snorting over his head and Nicholas eyeing the air above him suspiciously, like he was being toyed with by a ghost. I stifled a laugh, not wanting to encourage her.

Ethan was waiting, too, standing by a Save the Date poster for the eighth-grade dance. He looked away when he saw

Mystic and me, and he and Noah circled around me like I had leprosy or something, leaving hurt feelings in their wake. Carmen whinnied angrily after them.

Now, sitting on the plush and unstained carpet on Nicholas's floor, I look up from my algebra problem. "We don't know that's why Noah got detention. Maybe we're jumping to conclusions."

"Uh, he *stole* your unicorn," Mystic says. But her eyes drop as soon as the words are out of her mouth, and I see her sleeve is now securely covering her arm and all the bracelets hidden there.

I gaze up at the solar system hanging from Nicholas's ceiling. His parents have money. His sister, Sarah, goes to a fancy college. But Mystic, she's more like me: not much money, single mom, a dad in Florida who drinks too much. And she has a little brother to protect from it all. I wonder if anyone else knows she's stealing.

"Ethan's a dork," Nicholas says to get a rise out of Mystic, but she doesn't take the bait. He nudges her leg with the toe of his shoe. "Why are you all weirded out?"

Mystic's eyes shoot my way. "I'm not weirded out."

"Could have fooled me." Nicholas shrugs and gets up, tossing me his *Highwaymen*. "We need snacks," he says, and leaves the room.

This is my chance. "You've got like two minutes to talk to me."

"It's not a big deal," Mystic says, already on the defensive.

I feel my mouth gape open. "What? *Stealing?* That *is* a big deal. You know that."

"I'm not stealing," she says. "I'm just borrowing."

It's her casual tone that freaks me out. "Yeah, right. Then you won't mind if I tell Nicholas?"

"Come on," Mystic snaps, slipping into pleading mode. "I don't want him to know. It's seriously not that big of a deal. He won't even care."

"Then tell me," I say, holding my ground. "How long have you been stealing?"

"I haven't been stealing. It's just . . ." She looks away, then says quietly, "Brooklyn was so careless with this." She touches the bracelet under her sleeve. "It was sitting on the bench for a long time. Not just a second like she said. And I had this thought like, why does she get to have so many nice things? And she doesn't even take care of them. It's not fair."

"So it's fair for you to take it?"

Her eyes are vulnerable in a very un-Mystic-like way. "Well, no, but . . ." It goes super silent between us, until she says, "I'm going to give it back."

"You are?"

She nods. "It just felt so good on my arm." Mystic rolls up her sleeve, and we both admire Brooklyn's beautiful bracelet sandwiched between Mystic's handmade ones. "I thought it wouldn't hurt to keep it for a while. Make her miss it. Make her be more careful next time." Mystic pauses, her eyes on the pink stone. "I *was* tempted to deconstruct it and use it to make new bracelets. But I guess once I did that, there'd be no going back."

"Myst, you're really good at your jewelry," I say. Mystic's jewelry may be weird, but it's also good. I guess it's what you'd call original. "You don't need her dumb mass-market thing."

"But just think how good I'd be if I had materials like this."

"Yeah, but you make so much out of so little. Don't you think doing it your way is just . . . cooler?"

"You think so?" Mystic smiles at me.

"Yeah, I do." I smile back.

Mystic rolls down her sleeve, covering the bracelets. "Tomorrow," she says. "I'll leave it in the locker room tomorrow."

"Okay," I say, and, as if in triumph for my moral victory, my forehead pangs, throbbing right under my horn. I can tell Carmen feels it, too, because she whinnies from where I left her in Nicholas's front yard.

I gaze at Mystic's beautiful, hornless forehead like it's a bracelet left carelessly behind by a girl who doesn't appreciate it. And I understand why she did what she did. Because if I could steal that, I'd do it in a second.

Emails from Angela

I wake up to see my mom standing at the side of my bed, staring at me. It's unsettling.

"What's wrong?"

"I got a phone call a few minutes ago," Mom says.

I rub my eyes sleepily. "Yeah?"

"From a Dr. Stein in Los Angeles."

I bolt up in bed and almost fall over. My horn tends to unbalance me when I move too fast. "Um . . . who?" I ask nervously. How did he call her? I never gave him a phone number.

"He said he didn't want to email me back because he wanted to tell me the news on the phone." I can't read her face. It's tight, almost expressionless. "That's strange, I told him. Because I've never emailed this man. I've never even heard of him. But he's heard of me—and my daughter who has a horn on her head."

My heart is beating so fast. "Mom, what'd he say?" I know I'm in trouble but I'll deal with that later.

"About which part?" she says. "About you faking an email address for me? About you emailing him as if you *were* me? About—"

"About my horn!" I practically shout. "Can he do the surgery?"

She stares at me for a long moment. "First you skip school, and now you're sneaking behind my back with this. I don't know who you are anymore." She pauses. "We have a plan, remember?"

"We need a new one, remember?" I swipe back.

She purses her lips together tightly, then gets up and stalks out of the bedroom.

"Mom!" I call out after her. She doesn't answer, so I jump out of the bed and rush to the kitchen, where Grandma's eating cereal at the table, I'm sure wondering what all the fuss is about. "What did he say?"

"He said that I did an excellent job getting him all the scans he needed. He said that I was a wonderful mother who clearly cares very much about her daughter. Oh, and he thanked me for my patience and apologized for everything taking so long." Mom raises her eyebrow. "Because get this! I've been emailing with him since *May*! A whole four months ago. Did you know that? I sure didn't!"

"Who have you been emailing, Angela?" Grandma asks innocently.

"Well, that's the funny thing, Mama. I haven't been emailing anyone! Jewel has!" Mom's eyes pierce right through me.

I don't have any defense but desperation. It's weak, but it's all I've got. "Mom, what else was I supposed to do? Just because you think it's okay for me to have this horn for the rest of my life . . ." I'm surprised to find my voice wobbling. "It doesn't mean it's okay with me!"

"Jewel." Her voice lowers. "It's too dangerous. That's what all the doctors said."

"Not this doctor!"

"That's what concerns me." Mom shakes her head. "You don't understand."

"*I* don't understand?" I feel like a bowling ball is lodged in my throat. "I wish *you* could have a horn on your head. For just one day. Then you'd know what it's like to get stared at all the time. To almost kill someone because of this!" I point to the horn for extra emphasis.

"That was an accident—"

"It doesn't matter! It happened. Everybody is always going to see me as the girl who gored Noah Samuels."

"Oh, honey. No they're not."

I'm so frustrated I could scream. "Please, Mom, please! I'm sorry, okay. I shouldn't have lied. I know that. But that's how important this is to me! I've got one chance—maybe the only one I'll ever get—to do something about this." I stare into her eyes pleadingly. "Just tell me what he said."

Her pause makes me sweat, and when she finally speaks, she's cautious. "Something about how the research he's been doing is working. And that they're ready for the next stage." Her face crumbles. "He thinks he can do it."

Now I do scream.

"But Jewel, no."

"What do you mean, no?"

"I told Dr. Stein everything. He knows you wrote the emails. And now he knows how I feel about it. You need parental consent."

"Which. You. Have. To. Give. Me," I say, emphasizing each word. "Mom, *please*." I don't think I knew the meaning of "please" until right now.

"Jewel, we don't know anything about this doctor. Just because he says he might be able to do this doesn't mean he can do it *safely*."

"But I told you! Dr. Stein is different. Do you know how many doctors I've researched? How many I've emailed?"

Her eyebrows crease. "No, how many?"

"A lot."

"How many is a lot?"

"Seventy-four," I say, more quietly.

"Seventy-four!" she says, not quietly at all. "How long have you been doing this?"

"A long time," I say, not letting my eyes drift from hers.

When Mom turns away, I look at Grandma, who's staring at me in disbelief. Behind her, outside the window, is Carmen, and I wonder how much she's heard. I go to the window and close the blinds.

"Mom," I try again, lowering my voice.

She sighs and looks back at me. "Even if I said okay—which I am not saying—how are we supposed to pay for this?"

"That's the thing, Mom. I'd be part of his research project. We wouldn't have to pay. They'd take care of everything."

"You'd be a guinea pig," Grandma says.

I look at Grandma. The confusion on her face has cleared. "What does that mean?" I ask.

"They'd be experimenting on you," Mom says. "That's what that means. Our payment would be the risk you're taking. The risk *we're* taking. Something could go wrong. That's why we wouldn't have to pay."

"Yeah, but Mom," I say, tears forming despite my struggle to blink them away. "What if something goes right?"

"Jewel, honey, it's too risky. I'd rather have you with a horn than no you at all."

I slap the side of my horn angrily, but that hurts only me. The desperation in my stomach crawls up to my lips. "Did you tell him no?"

She nods. "I told him no."

The silence that descends upon us is heavy. I can't believe what I'm hearing. I can't believe she would do this to me.

Mom glances at her watch. "I've got to get to work. We can talk about it later."

"What's there to talk about?" I say despondently.

"When you have a child of your own, you'll understand this." She looks to Grandma. "Can you please talk to her?"

I stand frozen at the counter while Mom picks up her purse and heads toward the door. After it closes, I hear Grandma say, "Jewel," but it's like she's speaking to me from underwater. I go to our bedroom and shut the door.

Frantically, I open my laptop and pray for a connection. I click on my email and start typing.

Dear Dr. Stein,

I know you spoke to my mom this morning. And I know she told you no. I'm sorry. I shouldn't have lied to you. I shouldn't have pretended to be her. But please, please, don't give up on me. I've done the research. I know you're the only one who can help me. I'm going to change her mind. PLEASE DON'T CHANGE YOURS.

Sincerely,

Jewel Conrad

* * *

School drags like a snail across my day. I keep picturing my mom's sad but firm face as she tells me no. It plays over and over again. I've been able to check my email twice, but nothing back from Dr. Stein.

Why did he call her? How did he even get her number? I would have had to get her permission at some point, but it wasn't supposed to be yet. It wasn't supposed to be like this.

By French class, my mind is so spun that I hardly hear when Monsieur Oliver calls my name. "I'm sorry, what?"

"I thought we'd start with your essay, Jewel," he says.

"Start how?"

Monsieur Oliver grins. "*Alors,* will you come up and read your essay to the class, *s'il vous plaît?*"

My mouth goes Sahara Desert dry, and I can't move. What is he thinking? I sit in the back of the class for one reason—not be seen. And now—

"Jewel?" he says, and everyone turns. Josh Martin, Ethan, Brooklyn . . . I stall until all the stares break me down. Slowly,

I rise from my desk and channel a glacier as I step as slowly as possible up the aisle. *Please, please, don't make me do this!* I'm screaming silently at him with my eyes.

Unfortunately, Monsieur Oliver is a terrible mind reader, because instead of sending me back to my desk and apologizing for the inconvenience, he hands me my essay and gestures for me to turn around and face the class. "All right, little French fries," he says, holding up his hands. "*Écoutez.*"

As they quiet down, he whispers to me, "You can do this."

He steps away, and there I am, alone. Monsieur Oliver gives me an encouraging nod, and I take a deep breath and—honestly, I picture myself fleeing the room.

But I don't do that. Fleeing, screaming unicorn girl would be even more embarrassing than terrified, regular unicorn girl. So, slowly, I turn and face all those eyeballs. Staring at me. Staring at my horn.

Clearing my throat, I hold up my essay and begin. In French, I mumble: "I am a girl with a horn on her head. In case you didn't notice." I glance up. That was supposed to be funny, but no one is laughing. I clear my throat again and try to speak louder. "Some kids call me the unicorn girl. And I understand why. But see, I'm not a unicorn. I'm a girl. I'm just like other girls. Most people don't see that."

No one's reacting. Okay . . . now I'm starting to wonder whose French is even good enough to understand me. I mean, Josh can understand me. Maybe Brooklyn. But is it possible that, to the ears of most of my peers, all I'm saying is gibberish?

Still, I've never talked about my horn in front of people before, in any language. I've never told other kids what it's like to be me. It feels weird. Uncomfortable.

But as I somehow string the words together, I start to feel something else swelling inside me. These words, hidden in another language, are the most truthful ones I have ever spoken. The more I say, the more urgent it feels. My voice becomes stronger. By the end of the first page, I'm feeling it. I'm feeling that what I am saying is important.

It's an unfamiliar taste, this confidence on my tongue. When I look up, I'm feeling hopeful, somehow connected to these kids I've never bonded with before. My eyes are expectant. So is my heart.

But when my eyes fall on Brooklyn, my insecurities return. She's watching me, hands tucked under her chin, as still as porcelain. Is she really interested in what I'm saying or is she staring at the freak show that is me?

Deterred, I glance at Monsieur Oliver. He gives me his trademark encouraging smile, and I plug along.

My voice warbles through the next few pages, somewhat diminished. The swell inside me contracts, and by the time I reach the last few lines, I'm speaking so softly that I'm practically reading to myself: "There are moments when I forget about this horn and live in the dream of who I really am. In those moments, I can see myself clearly. And so I long for the day when I don't have this horn anymore, when everyone else will see me clearly, too."

I look up, and I'm met with silence. Do they know it's over? "*C'était magnifique,* Jewel," Monsieur Oliver says, beaming. "*Merci, merci,* for sharing *ton histoire* with us."

I hurry back to my desk, and Monsieur calls on Brooklyn to read her essay. As she strides to the front of the class, I sit down self-consciously.

Mystic leans across the aisle and whispers, "That was great! I hardly understood a word, but you were awesome."

I shake my head, mortified, as Brooklyn faces the class, smiling naturally. She doesn't clear her throat, or shuffle back and forth awkwardly. She reads her essay clearly, and everyone pays attention. Every eye is on Brooklyn, in a good way. Her pronunciation is decent. Her story is passable. But it's her confidence that hypnotizes. Everyone wants to hear what comes out of Brooklyn's mouth.

Suddenly I'm wading deep in the swamp waters of post-speech shame. There was a moment when I was thinking . . .

maybe. Maybe I could compete at the regional competition. Maybe I could stand on that stage in front of judges and strangers.

But now I realize what a mistake that would be. I can't be up there in front of all those people looking like this.

When the bell rings, Monsieur Oliver asks me to stay behind, so I wait by my desk, feeling embarrassed, and a little betrayed.

After everyone else leaves, he leans against the desk in front of mine. *"Alors,"* he says, his eyes shining. "How was it? I wanted you to see that you could do it."

I struggle not to roll my eyes. "It was a disaster. Didn't you see that?"

"Not true at all. You were on a roll, Jewel. I'm sure you felt it," he says. "I know it took a little time for you to get going, but there was . . . *un moment.* A moment, *vraiment. Tu comprends?"*

I look down. "Yeah, but a moment is not enough."

He chuckles. "It's good, Jewel. What you wrote is really good. And with some practice, you'll be able to present it like *un vrai savant."*

Me? A true scholar? His words reach my heart, and I want to believe him.

"I'll help you get ready," he says. "We have to submit a name and an essay to the Alliance by next week. What do you say?"

My eyes meet his, and I want to say yes! I want it to be *my* name and *my* essay. I want to be the one to do this. But he doesn't understand. My horn is what everyone sees. I can't compete with normal kids. There's no way.

My mind flashes to this old black-and-white movie that Grandma was watching not long after she moved in with us. It was about people in a freak show. Yes, believe it or not, there was a time when a freak show was a real, actual thing— where people with weird deformities would be on display in front of heartless, gawking strangers. These "freaks" would travel on circus trains from town to town, and every night they'd suffer a new array of strangers' eyes.

Grandma had fallen asleep on the couch and didn't know I'd come in to watch. When she woke up and saw what was happening, she grabbed the remote and shut it off fast, which told me something that I hadn't truly realized before.

I was a freak, too.

The movie made me wonder what my life would have been like in another time. I pictured the unicorn girl standing alongside the lizard man and the bearded lady, enduring the pointing, and the laughing, and the staring. It wouldn't matter how smart I was, or how well I spoke French. I'd just be one of them.

How much has changed, really?

If I didn't have this horn, I would say yes to Monsieur

Oliver right now. But I do have a horn. And the chances of that changing are dwindling by the second. Because even if Dr. Stein changes his mind, I know my mom will never change hers.

So I take a note from my mom's playbook. "No," I say, sad but firm. "I'm sorry. I just can't do it."

Ghosted

This is the worst day of my life.

My mom has destroyed my chances with Dr. Stein, which has destroyed my chances with the essay competition. I feel so dumb. Why did I get my hopes up?

I didn't want to go home, so, feeling like an empty shell, I followed Mystic and Nicholas to his house after school. We're in Nicholas's den, surrounded by shelves lined with hardcover books; paintings with actual paint on them; black-and-white photos of Nicholas, his parents, and Sarah at different ages; and a saltwater aquarium with a real live Nemo swimming inside.

Nothing here reflects *my* life in any way.

While Nicholas and Mystic play a video game, I open my email one last and final time.

Still nothing from Dr. Stein. I've been ghosted.

Gloomily, I pick up a copy of *Highwaymen* that I've read before, and try to block out my life.

The Watering Hole, with its long counter and assortment of wooden tables and chairs, looks like a regular Western saloon, just like the ones you see in movies. And it is—until you look closer and notice the small cabinet with a sign under it that reads BREAK GLASS FOR GRENADE. (Pro tip: there were no grenades in the 1800s.) Or the intricately shaped bottles behind the bar with labels like Dragon's Blood and Elixir of Sphinx. Or the bird perched at the end of the counter that happens to be a phoenix.

In the middle of this scene, Esmeralda sits at a table with Wesley and two of his baddies playing poker. That's Esmeralda's game, and the fact that she's willing to sit at a table with Wesley tells me the stakes are high. Her long green-and-black barmaid's dress is hiked up just enough to reveal the ace of spades tucked into the garter around her left thigh. Spoiler: Esmeralda cheats at cards.

What I would give to just disappear into Hot Springs and stay there forever.

"Shoot!" cries Nicholas.

"Nice one," Mystic says, her eyes glued to the screen where Nicholas's guy must have bitten it. She dumps her controller onto the couch and asks, "What's wrong, Jewels?"

I look up from *Highwaymen*. "What do you mean?"

"You've been really quiet."

"Very unlike you," adds Nicholas.

"I told Monsieur Oliver that I'm not doing the French competition."

"What!" Mystic says. "But you have to."

I drop my head. "I just can't."

"Wait, why not?" asks Nicholas.

I'm afraid to speak. I'm sure I'll burst out crying. I feel Mystic's hand on my shoulder. "Well . . . my mom ruined my chances with Dr. Stein," I say, looking up at her.

"What happened?"

"He called her."

"He called her? How?"

"Who knows? What I do know is I'm not getting this thing taken off any time soon." As I point to my horn, I spot Carmen standing in the rain outside the window.

"Huh?" Nicholas says. "What are you talking about?"

"Jewel found a doctor who could take off her horn."

Nicholas turns to me in disbelief.

"Yeah, this doctor in LA thinks he can do it. I was email-ing him pretending to be my mom. But then he called my actual mom and it all went . . ." I make an exploding sound.

"Oh, crap," Mystic says.

"Wait a minute!" Nicholas holds his hands up between us. "Is this for real? Why didn't you tell me?!"

"We all know your strange attachment to Jewel's horn."

"I don't have a strange attachment to—"

"Anyway." Mystic turns to me, ignoring him. "Do you think you can change your mom's mind?"

"I doubt it." Saying these words literally feels like a dagger in my heart. "She just doesn't get it. She doesn't know what it's like to be a freak."

"You're not a freak," Mystic says, forcing a smile.

I force one back. "And you're not a good liar."

"It's a pretty horn," she tries.

"It's a horn," I spit. "None of it matters now. My mom told him no, and he hasn't written me back since they talked, so . . ." I shake my head. I'm done talking about this. Time to move on.

Nicholas looks relieved. "Good."

Mystic pounces on him. "Nick!"

"I'm just saying. It's probably not a good idea."

"You sound *just* like my mom," I say.

"Um, I highly doubt we share the same reasoning about this."

"Oh, really?"

"It's actually serious, okay?" Nicholas looks right into my eyes. "Here's the deal. If you get your horn taken off . . . really . . . you could die."

"Dr. Stein is a *specialist*. He's not going to—"

"I'm not talking about the surgery, Jewel." He waves a hand, batting my words away.

"Then what are you talking about?"

"A unicorn can't live without its horn."

Mystic covers a smile with her hand.

"It's not funny, Mystic," says Nicholas. "It's true. Am I the only one who knows anything about unicorn mythology around here?"

"Um, yes," we say together.

"I'm being serious!" Nicholas says, now frustrated, too. "It's a well-known fact that unicorns can't live without their horns."

Carmen whinnies on the other side of the glass. I turn to the window and say, "I'm not a unicorn."

"How do you know for sure?" Nicholas says.

I put my hands to my face. Sometimes I wonder about him.

"You know who would love your horn?" Nicholas says.

"Esmeralda." It's just like him to use *Highwaymen* against me. He knows how I feel about Esmeralda.

Mystic looks confused, then says, "You mean that lady from the comic book?"

"Graphic novel," Nicholas and I say at the same time.

"It comes out every month?" she says. "Doesn't that make it a comic book?"

Nicholas and I look at each other. Mystic has a point. But Nicholas thinks that "graphic novel" sounds more legit than "comic book," so that's what we call it. Nicholas blanks the question altogether and turns things back to me. "Plus, without your horn, don't you think your nose would look big?"

"Cut it out, Nick." Mystic throws a sofa pillow his way. "He doesn't know what he's talking about."

"You're not really thinking about it, are you?" he asks, now seriously.

"Of course!" I exclaim. "If my mom would let me, I'd be in LA tomorrow."

"Jewel," Nicholas says, "you're the only one with a unicorn horn in the whole entire world. You need to keep it."

Mystic shakes her head. "Get a grip, Nick."

But his words seep into me. *What if I am a unicorn? What if I do need my horn?* I sneak a glance at Carmen and try to push these thoughts away.

Carmen is the unicorn. I'm just a girl with a horn.

One is distinctly magical. One is distinctly not.

Right?

* * *

At dinner I take the silent treatment to the next level. Okay, so this may not be the most mature thing I've ever done, but begging and well-reasoned arguments have gotten me nowhere.

Mom doles out our plates of chicken fingers, mac and cheese, and broccoli salad, bought with her discount at the Walmart deli. When she starts to cut up Grandma's chicken, Grandma clucks her tongue. "I can do that."

"It's easier for me," Mom says, cutting the strips into manageable pieces. Mom's right, of course. It's still not easy for Grandma to use her left hand.

"Angela, please. I'm not a child," Grandma says, annoyed, but she waits for Mom to finish.

When Mom sits down, she looks at me deliberately. "Eat."

I fold my arms across my chest instead.

"How was your day?" Grandma asks Mom, trying to lighten the mood.

"It was fine, Mama. Thank you for asking."

Grandma fixes her eyes on me. "Tell me something you got up to today."

I'm stuck. I hate ignoring Grandma. But I have to make my point. So of course the mood doesn't lighten. There's just more uncomfortable silence. After about a minute of that, Grandma breaks. "Okay, I can't take it. Somebody say something."

Mom heaves a gigantic sigh. "I don't know what there is to say right now."

Grandma looks at me again. "I hate to say this, darlin', but you're being childish."

"Me?"

"You're punishing your mom, and that's not fair."

Not fair! I make my wide eyes do the talking for me.

"Not fair," Grandma repeats, and we go back to eating silently. Mom glances my way, but then looks down at her food.

This is my last chance. I can feel it. I can either sulk away to my room and be disappointed for the rest of my life, or I can say something. It might not change anything—in fact, I'm pretty sure it won't—but a girl's got to do what a girl's got to do.

So I clear my throat and stand up. "I understand, Mom." She looks up at me, either surprised or wincing, it's hard to tell which. "I'm your daughter, and you don't want anything bad to happen to me."

They're both looking at me now. I take a breath and plow on. "BUT," I say. "This is *my* life. I'm thirteen years old. That may not sound old to you two, but thirteen years living with a horn on your head is a long time. If I don't try this, how will I ever do the things I want to do? Can you imagine me at the Eiffel Tower looking like this? And I want to see the Eiffel Tower. Up close. In person. I want to ride the elevator to the top and look over the city that I think might be the greatest place in this whole entire world. I don't just want to imagine it. I want to be there. I want to speak French with real Parisians. I want to eat croissants and see the *Mona Lisa*. And I want to be in a French competition for my school—and win." I pause, gathering myself together. "I have tried. I have endured a million stares. But there's just so much a person can take. So much a girl can miss out on. If I don't try now, I'm afraid I'll be disappointed for the rest of my life. I'll quit expecting anything good. I can already feel that happening." I search my mom's eyes. "So, don't be mad at me if I become that messed-up girl. Because the way I feel, I don't know who else I can end up becoming."

We look at each other for a long moment, but she doesn't say anything back.

"May I be excused?" I finally ask.

"Sure," she says, and puts her fork down.

I stand there for a second longer, hoping for something back. But I don't get it. I can feel that the subject is closed.

Going into my bedroom, I shut the door behind me. My head is pounding. Why doesn't she understand? This is my one chance. And she's going to let it slip away.

My collage of faraway places mocks me from over my bed. The Eiffel Tower. The Tower of London. The Taj Mahal. All places I'll never go. Growling, I grab the collage off the wall and throw it to the floor.

I'm so full of anger and sadness and frustration that I feel like I might explode. I yank down the cord to my window blinds—and almost have a heart attack.

Carmen is standing on the walkway outside my window. "You scared me to death," I say, breathlessly.

She whinnies and jerks her head up. Her eyes are agitated, and I wonder for the billionth time how it's possible that we can feel each other's emotions. I pull open the window and crawl out onto the sill. "What are you doing here?"

Carmen's head is thrashing. She's hardly ever like this. Placing my hand on her nose, I try to soothe her. "Carmen," I whisper, and she whinnies again. "Shhhhh," I say gently. "What's wrong?" I ask, but really, I already know.

I'm upset, so she's upset. It doesn't always happen this

way. Most of the time, she calms me when I'm like this. But when my emotions are so big, like they are now, she succumbs and feels them, too.

"Calm down. It's going to be okay," I say, even though it's not. But just being together, my hand on her face, our heartbeats seem to settle. We stay this way for a long time, until I say, "You know what you are, Carmen. You're supposed to have a horn. But I'm not like you." I lean my head against her nose and whisper, "I'm a girl."

As Carmen nuzzles me, I catch sight of the light turning on in Emma's room across the parking lot. Carmen may be my unicorn, but she doesn't understand me any better than Emma does. She doesn't know what it's like to be . . . different. "I just can't do it anymore," I say quietly. "I need to be normal."

I wipe a tear from my cheek. "I'm sorry," I tell her, and I mean it. Then I crawl back through the window and close it shut. But even when I pull down the blinds, I can still see her pointy profile standing there, watching over me.

Suspicions

The locker room is emptying out around us as Mystic and I change after PE. I'm feeling tired and moody from the night before, and spending the past hour on the volleyball court didn't help. Why Coach T. thinks it's a good idea to make a girl with a horn on her head play group sports is beyond me.

After slipping on my sweatshirt, I close my locker to see Mystic balancing a silver bracelet on her index finger. It has a little ornament hanging from it. "Is that the Eiffel Tower?" I ask, amazed.

"Yeah," Mystic says, somewhat proudly. "It's for you."

"Really? It's beautiful, Myst."

I go to slip the bracelet on my wrist, but it's too small.

"It's not for your arm," she says.

I look up at her.

"It's for your horn."

"My horn?" I look at it again, confused. "Why does my horn need a . . ."

"Hornlet? That's what I was thinking about calling it. Catchy, right?" She touches the metal Eiffel Tower, and it swings slightly. "I wanted to cheer you up about Dr. Stein. I mean, I don't know anyone else who gets to wear horn flair, so . . ."

She made this for me. She invented it *for* me. This is the first time she's ever made me something, so I know how special it is. But the last thing I want is to draw more attention to this horn I'll have forever.

"Too weird?" She bites her lip.

"No! It's nice. I just . . ."

"You don't want your horn, so why would you want a hornlet?" she says, pretty much reading my mind. Mystic goes to take it back, but I don't let her.

"It's nice, really," I say. "I'm just not ready to wear it . . . yet." I don't have the heart to tell her that I probably won't be ready to wear it ever. And I know that's a shame, because it's beautiful. It is so authentically Mystic.

"Totally get that," Mystic says, then reaches into her locker and pulls out another piece of jewelry.

"Brooklyn's bracelet!" I say. I was beginning to think Mystic might "forget" to bring it back.

"Yep. So beautiful."

"And so not yours."

"I know." Mystic gazes at the bracelet's pink stone and whispers, "I'll miss you," then goes and places it on a far bench. As she walks back, she opens her palms and says, "Did you doubt me?"

"Of course not," I say, but I'm relieved that Mystic is giving up a life of crime. As she closes her locker, a toilet flushes inside the locker room. Our eyes dart to each other's. We thought we were alone.

"Crap," Mystic mouths as Emma appears from around the stalls. Like a bracelet-seeking missile, she spots Brooklyn's bracelet right away.

"Where did this come from?" Emma asks, and picks it up. Frozen, we watch her admire the bracelet, then slip it onto her wrist. We're still frozen as she walks past us. Emma glances at me briefly, with what I take as a knowing smile, but after she's gone, I have no idea what she knows.

"She heard us," Mystic whispers, panic in her eyes. "She knows I took the bracelet."

"Maybe not."

"Did you see that look on her face?" Mystic says, then adds urgently. "What did I say? Like exactly what?"

"I don't know. Something about Brooklyn's bracelet."

"I said those words? I said 'Brooklyn's bracelet'?"

I frown before I can stop myself. "Maybe I did."

"Oh, crap, I'm screwed."

"*We're* screwed," I say, because I may not have taken Brooklyn's bracelet, but I'm a part of this. For all Emma knows, we're in it together.

At lunch, we watch as Emma ceremoniously walks in and presents the bracelet to Brooklyn, who is completely overjoyed as she puts it on her wrist. Emma doesn't look over at us, but I know she knows. She was in that stall listening to everything we said. I can feel myself sweating under my shirt.

We can barely eat, watching—but trying not to be noticed—to see if Emma says anything. It seems like she doesn't. She just basks in Brooklyn's gratitude.

"What's going on with you guys?" Nicholas asks, looking up from his drawing.

"Nothing," Mystic and I say, turning to him guiltily.

He scrutinizes both of us for a long second. "Yeah, right," he says, then goes back to his phoenix.

"Look," Mystic whispers, and I turn back to the popular table. Brooklyn is getting up. "Where's she going?"

I shrug my shoulders and grab my backpack as Brooklyn leaves the cafeteria. "I'll go see. Meet you in French."

In the hall, I follow Brooklyn, staying far enough behind so she won't become suspicious. She's heading toward the eighth-grade hall. If she catches me, I can always use the excuse that I was on my way to French class to use the internet.

Brooklyn turns the corner up ahead and by the time I get there, she's disappeared. Shoot!

Monsieur Oliver's room is open, so I resort to Plan B, to actually check my email. But as I step inside the classroom, I see Brooklyn standing by his desk. *Is she telling him?*

"Oh, hi," I say awkwardly.

Monsieur Oliver offers me a shallow wave, then he looks back at Brooklyn, so I sit down in front of a computer and try to listen to what they're saying. After a moment, Brooklyn books it past me into the hall. I guess she wouldn't be caught dead showing up early for class. My eyes flit to Monsieur Oliver, afraid of what she's told him, but he's just grading papers. Not looking at me suspiciously at all.

Trying to calm the paranoia that's building inside, I open my email.

Still nothing. One more thing not going right today.

* * *

After school, I find an empty seat on the bus and close my eyes. Boys yell and play games on their phones. Girls, quieter, talk seriously like they think they're already in high school. I float through it all like a ghost.

A group of girls moves down the aisle. I know their faces and some of their names. Megan Brotherton, Liz Wilson, someone I don't know, and Sonya Vai. They pass and don't even look at me. I'm just the girl with the horn.

It makes me think: *Would they even recognize me without the horn? How many people actually know what my face looks like? What if I really did show up one day all hornless and normal?* Everyone might think I was a transfer student from some other town. I could start over. Emma and I might even be friends again.

J + E = BBFF ☺

What?

It's written in black Magic Marker on the back of the seat in front of me. I feel ambushed. Dumbfounded, I stare at the letters. Fourth grade. Emma's marker. Her handwriting. My smiley face. *Am I actually sitting in our old elementary school bus?*

This is where we used to sit every day on our way home from school. Emma's the one who liked to say we would be Best *Best* Friends Forever. *Hold it together, Jewel.*

I look around, feeling exposed. Like my feelings are so big that they surely must be seen. But nobody is looking. Nobody knows how much I miss Emma. I miss sitting on the steps outside our apartments and talking for hours while Carmen watched over us. Emma was the only person in my life who ever saw my unicorn. Back then, we'd even call her *our* unicorn.

Emma's not on the bus today—probably at some club meeting or cheerleading practice—but if she were, I'd make her look at what we wrote. I swear I could make her remember. Gently, I trace the letters written by Emma's hand with my finger. It wasn't that long ago, but it feels like forever. But who am I kidding? I couldn't make Emma do anything now, especially be my friend again.

Everything's piling up on me. My mom telling me *no*. Dr. Stein ghosting me. Emma overhearing me and Mystic. Turning down the French competition. And now this. As soon as I see our apartment complex, I'm out of my seat and up the aisle.

"Well, look at you bust a move," the bus driver says, surprised to see me up front so fast. "Now, that's what I'm talking about." She's used to waiting on me because if Emma is on the bus, I always let her get off first so it won't be awkward.

I don't say a word, just stare at the doors. *Open. Open. Open.* When they do, I rush away from my bittersweet past.

Carmen is waiting for me in the parking lot, but I hurry past her without a word. I tear up the stairs, put my key in the lock, and open the door. A cheerful song from an old movie greets me when I get inside.

"Hi, sweetie!"

"Hi, Grandma!" I have to really work to muster that exclamation point.

"How was your day?" Grandma asks from the couch.

"Fine," I answer before slipping into our room and closing the door. I really, really hope she'll get the message and leave me alone for a minute.

I fling myself across my bed. How could everything be going so wrong all at the same time? For an instant, I picture myself on a stage at a French competition without a horn on my head. Ha! What a dream! I don't understand how I could be so good at something and never get to use it. It's just one more thing to slip away. Like my stuffed unicorn. Like Dr. Stein. Like my best friend . . . all gone and there's nothing I can do.

And now that Emma knows about Mystic and the bracelet—and knows that I knew about it—that's just another wedge to widen the gap between us.

There's a tap on the door. "Can you give me a minute, Grandma?" I call out.

The door opens anyway. It's Mom. "You all right, honey?" she asks.

"Why aren't you at work?" I ask, stiffening.

"I'm going now, actually. With everybody being sick, my schedule's a nightmare. I'll be late tonight." She sits down beside me on my bed and touches my cheek. "What's wrong, baby?"

"Everything," I say, the sadness sticking in my throat.

"Oh, Jewel," Mom says and strokes my hair. "I'm sorry."

I look down. I can't even meet her eyes.

"I know I'm always telling you to make lemonade out of lemons in life," she says. "That you can be whoever you want to be, even with a horn. And I know it bothers you. I can't possibly understand what it's like being you."

"You can't," I whisper, feeling completely defeated.

It's silent between us until Mom says, "It'll be okay."

I shake my head. "It doesn't matter."

Her fingers cup the bottom of my chin and lift my eyes to hers. "It *does* matter. It matters a lot how you feel. Don't you *ever* say it doesn't matter."

"No, you were right." I have no energy left for this fight anymore. "Even if I went to California, the surgery probably wouldn't work, and then I'd be even more disappointed."

Mom doesn't say anything.

"It's okay." I try to pull myself together.

"Jewel." Mom says, snaking her arm around my shoulder.

"I feel so stupid, Mom."

She pulls me into her chest. And that does it. I'm sobbing like a six-year-old.

Lemonade

When I wake up the next morning, for a blissful moment I forget. But my stuffed-up nose from all the crying reminds me of everything: Emma and the bracelet, Monsieur Oliver and the essay competition, Mom and her sad face.

Good things just don't happen to us.

That's what I finally got through this thick head of mine. Grandma injures her arm at the factory, Mom works at a job she hates, and I have a horn. So what if we have dreams of something better? It's just the way it is. People like us will never live on Park Street. People like us live here, like this.

As my feet touch the floor and I rise out of bed, I can tell that something has changed. My horn feels heavier on my head. It feels final. And I finally understand why Mom does what she does every day.

She has no choice.

She always wants me to make lemonade out of lemons because her life has been full of lemons. Sour, bitter, yellow things. Hopeless things, lemons. And my mom has never found a way to make lemonade.

I am like her now. I live in a lemonade-less apartment with a lemonade-less family, and that's the way it is. I decide one thing with certainty: Last night is the last time I'll cry for at least a year. Tears only belong in a world where lemonade is possible.

It's bright outside, too bright. I turn the clock between my bed and Grandma's and see that it's after eleven. Why didn't they wake me? It's Friday—a school day.

I hurry out of the bedroom and see Grandma and Mom huddled at the table, Grandma's arm around Mom's shoulders.

"Mom? What's wrong?"

She looks up at me. Tears streak her face like I can still feel on my cheeks from the night before. And my mom *never* cries.

"Sit down, Jewel," Grandma says, and I do.

"Grandma, what is it?"

"It's okay, baby doll. Just give your mama a minute."

Helplessly, I watch Mom struggle to pull it together. She pushes her hair back, and wipes her splotchy face with her palm. This must be bad if she let me miss school over it.

"It's okay," Mom finally says, giving me a weak smile.

"Um, it seems like it's not."

"It is," Grandma assures me.

"You're freaking me out!"

Grandma looks at Mom. "Sweetie, tell her."

Mom sniffs, and sits up straighter. "Okay," she says, then looks at me.

"Mom?" I whisper.

"Jewel, honey, I've got something to tell you."

I stare at her, waiting. *Tell me already!*

"I want you to know that what you want matters," she says, her voice breaking. "It does. And I never want *you* to give up on you."

"Okay, Mom," I say. *What is going on?*

"It's just . . . you're the most important person in the world to me. You're my baby. Without you . . ." She trails off and her chin starts to tremble. "I don't know what I would do."

"What your mom is trying to say," Grandma says, "is you are *her* miracle, and she only wants you to be happy."

"I'm happy," I say, trying to make it better. "I'm okay. Really, I love you, and I'm fine."

"No, you're not!" Mom says, and her face twists with a flash of anger. "I don't know why you have this horn on your head. I don't. I wish I did. And when none of the doctors could take it off, I just hoped you'd learn to be okay with it." Mom closes her eyes. I think of Monsieur Oliver, saying the same kind of thing. All these adults wanting to change me into some confident girl I'm not. "But you're not okay with it. And I can't make you okay with it. I'm just so afraid something bad will happen."

"I don't understand, Mom. What are you talking about?"

"I called Dr. Stein this morning."

My heart stops. "You what?"

"I decided that it wasn't fair for me not to get all the information. So I called him. He told me all about the surgery and what he thinks he can do for you."

"And?" I lean forward in my chair.

"He talked about your horn"—she makes a vague gesture with both hands—"*differently* than the other doctors. He said there would have to be more tests run to be sure. And he promised he wouldn't even try to remove it unless he was ninety-nine-point-nine percent sure it was going to work."

"What are you saying?" I ask breathlessly.

Her eyes meet mine. "I want you to try."

I feel a sudden rush of lemonade inside. Throwing my arms in the air, I scream through the ceiling. "Woo-hoo!" I'm jumping around the room now. *I'm going to get my horn taken off!* I hug my mom, and whisper, "Mom, thank you. Thank you. Thank you."

"Wait, honey," she says, pushing me back and holding on to my arms. "One more thing. I went in to see Mr. Perez this morning."

Whenever Mr. Perez comes up, it's never good.

"If Dr. Stein can do the surgery, you'll be in Los Angeles for a few weeks, and—I can't miss that much work."

I feel myself deflating. "You can't come with me?"

"But I can," Grandma says. And I realize this has been discussed and decided without me.

I look at Mom. "It's the best we can do," she says.

"We can do this, darlin'," Grandma says. "You and me."

Suddenly, every cell of my body floods with relief. Grandma wipes a tear from her cheek, and I see her hand is shaking. "Oh, my," she says, standing up.

"Are you all right, Mama?" Mom asks as we watch Grandma disappear into our bedroom.

Mom looks at me, and I look at her.

"Grandma?"

"Come help me with this!" she says, and we both hurry to the bedroom.

Grandma is sitting on the floor next to the closet, pointing to something inside. "I can't get it," she says to me. "Reach in there, Jewel."

I drop to my knees and grab the jar she's pointing at, buried at the back of the closet. When I deposit it on the floor between us, I hear Mom gasp.

It's full of money.

The jar is crammed with crumpled bills and tons of coins. Grandma rests one hand on the lid. "It's not much, but we'll need spending money for the trip."

"What . . . how?" Mom asks, stunned.

"My hope jar. My dribs and drabs, the little bits I've managed to cling on to from the little money I've made." She grabs my hand and looks up at Mom. "I just wish it was enough for you to go, Angela. I wish there was enough for you to quit your job and be done with Mr. Perez for good. I wish it was more."

"But Mama, we've had lots of rainy days before now."

"I know, but"—Grandma grins at me—"maybe I was saving this for a sunny one. Something good is happening for our girl."

I take the jar to the kitchen table and they watch as I count out the money. Three hundred twenty-four dollars and forty-seven cents. Wow.

"Mama," Mom whispers.

"So it's settled," Grandma says, the wrinkles on her face becoming exclamation points around her eyes. It's like God or Santa has spoken.

"So, when are we going?" I ask.

"Tuesday," Mom says back.

My eyes go wide. So do Grandma's. "Tuesday?!" we both say at the same time.

"Tuesday," Mom repeats.

Maybe it's the waves of pent-up energy, but we all three suddenly dissolve into laughter.

"Oh, boy," Grandma says, shaking her head.

Mom puts her hand on mine. Her eyes have never contained more love, I swear. "Let's get you ready for Los Angeles."

* * *

I don't go to school. What's there for me anyway? One more chance for the whole school to see me as the unicorn girl? No thanks.

I *could* go and tell Monsieur Oliver what's happening. Maybe I could do the essay competition after all. But what if I don't get my horn taken off? What if it doesn't work? Ugh! It's just too much for my pinball machine of a brain to process right now. He's probably already submitted Josh Martin's name anyway. I hate to admit it, but Josh would be an excellent choice. He's almost as good at French as I am. Almost.

Mom and I come to an agreement. If I email my teachers and get all my assignments for while I'm away, I can spend the next few days getting ready. The thought of not going to school again for weeks is like a gallon of lemonade in itself.

When I'm sure that Mystic is home from school, I call to tell her first.

"I can't believe it!" she says.

"I know, right?" I'm still glowing from the buzz of it all.

"Are you excited? Are you scared?" She asks about ten versions of these questions, which I mostly answer in the hyper-affirmative.

Nicholas is far less excited about the prospects of my surgery. He actually tries to talk me out of it. He reminds me of our future road trip to find all the magical creature geolocations on our map, and how it won't be as cool to visit those places if I don't have a horn. *What* is he talking about?

On Saturday, he bombards me further with texts like:

If you take off your horn, you won't be a unicorn.

If you take off your horn, you'll lose your magic.

If you take off your horn, I won't recognize you.

I text him back:

You're wrong.

What magic?

Of course you'll recognize me.

His words work on me, though. There's someone I still

have to tell. I don't want to, but the more I put it off, the harder it will be.

That night, I go outside and meet Carmen at the foot of the stairs. I sit so my eyes can be level with hers. The parking lot is empty of people, and a sole light flickers nearby. She nudges my face with her nose.

And I tell her.

After I'm done, I pull away and look into her eyes. "Please," I say. "Please understand. I have to do this."

But she doesn't understand. I could read that thought a thousand miles away. "Please, Carmen," I say again.

Carmen lets out a whinny and shakes her mane, and I feel uncertainty settle over me. I'm calm but she's not? That *never* happens. She's either super serene or upset along with me. I'm not upset now—I'm resolved, even excited. But Carmen stomps her hoof onto the pavement and throws up her head. "Carmen," I say, "It's okay."

But she's not.

When Mom finally calls me inside, I reluctantly leave Carmen at the steps. I've never felt so out of sync with her in my entire life.

Before I go to bed, I call Mystic one more time. I'm still unsettled by Carmen being so weird, and I think talking with Mystic will make me feel better. It does and it doesn't.

"You have to bring me back something cool from Hollywood," she says, right before we hang up. "And, hey."

"What is it?" I ask.

"It's just—going to be different. I mean, things will change. Like, between us."

Huh? "Nothing's going to change with us. And maybe it won't change with my horn, either. I mean, there's a chance he won't be able to do it," I say. "Don't tell anyone where I'm going, by the way. I don't want everyone to think it's about to happen and then I come back and it didn't work."

"You're not going out there for nothing," Mystic says, and I swear a part of her sounds worried. "He'll do it. And you'll come back different."

That's what I'm hoping for to the tip of my horn. But a part of me is afraid of being disappointed. A part of me is holding back, just in case.

Tuesday

"Come with me."

I say these words in the dark like a prayer. "Carmen, please come with me."

It's 4 a.m. and I'm standing by our car waiting for Mom and Grandma. "Please, Carmen."

I've been talking to her like this for twenty minutes, because the fear that she won't forgive me has been elbowing for space in my brain all night, and now it's pushed its way to the front.

"Come on," I say, stamping my feet because it's cold. Carmen stamps her foot back at me—because she's mad. "You have to understand."

When I hear Mom and Grandma coming out of the apartment, I lean into Carmen and whisper, "I'll see you in

LA, okay? Or at the airport. Or on the plane! Okay?" I put my hand on her nose, grasping for confirmation.

Mom is dragging Grandma's suitcase down the stairs as my lips brush against Carmen's soft cheek. "I know I don't deserve it. I know I've been a terrible friend. But I need you. Please, Carmen. Be there."

After we load the car, I stare at her through the backseat window. Our eyes stay connected until we pull out of the parking lot, and then . . . my unicorn is gone.

I face forward and grip my hands together. *She'll show up,* I reassure myself. *Carmen always does.*

When we get to the Atlanta airport, Mom wants to park and go inside with us, but Grandma tells her to drop us at the curb. She has a long ride back and a shift to work in just a few hours. Mom hasn't shed a tear since Grandma showed us her money jar. She's been extremely matter-of-fact about everything since then.

As I pull out our luggage, Grandma wraps her arms around Mom and says, "It's going to be all right, Angie." My mom nods curtly, but I can see everything she's trying to hide through her eyes.

Mom grabs my hands. "It's going to be *more* than all right," she says, unconvincingly. "You'll come back without your horn and I will love you all the same."

"What if I come back *with* my horn?"

"Then I'll love you even more." She tries at a grin but can't hold it for more than a second. "So long as you come back to me," she says, and takes me into her arms. She doesn't cry. She just holds me.

When she pulls away, I tell her, "Okay."

It's legit strange to see so many unchecked emotions on my mom's face. She's usually really good at hiding them. I wonder if she'll let it all out on the drive home without us.

As we enter the airport, Grandma and I turn one last time to wave to Mom, who hasn't gotten back into the car yet. Looking at her, I feel the same ache in my heart that I felt this morning with Carmen.

Grandma takes my hand and we walk inside, and—oh, boy. There they are. All the people. All the eyes. They find me seemingly by instinct. Every person who passes stares with that familiar mix of disbelief and pity. Wow, I don't think I've ever had so many strangers looking at me before.

Lacing her arm through mine, Grandma pulls me closer. "Don't let it bother you. They don't know you."

Easy for her to say. This. Is. Why. I'm. Doing. This. There are so many smaller reasons, but this is the big one. It's not that I don't want attention. I just don't want *this* kind of attention. I want to walk through an airport unseen. Or stand on a competition stage seen. But for who I am. Not because I'm the girl with the horn.

When the plane takes off, Grandma holds my hand again. Neither one of us has ever flown before. We're both excited and afraid at the same time. I'm in the window seat, and Grandma is in the middle next to a man wearing a suit and thick black glasses. Once we're in the sky, he pulls out his laptop and opens his little tray table. I watch how he does it so I can open mine, too.

He's fine now, but when we stopped in front of him and Grandma said, "I believe those are our seats," and pointed to the ones beside him—he was not what I'd call *overjoyed* to see me.

The captain announces that the seat belt sign is off and we are "free to move about the cabin," and Grandma elbows my arm. "They really say that!" she says. "I always thought they made that part up for the movies." We break into giggles. This is definitely the coolest thing I've ever done.

I can't seem to stop looking out the window at the clouds beneath us that resemble a collection of cotton balls. Puffy and white. Otherworldly. I almost expect Carmen to come running on top of them, chasing our plane across the sky.

I got a text from Nicholas this morning listing the places I need to look for from my window on the plane. Like Oxford, Mississippi, where the griffin came from, and Abilene, Texas, whence the harpy hailed, as Nicholas said. We'll be flying over the real Truth or Consequences, New Mexico, too (which was once the real Hot Springs), but I can't imagine how I will see any of these places underneath all those clouds.

"I hate that your mother is missing this," Grandma says, interrupting my thoughts of Carmen, Nicholas, and *Highwaymen*.

"Me, too." Kind of. I'm sorry Mom's missing the plane part, but I'm not sorry she's missing the rest of it. She doesn't like the staring either, and it's not like it's stopped now that we're on the plane. Every few minutes, I catch someone sneaking a glimpse of me over the back of their seat.

Grandma leans toward me and says quietly, "I've never seen so many different kinds of people in one place in my whole life," and I realize that Grandma has been people-watching them like some of them have been people-watching me. Her eyes wander to the next row, where a woman is typing on her laptop. A turquoise hijab covers her head and wraps around her neck in a stylish way. There's a girl in my school who wears one, but I don't think Grandma has ever seen a hijab-wearing person in real life. She just nods, taking it in, then turns back to the window.

I watch her gazing at the impossible clouds. The light reflects off her face, and she looks ten years younger. "Do you think they'll come over with one of those carts and offer us a drink soon?" Grandma whispers.

Peering around the seat in front of me, I don't see any carts yet. "Are you thirsty?"

She shakes her head. "No, I just want them to do that."

I grin, glad she's the one coming with me.

Everything's happening so fast that I can't quite get my head around it. I touch my horn with my fingers. I don't want to get my hopes up too much in case Dr. Stein can't do it.

But who am I kidding? My hopes are higher than this plane in the sky.

* * *

People at the LA airport stare less than people at the Atlanta one, which is a relief. I guess they're used to freakier people out here.

At the bottom of the escalator, several men stand holding signs with people's names on them. The one who wears a fancy blue cap and a navy suit is holding a small cardboard sign that reads CONRAD. I grab Grandma's arm and point to him. "That's our guy," I say excitedly.

"Are you Jewel?" he asks when we walk up. George, as he introduces himself, is probably a few years younger than Grandma and has salt-and-pepper hair and a gray mustache. He smiles at me and doesn't look at my horn even once, which makes me immediately like him.

George takes us to baggage claim, and when we spot our brand-new-to-us suitcases (thank you, Goodwill!), he pulls them off the conveyer. "Follow me, ladies," he says, and we hurry to keep up.

The automatic doors slide open, and we walk out into the California sun. It was cool when we left Atlanta, but here, it's warm. I tear off my sweater. *We're here!*

George is halfway across the pedestrian crossing when a man cuts in between us and practically pushes Grandma and me back onto the curb.

I see the camera in his hands and freeze.

"Hey, unicorn girl!" he says, snapping a picture of me.

"George!" Grandma calls, and I see him turning from across the lanes, the traffic filling in between us.

"That's some horn you've got!" the man shouts. "I didn't believe it. Took a runner on this. But wow! Is it real?" More clicks of the camera.

I'm paralyzed. This reminds me too much of the man with the camera who showed up when I was little. It was scary then. This is scary now. There's no normal life with a horn when there are people like him in the world. See, this is why I could never be onstage with this thing on my head. This is why I couldn't go to Paris. One aggressive opinion about my horn, and I can't move.

Grandma pushes me back and plants herself between us. As she scolds him, I see George raise his hands and wade into traffic like he's parting the Red Sea or something. He pulls the man aside and without a word, corrals us onto the crosswalk and over to our suitcases.

The man isn't far behind. As he runs in front of us, clicking away, George whips his hat off his head and places it onto mine. The brim sits high on my horn so it doesn't hide the horn entirely, but it helps a little. "If there's one thing I hate about Los Angeles, it's the paparazzi," he says.

Gosh. If there's one thing I love about Los Angeles, it's George. "That's a paparazzi?" I ask. "He's kind of . . ."

"Aggressive? Obnoxious? Subhuman?" offers George.

"I thought they weren't allowed to make pictures of children," says Grandma as we keep up with him.

"They're not," George says. "But that doesn't stop the scummier ones."

Finally, we're at a nice black car. We get in the backseat, and after George loads our bags in the trunk, he steps into the driver's seat. It's like we're famous! Like a movie star, I shrink down in my seat so the man can't see me.

"Don't worry, Miss Conrad," George says, winking at me in the rearview mirror. "Tinted windows. You can see out, but he can't see in."

"Really?"

George nods. "Absolutely."

As George backs the car out of the parking space, I see the man through the back window. He stares after us, his camera hanging limply at his side.

"It's okay now." Grandma pats my leg.

"Don't worry," says George. "There're nice people here, too." He smiles at me in the mirror, and I know I'm looking at one.

George takes a ramp that leads to a big wide expressway that crosses over a bigger expressway—and there's Los Angeles. Across the sky, airplanes come in for landings. Ahead of us, cars are everywhere. Around us, there are so many of everything. My first faraway place! I lean back against the cool leather seat.

And breathe.

George points out lots of sights for us, like the Coliseum where the USC football team plays, and the Staples Center, where the LA Lakers play. I think George likes sports. When I comment on how crowded the expressway is, he says they call them freeways out here, and that they're almost always this busy.

After we've been on three of these car-packed freeways, George exits on what seems like a regular street. Although how regular can a street be when it's lined with palm trees?

George parks in front of an old building that looks like a house but he tells us are apartments.

I'm about to follow George up the path when I notice that Grandma has gone frozen on the sidewalk and is staring strangely at the sign in front of the building.

"What's wrong?" I ask. "Are you okay?"

"We're staying at the Garbo," she says reverently.

"Uh. Yeah." I'm missing something. "What's a Garbo?"

"What's a Garbo?" Her voice rises an octave. "Greta Garbo. *The* Garbo. One of the greatest movie stars of all time." I'm feeling like a bum for not learning anything about Grandma's old movies right about now. "From Sweden? Her most famous line was: *'I vant to be alone.'*" Grandma's eyes wander up the street to the signs in front of other apartment buildings: the Fairbanks, the Chaplin, the Harlow, the Barrymore.

"Holy . . ." escapes her lips. "We sure are in Hollywood."

"Most of these apartments are named after silent movie stars," George tells us. "They shot lots of silent movies in this part of town back in the day. One of the earliest silent movie studios is just down the street."

"Why would they make movies without sound, anyway?"

George chuckles. "It was a technical issue."

"Did you watch them when you were a kid?"

"No!" Grandma cries. "That was a hundred years ago. George wasn't alive then." She shoots me a look. "And neither was I, so don't ask."

"Noted." I gaze at the signs along the street and marvel at the sparkle in Grandma's eyes. This must be her ultimate faraway place. Coming here for her is like going to the Eiffel Tower for me. Her Greta Garbo is like my Esmeralda.

Inside, the Garbo is old, maybe as old as silent movies. There are two bedrooms, a kitchen, a living room, and a small backyard that's shared with the other three units in the building. Grandma is disappointed that there isn't a picture of the actual Greta Garbo anywhere.

"Sure missed a bet on that one," she says, and George agrees with her.

As Grandma walks back outside with George, I choose a bedroom and lie down on the bed.

I touch my horn.

This is happening.

I am finally here.

Meeting Dr. Stein

"Look who's here," Dr. Stein says when he finally comes into the exam room where we've been waiting. "Hello, 'Angela.'"

My face gets so hot so fast it could cook a burger. "I'm sorry, I didn't mean to do anything wrong. It's just that I didn't think anybody would listen to someone my age and—"

"I'm kidding," he says, breaking out in a grin. "A girl who goes to such lengths to communicate with me is pretty determined, I know that much." He pauses and looks at my horn. "I'm Dr. Stein."

"I'm Jewel," I say back.

"And I'm her grandmother, Ruth," Grandma says.

"Nice to meet you, Ruth." He turns back to me. "How do you like Los Angeles so far?"

"I like the palm trees!" I say. It sounds silly and I immediately regret it.

But Dr. Stein's eyes are kind. "I like the palm trees, too. They take some getting used to, though, huh?"

"Where are you from, doctor?" Grandma asks.

"Boston. I'm a long way from home."

"So are we," says Grandma.

Dr. Stein's eyes return to my horn. Not in a weird way, for once, but in a curious one. "Your mom, the real Angela, said you don't remember being without your horn. It's pretty impressive, I might add."

"Yeah, it's a real horn all right."

"That it is." He examines my horn from all angles. No stranger has gotten this close to it for a long time. "Today, I want to take some measurements and do some preliminary tests." He leans in, looking closer. "May I touch it?"

He waits until I squeak out an "Okay," and then touches the tip of my horn, gently. "Tell me if this hurts."

He taps along the side of my horn, and I assure him that it doesn't. My horn isn't sensitive like that. He keeps looking, touching, and measuring, then finally sits down and goes through the plan with us—the tests and scans he'll need to do to see if the surgery can actually be done.

I get nervous. "Do you still think it'll work?"

"I'm hopeful, but let's not get ahead of ourselves," he says. "We'll know for sure in a few days."

* * *

"Your grandma told me about the tests," Mom says to me over the phone.

"I'm going back in tomorrow," I say, sitting under the lemon tree in the backyard of the Garbo.

"But how are you doing? You haven't had an earthquake, have you?"

"No, Mom. No earthquakes yet." I think she's kidding, but I press my palm into the ground anyway. Feels solid enough.

"And you're doing your homework?"

"Yes!" You'd think she could lay off the regular-mom stuff while I'm out here, but I guess not. "I'll stay caught up, I promise. Try not to worry."

"I'm not," she says.

"Then stop pacing."

"How did you know that?"

"Because you always pace when you're worried."

We talk for a while longer before Grandma comes out and reaches for the phone. "Calm her," I whisper, and Grandma winks.

As Grandma walks inside with the phone, I lie back against the (completely still, supportive) ground and stare up at the squirrels playing tag on a power line. It's hot, but not humid like back home, and a light breeze tickles my arm even though the sun is blazing above the lemon leaves.

Lemon leaves! You could make lots of lemonade from the lemons on this one tree. That's a Los Angeles lemon tree. Those are California squirrels. I can't believe it's really happening!

Tomorrow, they'll start doing more extensive tests on me. If this works, things will change. But how? I don't remember not having a horn. What will it be like if strangers don't stare at me anymore?

My fingertip touches the end of my horn. It's not sharp, but it's a point, and it can do damage. It *did* do damage. Without a horn, I wonder if Noah might forgive me.

Over the next few days, I toggle between Dr. Stein and his research assistants, who run all kinds of tests on me. Some I expect, like MRIs and X-rays. Others I don't, like memory and vision exams.

We talk to Mom every day with updates, but the update I'm waiting for hasn't happened yet. Whenever I ask Dr. Stein if he can do the surgery yet, he says, "That's why we're doing these tests. To find out." And when I press, he adds, "Patience, grasshopper."

Grasshopper? Last time I checked, grasshoppers had antennae, not horns.

As the days pass, seeds of doubt start to grow. What if it *doesn't* work? What if this has all been for nothing? What if I have to go back home like this? *What if, what if, what if...*

And Carmen isn't here to make it better. It's been days, and she still hasn't shown up. I mean, maybe it's hard for Carmen to get all the way to California. But somehow I thought Carmen could go anywhere.

I know she's mad. I know she doesn't understand. But I need her. I find myself looking for her around the corner of every hallway, behind the doors of every exam room.

By the time the tests are done, I'm feeling Carmen's absence acutely. It's ironic, right? I've avoided her for the past two years, and now I want her back so badly. If she would just get here, I feel like I would calm down.

I remember how in elementary school, Carmen would stand by my desk for an encouraging nuzzle whenever I took a test. No doubt her soothing presence actually made me get better grades. I wonder what Nicholas would think of that! I forced myself to power through exams without her in middle school, but I always knew she wasn't far, standing in the hallway, waiting for me. She was there whenever I needed her, even if I acted like I didn't want her around.

I shouldn't be surprised that her absence during all these

medical tests has unsettled me. By the time we're waiting for the final results in Dr. Stein's office, I'm a nervous wreck.

His seventh-floor window looks out onto a light blue sky streaked with white clouds. The clouds are so thin and wispy they look like they've been stretched out by a cosmic rolling pin.

"What if we've come here for nothing?" I say quietly.

Grandma grabs my hand. "Stop worrying. You're acting like your mother." But she's worried, too. I can see it in her eyes.

When the door opens, Grandma releases my hand, and we both turn to see Dr. Stein walking in.

"Sorry, sorry," he says and passes us to sit down behind his desk. "I know you've been waiting for me." He opens the folder he was carrying but doesn't look at it. He looks at us.

"Well . . . ," he says, and pauses.

I can't take the silence. "Dr. Stein!"

His dimples deepen in a way that makes my heart thump. "We can do it, Jewel," he says. "We can take off your horn."

"Oh, thank goodness." Grandma lets out a breath like she's been holding it since we landed in LA. "Doctor, you almost gave me a heart attack!"

"I'm sorry, Ruth," Dr. Stein says. "I just wanted to build some suspense. I guess Hollywood has rubbed off on me."

"Are you sure?" I ask, forcing his eyes to mine.

Dr. Stein nods. "As sure as I can be until we get in there. It's a difficult procedure. There are no guarantees with any of this. But I told your mother we'd only do it if the chances of success are great. And they are." He looks at Grandma. "Should we call her?"

"Yes, let's," Grandma says, and reaches for her phone.

"How will I look?" I ask, because that's what I really want to know.

"There'll be some reconstructive surgery and skin grafts, but mostly, Jewel, you'll look like . . . you don't have a horn."

I take this in as I hear Mom's voice come over the phone. She's been expecting our call. There's a mixture of happiness and fear in her voice when Dr. Stein tells her the news.

While they talk about the plans for my surgery, I stare out at the wispy clouds. *It's going to happen.* The thought burrows in, making me feel lighter, like I could skip across those clouds out there.

I imagine hornless Jewel. Normal Jewel. Jewel, who can go into any classroom without kids staring. Jewel, who can stand on any stage and read a French essay. Jewel, who can go any-where . . . *anywhere* . . . without all those eyes.

I'll get used to it. I'll get used to being different. I mean, I'll get used to being . . . the same. And Carmen will get used to it, too. She has to.

The Night Visit

It's the night before the surgery and I'm alone in my hospital room, texting with Nicholas.

Him: *There's still time. Run for it!*

Me: *Too late.*

Him: *What about your nose? Could look BIG.*

I check, feeling my nose, instead of texting back.

Him: *Who will you be without your magical horn?*

Me: *ugh NOT MAGICAL!*

Him: *What if it is?*

Me: *Tell me one magical thing it's done for me? IRL.*

Him: *Brought us together.* 😛 🎋 💕

I send him this: 🗿

Me: *Sometimes I swear you only like me for my horn.*

Him: *I do like your horn.*

Me: *I know.*

Him: *But I like you too.*

I start to text back, but then stop. What is he saying? Does Nicholas *like* me, like me? Is he saying—

Him: *Not that way.*

Me: *I didn't say anything.*

Him: 😐

Me: *Oh, shut up.*

Him: 😄

Me: *Why are you acting like this?*

Him: *To get your mind off things.*

Okay, Nicholas, not a bad idea.

Him: *Look outside.*

Me: *Huh?*

Him: *Out the window.*

I walk to the window of my ninth-floor hospital room, half expecting to see him there. But instead my breath gets stolen by the beauty of the lights. It's night, but it's never dark in this city.

Me: *OK, what am I looking at?*

Him: *Humanity. Think of all the people out there. No one with a horn. You're an original. What if you regret it?*

Me: *I won't.*

He doesn't text back for so long that it seems like bait.

Me: *You there?*

Him: *Yeah.*

Me: *Thanks.*

Him: *You scared?*

Me: *A little.*

Him: *I can text all night.*

It's almost midnight for him, and he's got school tomorrow.

Him: *Gonna miss weird Jewel.*

I grin.

Me: *I know.*

Nicholas keeps me company for a little while longer. When we say good night, I lie back in bed feeling lonelier than I've ever felt. Wow, I'm *really* not used to being so alone. Carmen has always been with me.

I get up and study my horn in the mirror, this horn that has always connected me to her, and realize this is one of the last times I'll ever see it.

I go to my suitcase and pull out a little pouch that holds the hornlet that Mystic made for me. In the mirror, I watch myself slip the wire chain with the Eiffel Tower ornament onto my horn.

The Eiffel Tower dangles dreamily, just how Mystic must have designed it. My horn, adorned, for the very first and very last time. I watch a small smile inadvertently escape my lips.

This thing has defined me for all my life. I take a selfie. My last picture with a horn. The last time I'll ever look like this.

I don't think Nicholas is right about unicorns not being able to live without a horn. First, I'm not a unicorn. Second, without it, I'll start *living* for the first time. But a lasso of melancholy wraps around me as I touch my horn now. It's smooth and pointy, like it's always been, and tomorrow it will be gone. As much as I want this to happen, I truly can't imagine who I will be without it.

I slip the hornlet back in the pouch and into my suitcase. Crawling into bed, I take an issue of *Highwaymen* from beneath my pillow and read it by the light of the un-night night. I'm not sleepy. I'm too nervous about tomorrow.

* * *

I don't know what time it is when I hear a familiar sound coming down the corridor. I reach for my phone, but the battery's dead.

The *clomp, clomp, clomp* beats out a steady rhythm on the hallway tile, and a tingle rushes through my heart. I jump out of my bed.

She's here!

At the door, I look around the corner. I'm not the only one. Other kids, some with bald heads, some with arms in casts, all with big eyes, peek out from doorways.

I don't know how they see her, but they do. All of them are staring at Carmen.

They gaze at her flowing white mane, her sapphire blue eyes, her long pointed horn. They've never seen a unicorn before. They've never seen something so beautiful.

I wait at my doorway as the other children form a procession behind her. Carmen moves down the corridor majestically, like a queen, like the wild creature she is. When she stops before me, the children stop, too.

"Is it a real unicorn?" a little boy whispers, and I smile at him.

"Yes," I tell him. "She's real."

I gaze into Carmen's bottomless blue eyes. "You came," I say, feeling the deep relief inside.

She whinnies and shakes her head.

"I'm so sorry."

Carmen dips her horn down to touch mine, and it's fierce like an electrical current, but painless. It runs through me and back through her, as if we're an infinity symbol. Never-ending and always connected. I stand there, taking it in. Being one with Carmen like this, one last time.

The current breaks when I finally pull away. Reaching

out, I grab her tangled mane and pet her velvet nose. "Don't be mad," I beg, and tuck my head against her strong, muscly neck. "Please understand."

I don't know how long we stand there together. Maybe a long time. I'm startled when I hear footsteps coming toward us.

Untangling myself from Carmen's mane, I see Beaumont, the sheriff from *Highwaymen*, standing before us. His charcoal cowboy hat rests on his head and his sheriff's badge shines under the fluorescent lights. Beaumont holds up his right hand so it faces me like a stop sign.

"Truth," he says, then opens his other palm in the same way. "Or consequences."

I look at Carmen and it comes out of my mouth before I even decide. "Consequences," I tell him.

* * *

"Jewel."

I feel like I'm underwater. Like someone is trying to reach me through rippling waves.

"Jewel, honey."

Slowly, I open my eyes to see Grandma standing over me. "You're awake," she says, with a relieved smile. "How do you feel?"

I groan. My head feels like fire.

"Let me get the nurse," she says and disappears.

Where am I?

Squinting out the window at the strange blue sky, it comes back to me. I'm in a hospital. Far from home.

I reach for my forehead to put out the fire—and my hand moves through my horn. I touch what feels like a bandage. And I remember why I'm here.

Sitting up too quickly, I wobble unsteadily. My head is so light and so heavy at the same time. I prop myself up on my elbow as Grandma hurries back with the nurse.

"Hi there, Jewel," the nurse says with a smile. "It's so good to see those pretty eyes of yours again." She gently guides my head back toward the pillow. "Lie back down now."

"Wait!" I say to Grandma. "Can someone please bring me a mirror?"

"One mirror coming up," Grandma says, and scurries toward the bathroom.

I go to touch my forehead again and the nurse stops me. "You don't want to be touching it now. There's a lot of healing to do."

Grandma comes back with the hand mirror, and I grab it and gasp. It's shocking when what you've been wishing for actually comes true.

My horn is gone.

Moving the mirror around, I catch as many angles of

my face as I can. There's a big bandage there, but nothing else. Nothing protruding. If I want, I can press my nose up against the mirror with nothing between me and it. No horn. I wave my hand across my reflection in the space where it used to be.

"What do you think, sweetie?" Grandma asks.

I lift up my chin, and my head doesn't feel like itself.

"I bet it feels different."

I can't seem to take my eyes away from the mirror and the image of hornless me. "Really different," I say, staring at the place where my horn used to be.

"How are you feeling?" the nurse says from behind Grandma.

"I've got a headache. A bad one."

"That's not surprising. We're managing the pain with meds, but it might be uncomfortable for a while."

Uncomfortable is an understatement. If I'm on pain meds and it hurts this bad, I'm scared to think what it would feel like without them. But when I look in the mirror, none of that matters. "I can't believe it worked," I say, completely awed, taking in what until now seemed impossible.

It's hard to believe my eyes, but it's true. My horn is *gone*.

Maps and Minotaurs

Grandma stands behind me as we ride up the long escalator toward baggage claim in the Atlanta airport. It's good to be on my feet after the long flight, but my stomach feels tight because we're almost home. I haven't seen my mom for three whole weeks.

I'm wearing the LA Dodgers hat that George gave me when he picked us up this morning. We had to adjust the snaps to accommodate my bandage underneath, but with the hat on, the bandage is almost invisible. The plane ride home was so much different than the plane ride out. This time no one stared at me—which felt both good and strange.

When I stepped off the plane, I searched for Carmen. I've missed her. I still wonder if I saw her that night in the hospital or if it was a dream. Either way, I haven't seen her since. I've been telling myself that maybe she couldn't make the distance to Los Angeles. Maybe Carmen can't do *everything*—I'd never tested distance before like that. Thinking that had calmed me down, and I figured she'd be waiting for me when we landed. But she isn't.

Mom is, though! I spot her as the escalator lifts us higher. She's standing behind the rope barrier where people are allowed to wait for passengers coming off planes.

She looks right through me.

Hornless, and hidden under my new cap, I'm a stranger to her. When she sees Grandma, she gives a confused wave before her eyes dart back to me. And her face crumbles.

We talked with Mom a lot while we were in LA, but we never texted her a picture. That was my idea—I didn't want her to see me until I really looked different and we were together. But from the look on her face now, waiting may have been a mistake.

We rush to her and I hug her over the rope line. "Mom, what's wrong?" I ask, because she's crying now.

"Oh, my sweet girls," Grandma says. I look at her for a clue about how to read this moment. Why is Mom freaking out? But Grandma's face is calm and almost bemused, and for the millionth time I'm reminded that Grandma is Mom's *mom,* and their relationship is its own special thing.

"Mom, don't cry." I slip under the barrier, and she hugs me again tighter than ever. By the time she lets me go, Grandma has made her way around the rope. She puts her arms around my mom, calming the waves inside like only a mother can.

"I'm sorry, I'm sorry," Mom finally says, pulling away and wiping her eyes. "I was just so worried. I missed you so much."

"We missed you, too, Mom."

I wait for her to say something else but she doesn't. She just stares at my forehead.

"Is it okay?" I ask uncertainly.

She keeps looking. "You're wearing a hat," she says, and lets out a gulping laugh.

"Cool, right?"

"It's really gone," she says, dumbstruck.

"Do I look totally weird? Is that why you're crying?"

She takes a deep breath, and in her eyes, I see my mom come back to herself again, but with a wonder I've never seen before. "Oh, Jewel," she says. "You look beautiful."

* * *

I'm excited to get home, so sure that Carmen will be waiting for me by the stairs. When we finally drive into the parking lot and she isn't, my heart kinks up like a twisted garden hose. Where is she?

We lug our suitcases upstairs, and after we step inside our apartment, I stop and look around. It's the same lumpy sofa, the same water spot on the kitchen ceiling, the same refrigerator that hums too loud, but it all somehow feels different.

Grandma gives me some time alone in our room to unpack. I pull out the box that Dr. Stein gave me before we left and place it on my bed. Opening the box, I look inside again at my horn. *Where am I going to put this?*

When I asked if he wanted to keep it for his trophy case, Dr. Stein looked at me oddly and asked, "Wouldn't that make me weird?"

I guess it would. Good on Dr. Stein.

We're not done with him yet. There are lots of rules like: Get enough sleep and don't do anything too strenuous. And of course, if something feels wrong, we have to call him right away.

Nothing feels wrong so far, just different. At least now I can finally walk around without having to catch my balance on a wall or a chair. I can hug Mom and Grandma without worrying that I might hurt them. But sometimes it feels like my horn is still there, especially when I wake up in the morning. Dr. Stein says it's like having a phantom limb—people who lose an arm or a leg often feel it after it's gone.

The weirdest is when I catch myself in a mirror. I've done hundreds of double takes because the image looking back at me doesn't seem real. Hornless Jewel is still a stranger to me.

I close the box and decide to store my horn in the closet where Grandma's money jar used to be. For what, I don't know, but it's not the kind of thing you throw away.

And yay for Grandma's money jar! Everything is expensive in LA. But there was enough to buy a bracelet for Mystic in a tourist shop on Hollywood Boulevard. And the picture of Grandma next to Barbara Stanwyck's star on the sidewalk didn't cost a thing, but the smile on her face was priceless.

I text Mystic and Nicholas, letting them know that I'm back, but the next two days are just for family. Mom's taking time off from work because of all the overtime she put in while we were away. We pop popcorn, watch movies, and even get a pizza delivered. What a luxury!

On Saturday, Mom goes back to work and Mystic comes over to hang out before I have to go back to school on Monday. She's pretty stunned when she sees her hornless friend.

"Whoa!" is her first reaction when she comes through the door.

We hang out in my room and I tell her about everything. I give her the bracelet—a chain with a gold star—and she loves it! Then I show her the almost-healed place on my stomach where they took skin and attached it to my forehead. She thinks it's gross and I agree.

"How's everything else?" I ask, angling for some intel about Emma and the Brooklyn bracelet situation. We never texted about it while I was away.

"I got a C– on my last French quiz," Mystic answers.

"How could you get a C–?" I ask, because even for Mystic that's extreme.

"It's your fault because you weren't here to help me," she says, teasing, "and French is sorely messing with my GPA."

"I'll help you," I say, but her expression turns worried. "What's wrong?"

"Um. Well . . . ," She pauses, and I can sense there's something she doesn't want to tell me.

"Did Emma say anything about the bracelet?" I ask, ready for the worst.

She doesn't answer at first, but then her forehead smooths and her worried look disappears. "No, I think we're in the clear on that."

"Whew, what a relief," I say.

"I know, right?"

"So what's wrong?"

"Oh, nothing. Never mind. What's under that bandage anyway?"

"You don't want to know!" I say. "It's kind of like Frankenstein."

"It can't be that bad."

"Ah, it's pretty bad." Slowly, I reach for the bandage, and Mystic leans forward as I gently peel it off. To her credit, she doesn't flinch.

"Not as bad as Frankenstein," she finally says.

"Thanks. But so much for my triumphant return."

"Don't say that," Mystic says. "You're way triumphant."

"Maybe I can wear a hat."

She's silent for a minute, then jumps off the bed.

"Where are you going?" I ask as she speeds out of the bedroom and says something to Grandma in the kitchen. In less than a minute, they both return. Mystic is carrying a pair of scissors.

"What are you doing?" I ask, feeling downright suspicious, because . . . scissors.

"I've got a great idea," Mystic says, and I look past her to Grandma.

"She does," Grandma agrees.

"I promise, it's going to look even better," Mystic says, and sits down across from me on the bed. She holds the scissors in front of my eyes and says, "Bangs," like it's the answer to the universe.

"Bangs?"

"Bangs," Grandma repeats. "Why didn't we think of that already?"

"Shouldn't we wait for Mom?" I ask, putting my hand to my forehead.

"Let's surprise her!" Grandma says, and she and Mystic gaze at me eagerly, waiting for the next move.

"All right," I say and grin. "Do it."

"Okay, hold still." Mystic lifts the scissors near my eyes. Her Hollywood Boulevard bracelet dangles from her wrist alongside her usual stack.

"Wait! Are you sure you can do this?"

"My mom cuts hair, remember? I've watched her do it a thousand times."

Before I ask if watching is the same as doing, Mystic grabs a section of my hair and cuts straight through. My mouth falls open as a bunch of hair comes off in her hand.

"Oh, yeah," Mystic says, then makes more clips here and there like she actually does know what she's doing. When she's satisfied, Mystic pulls back. She and Grandma study me like I'm a science experiment.

"What?" I ask because I can't tell what they're thinking. "Is it horrible?" I leap off the bed and steel myself before I look in the mirror.

Jewel.

I see myself as if for the first time. The bangs change everything. I see my eyes, my lips, my nose. My Frankenstein forehead is completely hidden. And guess what? Nicholas was wrong. My nose is not big. Not at all.

I can't stop staring. I look normal. I might even look good.

"Who's the fairest of them all?" says Grandma, and I turn to her and Mystic.

"Wow, you look amazing, Jewels," Mystic whispers.

"Wait until your mom sees," says Grandma, her eyes shining.

"Wait until everybody sees," adds Mystic, starting to laugh.

"What's so funny?"

"It's just . . . nobody's going to know who you are. I bet they won't even recognize you. You'll be like the intriguing new girl."

Intriguing? I'll just settle for "new girl."

"Hey, don't get me wrong, I thought you were the intriguing horn girl, too," Mystic says. "This is just a different look."

I smile at her. That was a way-cool thing for her to say. My eyes catch me in the mirror again. I *do* look different. So much that I'm not sure I even recognize myself.

* * *

The next day I'm in Nicholas's room looking at the new red flag we just pinned onto his wall map. A Minotaur—part man, part bull—showed up in the latest issue of *Highwaymen,* and from our calculations, it hails from Isabela, Puerto Rico. Who knew that Minotaurs lived in the Caribbean?

I can feel Nicholas staring at *me,* though. When he opened the front door and got his first glimpse, his eyes bugged out and his jaw literally swung open.

"You actually did it," he said, with a kind of disbelief that instantly annoyed me. He's been a big gaping fool ever since—and fifteen minutes of being gaped at turns out to be quite a long time.

But he did wait for me to do our map project together, which was cool of him. He's had this *Highwaymen* for over two weeks (as he's reminded me three times) and that's a really long time for Nicholas to wait when it comes to Hot Springs.

I'm pretending to study the map, but out of the corner of my eye, I see him still gaping. If he would just stop doing that!

"I guess I'll get used to it," he manages.

"Oh, phew," I say dryly. "I've been worried about how this would affect *you.*" I really *was* a little worried about how he would react, but now I'm about over it.

"Hey, I look at you more than you do. Don't you think it's important that I get used to it, too?"

I shrug and say, "Maybe."

"Do you miss it?" he asks.

I gaze out the window into Nicholas's front yard. Whenever I'm here, that's where Carmen usually waits for me. "No, I don't miss it," I say, but it's more complicated than that. Truth is, there have been a lot of feelings rushing through me ever since the surgery. I'm like a mood ring, alternating between feeling excited, confused, relieved, happy, lonely, and all kinds of strange colors in between.

"I do," he says, almost smugly, and suddenly the mood ring inside me flips to red.

"Stop looking at me like that!" I snap.

"Dude, chill!" he says. "I'm not looking at anything."

"You're looking at my bangs! You're looking at my forehead! You're looking at where my horn used to be!"

"No, I'm not."

Oh my gosh, the fake innocent look on his face. No. "I'm going home."

As I leave his room, Nicholas yells after me. "What did I do?" I speed down the stairs without answering and his tone changes. "Fine. Free country. Whatever."

Ugh!

It's started raining outside and I don't have an umbrella. It's miles to home but I start walking. Better rain than Nicholas.

I knew he was going to be a jerk about this, so why am I

surprised? He *is* a jerk. If I never had a horn, we would have never been friends. And now that I don't have a horn, we don't have to be.

I'm halfway down Park Street when I hear footfalls behind me. "Jewel! Wait up!"

Stubbornly, I walk faster, but Nicholas's legs are longer than mine, so it doesn't take him long to catch me.

"Where are you going anyway?"

I keep walking. "Away from you."

"I probably deserve that," he says, now by my side.

"You do."

"I know. Just stop walking, okay?"

I turn to him. "I always knew you only liked me for my horn. And now you've made that perfectly clear."

"No, I don't. It's just that I *liked* your horn. It was cool. I don't know why that makes you so mad."

"Because I'm not my horn!"

"I never said you were," he says.

"But that's what you thought."

He shakes his head. "It's just . . . you know me—I like magical creatures."

"I'm not a magical creature, Nicholas." I look toward town. I could keep walking. But I don't. I stand with him on the rainy sidewalk.

"I know," he says quietly. "It's just, it was *your* face," he mumbles. "*Your* horn. That's what I liked about it. That it was you. So, I'm sorry. I mean it."

I stare at him and wonder if I might have overreacted. I mean, it *is* weird seeing me this way. What if it takes him some time to get used to the new me?

Then he adds, "And I really missed you."

The mean part of me thinks, *Well, of course he did, he's my best friend.* But then again, he doesn't usually say stuff like that. And he waited over two weeks so we could put that dumb red flag on the map together. That's big in Nicholas World.

"I missed you, too," I say back.

He smiles, then looks up, opening his palms to the sky. "And it's raining," he says, like he's just noticed, and I laugh.

On our way back to his house, I tell him about LA. I tell him about George and the Garbo and Dr. Stein. I tell him everything, except about seeing Carmen in the hospital. I wonder if I will ever tell anyone about Carmen again.

Back inside, we towel ourselves off and Nicholas gives me a dry T-shirt to wear. In the bathroom, I slip his shirt over my head—so easy to do without a horn!—and my eyes land on the mirror. Still no horn. No wonder Nicholas was staring at me.

Even I can't get used to what I look like now.

* * *

I'm nervous about school tomorrow. What if everybody stares at me like Nicholas did? And then there's French. I won't lie, a part of me has secretly been holding out about the essay competition. Maybe Monsieur Oliver has waited for me. Maybe he feels so strongly that it's supposed to be me on that stage that he didn't submit Josh Martin's name to the Alliance. It feels almost too good to be true—to be hornless Jewel *and* French Rock Star Jewel all at the same time. But why not? Anything's possible now!

As I get ready for bed, I do what's become a ritual ever since I got home. I open the blinds, hoping Carmen will be standing outside the window. But she isn't. "Come on, Carmen. It's not so bad."

Carmen will forgive me. I tell myself. *I just have to be patient.*

From across the parking lot, the light in Emma's room comes on, and my thoughts shift to her. Emma hasn't seen me yet. Will she recognize me? Will she . . .

"Knock, knock," Mom says and comes in.

I pull down the blinds and hop into bed. That's another thing I'm into now—jumping around! It always hurt my horn to do it before, but now I'm like a bouncing rabbit.

"You feeling okay?" she asks.

"Tired. But good." She sits on my bed and pulls up the

covers. "Are you tucking me in again?" She's been tucking me in like a little kid ever since I got home.

"Yep."

"You're weird," I say.

"I'm okay with that. Sleep well, my sweet girl," she says, and kisses me on the forehead. She hasn't been able to do that since I was a baby, so now it's like she's making up for lost time. It turns out I like being kissed there.

The New Girl

"Who's the new girl?"

I actually hear somebody say that as I follow Mrs. Whatley out of the school's main office and into the hall. I had to check in with her because I've been away for so long.

"How was Los Angeles?" she asks in an odd, chatty tone. "I was there for a teaching conference several years ago. Did you get to see the stars on Hollywood Boulevard?"

"We didn't see any real ones, but we saw lots on the sidewalk."

"And your doctor? Did you like him—or her?"

"Him." I nod. She's never talked to me this much in my life. "Dr. Stein. He was good. Really good. I liked him a lot."

As we climb the stairs, a couple of girls steal glances at me like they're trying to figure out where they know me from. The stairwell is plastered with sparkly posters about the eighth-grade Under the Sea dance.

When we get to the second floor, Mrs. Whatley looks at me. "I just can't get over it. You really look different."

It's so strange, her being this nice to me. "Really?" I ask.

"In a good way. Not that your . . . you know . . . was a bad thing, but it might have gotten in the way of seeing the real you."

Huh. The real me. That's what she thinks she's seeing now. I don't feel more real though. I just feel like me.

I keep pace with her down the hall to homeroom, but when she grabs the doorknob, she stops and looks at me funny. "You okay?"

My heart is suddenly racing because nobody's really seen me yet. Only the people who knew I was getting my horn removed. To everyone else, I'm hiding in plain sight. When I walk through that door, I'll become a different Jewel. Hornless Jewel. Normal Jewel. Known Jewel. I'm not ready.

The bell rings. "Wait here," Whatley tells me, and steps inside.

I pull my Dodgers hat out of my backpack. With it on, I feel less naked, less exposed.

The door opens, and Monsieur Oliver steps out, followed

by Mrs. Whatley. He tries not to stare, but he does. Right at the spot where the "LA" is on my hat. Right at the spot where my horn used to be.

"Bonjour, Jewel," he says and smiles. "You ready to come in?"

He and Whatley gaze at me expectantly. I guess I can't stand in the middle of the hall forever.

"Sure," I say weakly, and follow him inside.

"Class, let's welcome Jewel back," Monsieur Oliver says as I make my way to my desk.

Everyone turns. Eyes widen. Murmurs erupt. Someone gasps.

"What happened to your horn?" Eduardo Alvarez blurts out.

There are giggles. Louder murmurs. Monsieur Oliver raises his hands. "Eyes up front, people. Let Jewel have some space, please."

By lunch, I'm still wearing my baseball cap and wishing to become invisible. At least when I had my horn, people pretended not to look when they were looking. Now they don't hide it at all. The news that the new girl is the unicorn girl has spread like wildfire.

By the time I get to our table, I'm relieved that Nicholas and Mystic are already there. I plop down my tray and sit with my back to the rest of the cafeteria.

"What's wrong?" Mystic asks.

"It's freaking me out. Everybody's staring at me."

"Everybody's always stared at you," Nicholas says.

"Yeah, but not like this."

Just then, over at the nerd table, Tall Ethan stands up with a big piece of poster board in one hand and a black top hat in the other. Ethan puts the hat on his head and turns toward the popular table.

"What is that idiot doing?" Nicholas says.

I glance over at Noah and can tell he's thinking the same thing.

Ethan approaches Brooklyn, who's apparently the only person in the cafeteria not paying attention to what's happening. Emma nudges her, and Brooklyn looks up to see an extremely tall boy with a top hat making him even taller, holding a sign:

WILL YOU GO TO THE DANCE WITH ME?

Laughter erupts from the popular table and ripples out like a wave. Brooklyn doesn't laugh, but she does say something to him and shakes her head no. Ethan just stands there staring at her awkwardly. The cafeteria is awash with embarrassment.

Why isn't he moving?

"I can't look," Mystic says, and covers her eyes.

Noah's out of his chair now. He hurries to his friend, takes the poster out of his hand, and leads him away.

Brooklyn looks relieved behind him, but Emma laughs, and I want to tell her to stop. Doesn't she realize how hard this must be for Ethan?

What was Ethan thinking, asking Brooklyn to the dance at all, let alone in public like that? It's all terrible, but secretly I'm glad he drew the attention away from me.

"Excuse me?"

I turn. Next to me is a kid I don't know, young but strangely confident and holding out a newspaper tabloid. The cover is of two photos of me, a before and after. One is from when we arrived at the LA airport with my horn in prominent view. The other is outside the hospital without my horn, with a big bandage on my forehead.

How is this possible? I never saw anybody taking pictures of me outside the hospital.

The kid clears his throat and holds out a pen. "Would you sign this?"

Nicholas's chair scrapes loudly as he stands and stares down at the kid. "Are you kidding me?" he says. "Get out of here!"

The kid holds his ground for all of three seconds before he comes to his senses. Nicholas may be a weirdo at our freak table, but that just makes him seem scarier to this extremely normal-looking kid. "Whatever," he mumbles and slopes away.

Nicholas sits back down and returns to his lunch like nothing happened.

Mystic grins. "Our hero."

"Yeah, right," Nicholas says.

"Wow," I whisper, stunned. My eyes follow the kid as he rejoins his lunch table. "What *was* that thing?" I turn to Mystic, panicked. "What does it say? Oh my gosh. Is this ever going to be over?"

Mystic doesn't say a word. She just gets up, walks straight to a table of sixth graders, and plucks the tabloid from the kid's hands. "Hey!" he yells, but that's about the apex of his outrage. She walks back and places the paper in front of me.

I stare down at me—and me—on the front page. This is why I couldn't travel with a horn. This confirms every fear I ever had about the world seeing me like that. "How did this happen?"

"It'll pass," Mystic says.

"But . . . this is everywhere. Everyone in the world is going to know about me."

"Then you'll never have to explain yourself," Mystic says. "Don't worry. Nobody stays a celebrity for long."

A celebrity? More like a sideshow.

I start to read what they've said about me. About being the unicorn girl. About the miracle surgery that made me normal. It may be intrusive, but it's actually not far from the truth. "Ugh," I say, and look up at Nicholas and Mystic. "What do I do now?"

"Be you," says Nicholas.

Mystic nods. "Yeah, be you."

I sigh. "I'm not sure what that even means."

"You'll figure it out," Nicholas says. "Isn't that what all this"—he karate-chops the air in front of his forehead—"was about anyway?"

"Yeah, but I just thought it was going to be easier."

"All the best things aren't easy at first."

Nicholas looks at Mystic, impressed. "Nice one, Myst."

He's right. So is she. Nothing feels easy about today. But I've been wanting this for so long. So I can either sit here and be afraid of a sixth grader and hide under a hat, or . . .

Slowly, I take my Dodgers hat from my head and brush my bangs forward. Mystic gives me a thumbs-up. Turning, I look out into the cafeteria. Lots of eyes are staring back, but a single pair catches mine. She's looking at me and I'm looking at her. Emma.

* * *

In French class, I sit at my desk in the back without my cap on, thinking maybe I look like a regular girl. As everyone comes in, I meet their stares without looking away, which makes me feel uncomfortable and brave at the same time. Mystic slips through the door and sits beside me right before the bell rings.

When Monsieur Oliver arrives, he smiles at me, and in that moment, I decide: I'm going to talk to him after class about the essay competition. I'm going to plead my case, and hopefully he'll find a way to still let me go.

As he hands back marked-up quizzes, he says, "*Pas mal,* for a pop quiz. But 'not bad' is not really good enough, *n'est-ce pas?*" A quiz sheet lands on Mystic's desk with a big fat red C on it. She points at the grade and mouths, "Your fault," and I grin.

"All right, *tout le monde,*" Monsieur Oliver says, returning to the front of the class. "As most of you know, the essay competition is around the corner." His eyes find mine, and I feel my stomach leap to my chest. What if he *did* wait for me after all? It's possible. It feels possible. I mean, look at me. I'm hornless. I'm ready. I'm—

"And Brooklyn is going to need all of our support to get ready."

Brooklyn? My stomach drops like a runaway elevator from the twentieth floor. *Brooklyn!* My eyes dart to Josh, who doesn't seem upset at all. If anyone should be going instead of me, it's him. Not Brooklyn!

Monsieur Oliver keeps talking but my mind can't keep up. I turn to Mystic, who is looking incredibly guilty. I mouth, "Why didn't you tell me?"

"I'm sorry," she whispers. "Really sorry."

I look away to see Brooklyn staring at me. What, to gloat? If she weren't a best-friend stealer and general selfish popular girl, I might confuse her look for a guilty one, too. How could she not know I wanted this more than anything? But I think by now I know better. Our eyes lock for a long beat before she turns forward again.

When class ends, I'm frozen at my desk. I'm angry at Mystic and Monsieur Oliver, too. *How could she not have told me? And how could he have chosen Brooklyn?*

"Don't be mad. I just didn't know how to tell you," Mystic says. "I knew it would upset you."

Well, duh.

She stands there waiting for me. "You coming?"

"No, not yet," I say, not looking at her. "I'll see you later."

Mystic waits for an awkward moment, then says, "Text me, okay?"

"Okay," I say, and let her walk away. As the room clears out, I slip my notebook into my backpack like I'm moving in slow motion.

When I stand up, Monsieur Oliver is waiting by the door. "I thought Mystic would have said something," he says. "I could tell you were surprised. I didn't want you to be."

"Yeah, I was kind of hoping . . ." The words get stuck in my throat. "I guess I thought it would be Josh, not Brooklyn, if it wasn't going to be . . . it doesn't matter, never mind."

"Josh had a conflict. And Brooklyn really wanted to do it."

What, did she ask for it?

"You were pretty clear about not wanting to go," he says.

"I know. I know." It's uncomfortable between us and I don't know what to say next. I'm relieved when he speaks first.

"How does it feel?"

"Not getting to do the competition?" I ask. It's all I can think about.

"No, not having your horn."

Oh. That. Now that it's gone, people seem to feel free to talk about it. "Good," I say. "Different. And the same. People are still staring at me though."

"They'll stop. I think you caught everybody by surprise. I wish you had told me. The office said you'd be out for a while, but they didn't say why."

"Yeah, it all happened kind of suddenly."

"Well, I'm glad. I mean, I knew you weren't happy." I must be giving him a quizzical look because he adds, "I read your essay, remember?"

"Oh yeah, right." I think about the words I wrote—how they poured out from my heart. How desperate I was to be like I am now. I stall under his steady gaze, then decide, what do I have to lose? "Before I left," I say, "when I knew that I might have the surgery, I wanted to email you to see if I could still compete in the competition. But there was no way to know it would actually work. The horn surgery, I mean. Not until I got to LA, not until they did all kinds of tests. It was complicated, and . . ." *Too many words. Get to the point, Jewel. Why am I so scared to say this? Just say it!* "Is there any way I could still do the competition?"

The knot in my throat tightens as Monsieur Oliver sighs. "Yours was the best essay, Jewel. *Sans doute.* It's a rare student who has so much natural ability in the language. And you work hard, too, I know that." He pauses. "I guess what I'm trying to say is that you deserve to go to the competition, but—"

"But Brooklyn." I say it before he does.

He nods. "But Brooklyn."

I look down. This hurts. It's not the answer I was hoping for.

"If it's any consolation, I'm sorry it's her and not you," Monsieur Oliver says.

"Thanks," I answer softly.

"But I'll deny it if you repeat that." His eyes crinkle. He knows I'd never say a word.

"I guess my essay wouldn't work now anyway. I'm not a girl with a horn anymore. It wouldn't be true."

"I bet you could rewrite it. From the perspective of the girl who used to have a horn, *n'est-ce pas?*"

"Peut-être," I say. But why? There's nothing to rewrite it for.

"So, we'll support Brooklyn, right?"

When he says this, I won't lie—I cringe inside. But I put my best hornless face forward, and say, *"Absolument,"* even though I know that's going to be an uphill battle.

* * *

Less than two hours later, I'm on the bus, sitting alone. That hasn't changed. I press my head directly against the glass for the first time without my horn blocking the way. It's a little thing, but it's a thing. I come across hundreds of them every day. *Tap. Tap. Tap.* Ever so slightly I turn my head back and forth, tapping my invisible horn against the bus window, and close my eyes.

It sucks so bad that Brooklyn is taking my place in the essay competition. Now that I don't have a horn, I could do it. But like other things in my life, Brooklyn gets this, too.

And why didn't Mystic tell me? She found me at the end of school and apologized, saying she didn't know *how* to tell me. But still. She should have.

When I open my eyes, I see Emma sitting several rows ahead. The back of her ponytail bounces gently to every bump and lurch of the old bus.

When we stop in front of our apartment complex, Emma is down the aisle and off the bus before I'm barely out of my seat. As I approach the bus driver, she says, "Lookin' good, Jewel," and smiles at me. One of her front teeth is missing. I never noticed that. How could I? She's never smiled at me before.

"Thanks," I say swiftly, and pad down the stairs. My whole life, as long as I've been going to school, Carmen has met me at the bus every afternoon. And most of that time, I wanted her to be there. There's a pang of guilt in my stomach as I think about how I've treated her for the past two years. She didn't deserve to be ignored, or told to go away.

The image of Carmen is so alive in my mind that I almost expect to see her as I step onto the sidewalk.

She's not there, but what I do see takes my breath away.

Emma is waiting for me.

Emma

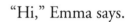

"Hi," Emma says.

"Hi," I say back as the bus lumbers away.

"How are you doing?" she asks, not moving, just looking at me.

What's going on? Why is she talking to me? Why are we standing here? This is so weird that I—

"What's wrong?" she asks, like everything is normal, which it is not.

"Well, you're talking to me, for starters."

Emma flips her hair over her shoulder. "It's about time we started talking again, don't you think?"

"I guess . . ."

She starts walking to the apartments. It feels silly to follow her, but we both live here.

"You look really good, by the way," Emma says, glancing my way.

"Thanks," I say, but that's all I can manage. My hands are clammy and my mouth feels dry.

"What was it like in Los Angeles?"

"Fine."

She stops at the stairs that lead up to her apartment. "You went all the way to LA and it was just 'fine'?"

"No, it was good." There, more than one syllable. "I like palm trees."

"Palm trees?" She cocks her head. "What about movie stars? Did you see any movie stars?"

I shake my head. "I don't think so."

"That's too bad."

"I guess we weren't in the right places for that. I was mostly in the hospital, but we stayed in this place called the Garbo, which was pretty cool."

"What's a Garbo?" she asks.

"This old movie star who Grandma likes."

"Did you meet her?" she asks, brightening.

"I don't think she's still alive."

"Oh," Emma says, and then goes quiet.

Words used to flow so effortlessly between us, and now it's like we're strangers. The Emma I knew would giggle and make funny faces. This Emma feels older. More serious. Totally different.

Maybe I'm different, too.

"Well, I'm glad it went okay," she finally says and heads up the stairs. When she gets to her apartment door, she turns and smiles down at me. For this, I am not prepared. An unexpected surge of emotion runs through me. I gaze up, soaking up every ray of that smile, until she turns and goes inside.

I don't even remember getting from the parking lot to my front door. *What just happened? What does this mean?*

When I open my door, Grandma's standing at the kitchen counter. "You look happy," she says. "Good day?"

I think about this day, my first at any school without a horn on my head. Nicholas stood up for me with that kid at lunch. Monsieur Oliver couldn't give me what I wanted, but he did it in the nicest of ways. And Emma. That wasn't expected at all. "Yes. Good day," I say, and Grandma smiles back at me.

The rest of the week, Emma doesn't take the bus. And at school, she acts like we never spoke. It makes me think of how I treated Carmen. It's awful to be ignored, but I probably deserve to feel this way. Karma sucks.

By Friday, I'm starting to wonder if Emma even talked to me at all. Could I have wanted to be friends with her again so badly that I made it all up? So when she plops down beside me on the bus after school, I'm surprised. And happy. And confused.

"Who did your bangs?" she asks. "It's a good look for you."

That's the first thing she wants to know? *O-kayyyyy.* "Mystic, when I got back."

"Mystic, huh?"

Am I imagining it, or did she say Mystic's name funny? It makes me wonder if she *did* hear us in the girls' locker room that day, if she *does* know it was Mystic who "borrowed" Brooklyn's bracelet.

"Hey, listen, what are you doing this afternoon?" Emma asks, like the past two years never happened.

"I have some French homework, but—"

"French homework? You sound like Brooklyn," she says, rolling her eyes. "That can wait, can't it? Come over."

"Sure," I say. She scrolls through her phone and I feel tingles of excitement bubble up—nerves, too. I haven't been to Emma's apartment in two years, either.

Sneaking a peek at Emma's phone, I watch pictures fly by, freeze, and fly by some more. Most are selfies of Emma or Brooklyn or other cheerleaders. When she catches me looking, I turn away, pretending I wasn't.

"Why aren't you following me?" she asks.

"Huh?"

She holds up her phone. "Why aren't you following me?"

"Oh, my phone's messed up. I can't download apps."

From the look on her face, I might as well have told her that somebody died. "Let me see it."

I retrieve my useless phone from my backpack. "Password," she says.

"One, two, three, four."

"Seriously?" As I start to explain, she waves it away. "Never mind. We'll deal with that later."

She stabs at my phone like some kind of telecommunications surgeon, and I watch, amazed, until the corners of her lips turn down. Literally. I'm tempted to say, *Turn that frown upside down* when she looks at me, bereft. "Your phone's messed up."

I know.

We get off the bus and I follow Emma to her apartment. As the familiar aroma of fried chicken hits my nose, I'm taken back to all the dinners with Emma and her mom at their kitchen table. Emma's mom is an excellent cook.

"Emma, didn't you get my text? I'm—" Her voice trails off as soon as she sees me. "Jewel. Hi," Emma's mom says, wiping her hands on a kitchen towel. "It's so good to see you. Your mom told me about your trip. You look really good."

"Thanks," I say, and stand awkwardly until Emma grabs my arm and drags me into her bedroom.

"We've got stuff to do," she tells her mom.

"I'll be gone for about an hour. Have some chicken if you're hungry."

"Okay, we're good," Emma says, and closes the door behind us.

Emma's room is so different. Her blue walls, once pink, are now covered with posters, mostly of boy bands. The burgundy bedspread is a far cry from her Tinkerbell one. "I like your room now," I say.

"Yeah, it's okay." Emma twists her hair into a messy upknot and sits down on the bed. "My dad's getting me a new desk, *finally*, so . . . pretend that one's not there."

"Your dad's around?" I know for a fact that Emma's dad left town when we were in first grade. I remember how sad she was about it—and how angry.

"No, he's still in Texas, but we talk like all the time. He's married now, to Josie. She has two kids, the cutest little girls ever, omigod, and they want me to come visit next summer."

"That sounds good."

"We'll see," she says. "So, okay, who are you going to the dance with?"

"What dance?"

"Uh . . . the *eighth-grade dance*," she says, her eyes wide in disbelief.

"Oh yeah, that dance. Nobody," I say. "When is it again?"

"Saturday. A week from tomorrow. How do you not know when the dance is?"

"I guess I've had a lot going on."

"I guess." She looks at me. "Then you don't have a date? Really?"

"Really. Who are you going with?"

"Thomas Kelly."

"Thomas Kelly?"

"He's not a jerk . . . anymore," she says with a sly smile.

Um, I know for a fact that Thomas Kelly is still a jerk. Just last month, he stole the stuffed unicorn she gave me! I guess in the past year he did grow about a foot and got hot. Does that make him not a jerk anymore?

"I'm sorry, but Thomas Kelly is still a jerk," I say.

She stares at me, making me regret my bluntness. "Nah, he's all right. Better than he used to be."

I'm still standing awkwardly by her door, wondering if this was a good idea at all. Is it too early to leave yet?

"You know," Emma says. "I'm in charge of the dance committee, and I was thinking, you want to help us out? Marianne broke her ankle, so we're down a member. And there's so much more we have to do."

"How'd Marianne break her ankle?"

"Gymnastics." Emma rolls her eyes in what I'm coming to recognize as her new signature move. "I guess she landed on it wrong or something. Anyway, you're good at drawing and excellent at glitter, so I was thinking . . . maybe you would join the committee?"

"You want me to be on the dance committee?"

"Uh, yeah. We need you, J! And it'll be fun."

"I guess I could. What do I have to do?"

"Just come help us after school next week. And since you don't have a date, you could be in charge of the refreshment table. Marianne was on refreshment duty."

"*At* the dance?"

"If you're on the committee, you have to be there, J." Emma grins. "Plus, it's the eighth-grade dance and you're an eighth grader! Of course you've got to come."

* * *

I hear the click of a camera and turn, startled, toward the sound.

"Sorry," Mystic says, handing me her phone so I can see

the picture. "You just looked so happy." There I am, bangs, no horn, with the most chill look on my face.

I'm glad Mystic can't read my mind to know I was thinking about Emma. After I agreed to be on the dance committee, Emma pulled out this big notebook and showed me her Under the Sea designs for the dance. I drew her some mermaids like she needed, and they weren't too bad! Sure, Nicholas's mermaids would be better, but Nicholas wouldn't be caught dead drawing mermaids for the dance committee. I stayed over for dinner with her mom and we even watched some YouTube. It was a legit hangout.

That was yesterday. Today Mystic and I are at Tina's Treasures, the thrift shop in town, scavenging for cheap trinkets for her jewelry before meeting Nicholas at the gazebo later. There are only three dollars in her wallet, but Mystic can make three dollars go a long way.

"What's on your mind, smiley?" Mystic asks as she takes her phone back and eyes the picture.

"I don't know," I lie.

Mystic and I went to elementary together, but we weren't friends then. She knows I was best friends with Emma, and she blames Emma for hurting me. I have the sense she'd somehow be both jealous and protective if she knew Emma was back in my life now.

I look out the window at the crowded town square. Saturdays are the busiest days for tourists at the peak of leaves-changing season. Even though I've lived here all my life, I've never been to the square this time of year. No way with a horn on my head.

"What about this?" Mystic says, holding up a crystal teardrop. "I could make a hole right there, and put this wire through it." In her other hand, she's got some beads, silver wire, and a string of leather.

"I love it," I tell her.

It's strange. It used to be so easy with Emma, and Mystic had a moat. Now it's the opposite. I have to parse my words with Emma, but with Mystic, I just speak without thinking.

We walk out into the brisk afternoon and head toward the gazebo on the other side of the square. The sidewalk is so crowded that it's hard to get through. We wind our way through tourist after tourist, stranger after stranger, until suddenly, I stop and gaze around in astonishment.

"Do you see this?" I ask, stopping and forcing people to circle around us.

"See what?" Mystic looks around. "The million tourists? Why are we stopping?"

"They're not staring at me." I rotate completely around, my eyes landing on face after face. All these people who've never seen me before, and not one of them looking at me at all. Their eyes pass right over me like I'm just a regular teenager here to cause trouble and shop in thrift stores. "I'm invisible," I say. It sounds so silly, but it honestly feels like a great achievement.

Mystic grabs my elbow and pulls me to the side. "Welcome to ninety-nine percent of the human race."

A mother with a tiny daughter approaches. I make eye contact with the little girl, but her eyes don't linger curiously. Her mother doesn't even notice me. It's almost like I'm not even there.

I gaze up at the gold, orange, and red leaves dangling from every tree in sight. It is beautiful. I guess I never noticed it before.

As we escape to the gazebo, Mystic looks back at the masses with disdain. "It's not that great to be invisible, trust me." We step into the empty gazebo and sit on the leaf-covered white benches.

I grin. "No, it's pretty great."

"Just wait until you want a boy to notice you and he doesn't."

"Oh," I say, coming back to Earth. She's talking about Ethan. "You won't always be invisible to him. Brooklyn's *that* girl. He'll see who she really is someday."

"Maybe," Mystic says, clearly unconvinced. "Do you like anybody?"

"Ah . . . I don't know. I mean, I had a horn until last month. It seemed kind of pointless—get it?" I crack up at my own weak pun. "Who's going to like a girl with a horn?"

"But you don't have a horn anymore," Mystic says, narrowing her eyes. "It's not Nicholas, is it? That would be weird. He's our friend."

I laugh. "If I liked him, I would have kept the horn on."

Mystic's eyes drift over my shoulder. "Speaking of."

I turn to see Nicholas jogging toward us. He reaches the gazebo and jumps over the rail. "Too. Many. People," he pants.

I grin. "It's kind of beautiful, right?"

Nicholas gives me a look like I'm insane. "Ice cream line is way long," he says. "What should we do? Cones or Factory?"

Nicholas and Mystic jump into a debate about which place is better and worth the wait, Fudge Factory or Cones on the Square.

I swing my head around. In the gardens on the other side of the gazebo, I could have sworn I saw—

"What's wrong, Jewels?"

I look at Mystic. "Ah, nothing," But that's not true. Out of the corner of my eye, I could swear that saw I her.

"You look like you saw a ghost or something," Nicholas says.

I feel cold, like maybe I did see a ghost. It was a flash of white. Fast, fleeting.

I gaze at the gardens again. Nothing. Just a squirrel scampering up a tree. Not a unicorn in sight.

The Unspooling Black

Carmen. I've been thinking about her nonstop since the gazebo. I can't be sure that I saw her, but I know I felt her. So many times in my life I've sensed Carmen before I actually saw her. I'd feel a rush of reassurance, a wave of calm, and then I'd look up and there she was. The feeling I had on Saturday was neither of those, though. It was more like a rush of panic.

By Monday, I'm agitated, distracted. I'm in no state to be holding an actual pig's heart in my hand. But it's science class and this is dissecting day.

Gloomily, I stare at the heart in my rubber-gloved hand and imagine it beating inside a real pig who frolicked through fields of green grass and clover—though these days, most pigs probably never frolic through either. I hope this pig did. I hope this pig was up to her corkscrew tail in clover before she bequeathed her heart to me.

"You going to put it in the tray?" Ethan asks, and I gently place the heart in the pan. Tall Ethan is my dissecting partner. Our science teacher, Ms. Meyer, paired everyone up and put me and Ethan together.

Ms. Meyer tells us to pick up our scalpels, and I'm hoping Ethan will make the first cut, but when I see his face turning green, I reach for mine. I do exactly as Ms. Meyer says, pressing down with the blade and separating the flesh of Clover's heart.

"Are you okay?" I whisper to Ethan because, really, he doesn't look it.

A cry erupts from the front of the class and I can't tell if it's a boy or a girl until Thomas Kelly holds up his arm. A rivulet of blood runs down his hand.

"Already?" Ms. Meyer sighs. "Come on, Thomas, let's get you to the nurse's office." As she presses a paper towel over the bleeding wound, I grin inside. No matter what Emma says, Thomas Kelly is a unicorn-stealing jerk. And now I know he's a big baby, too.

"Quiet while I'm gone, please," Ms. Meyer says to the class. "You may continue following the instructions at your station. Just don't anybody else cut yourself, okay?" She says this in a weary tone usually reserved for teachers much later in the school year.

As she leads Thomas from the science room, Ethan and I sit back on our metal stools. "Couldn't have happened to a nicer guy," I say with a snort, suddenly feeling better than I have in days.

"If he bleeds out, maybe she won't come back," Ethan deadpans.

I drop the scalpel next to the tray holding Clover's heart and grin. "I didn't know you were funny."

Ethan cracks a grin back. "My mom says I have a dry sense of humor."

"Cool." I nod, not knowing what to say next.

After a moment, Ethan breaks the silence. "You look nice, by the way."

"Ah . . . thanks?"

"I mean about your horn," he adds hastily.

"I know," I say, then, "I'm sorry about what happened with Brooklyn."

He lets out a sigh. "Yeah, me too. I guess I was being kind of dumb. But a guy's got to try. That's what my dad says."

"Yeah, I guess," I say. *Dude, you need to stop listening to your dad.*

"That's what you did, right?" he continues. "You tried, and it worked. That's got to feel good."

"It does." My hand moves to my bangs. But then I think of Mystic. "You know, there are other girls."

He looks at me strangely.

"Oh, I don't mean like me or anything." I can feel myself blushing.

"Got it. I won't ask you to the dance."

"No, that's not what I'm saying," I say. Now I'm totally flustered. "Sorry. I didn't mean to make it worse."

"Don't worry. You can't make it worse. It's already worse." Ethan's eyes register something behind me and I turn to see he's looking at my backpack. "I'm sorry your little unicorn's gone."

"Like I said. Thomas Kelly is a real nice guy."

Ethan starts to say something, then stops himself. His eyes land on our dissecting tray, where Clover's naked heart lies in the cold, sterile pan, and he takes a breath. "I don't feel so good," he says. "Gosh, if I can't handle this, how can I ever be a fireman?"

"Why do you want to be a fireman?"

"My dad's a fireman. So's my uncle. Kind of runs in the family."

So this is what it's like to have a dad. Sounds like a lot of pressure. "Don't worry. I'll do the rest."

Picking up my scalpel again, I slice through the veins leading to the heart ventricles, exposing their tubular interiors, and then into the heart chambers themselves, while Ethan dutifully notes our findings. At the end of class, when I dump Clover's heart unceremoniously into the trash bin, I feel a little heartless myself.

As usual, I head to my locker at the end of the day, where Nicholas is waiting. "Want to come over and do homework?" he asks. I know he really means "Want to come over and talk about *Highwaymen?*" and usually I'd be completely down for that. But today is the dance committee meeting, and I promised Emma I'd be there.

"I can't."

"Why?" he asks.

I don't want to tell him about the dance committee for some reason, so this comes out: "I have French club."

"French club?" he says, frowning. "Since when do you have French club?"

I don't. There is no French club, but after the first lie, the second one's easier. "It's new."

"How are you getting home?" he asks, and that's a problem. Emma's mom is going to pick us up, but I can't tell Nicholas that.

"Ethan," I blurt out. "He's in French club, too. I'm getting a ride with him." *STOP TALKING, JEWEL.* Too many details. I stand there staring at Nicholas with a frozen smile on my face.

"You're being weird," he finally says. "So . . . have fun at *French club*." Nicholas's eyes stay glued to mine for a second too long before he hikes his backpack over his shoulder and moseys down the hall.

Phew. That was close. No. That was wrong; I know it was wrong. But I promised Emma, and Nicholas wouldn't understand. At least, that's what I tell myself as I head downstairs to the dance committee meeting.

* * *

"That looks rad, J."

I look up from the mermaid I'm working on to see Emma standing over my shoulder. "Thanks. They're turning out okay, I think."

Emma sits down beside me and picks up one of the mermaid stencils I cut out. In front of us, glittery cardboard mermaids swim across a blue paper ocean on the gym floor.

"You don't think it's a little too Ariel?" I ask.

"What's wrong with Ariel?"

"Nothing, I guess." I think about Nicholas and how he's not a fan of Disney creatures. His mermaids would definitely not look like this.

When I first got to the gym, I sat on the bleachers with everyone else as Emma went over what we have to do. There were twelve of us all together, a weird mix of cheerleaders and art kids. I was kind of annoyed to see Brooklyn here, but I guess you don't get one without the other.

"It's the final push, people," Emma said, like she was leading an army to war. "The dance is only five days away. You guys get that, right? Tomorrow, I don't want to turn around without seeing a poster about this dance. We need to sell more advance tickets, and we won't do that unless *boys* do what they are supposed to do. So let's make a lot of these!"

Emma held up a poster that said ASK HER NOW, spelled out in blue and gold glitter. A cringing image of poor Ethan popped into my head.

"But since boys are generally unreliable and we're all obviously feminists here," Emma went on, "I thought we'd try some parallel messaging. She held up another poster. ASK THAT BOY it read, which made some people laugh. "Hey," Emma scolded lightly. "Under the Sea is going to be the most successful eighth-grade dance in school history, and gender parity is not a joke, so whatever works, right?"

"You guys need water?" It's Brooklyn's voice behind us now, bringing me back to the moment, but I pretend not to hear.

"Yeah, thanks Brook," Emma says, and takes a bottle.

"Jewel?" Brooklyn says. And I do believe this is the first time Brooklyn has ever said my name.

I hold up my hand without turning around. "Sure," I say, and she places a bottle into my palm.

You'd think she'd get the message and go away, but she doesn't. Brooklyn sits down beside Emma and inspects my mermaids. "Wow, you're really good," she says.

"Thanks," I say begrudgingly. Doesn't she know it's not cool to suddenly start being nice to somebody *after* she's had her horn taken off?

Emma and Brooklyn talk dance committee business while I decorate one of my cutout mermaids with paint and glitter. This one has blue eyes, green hair, and . . . I almost give her a unicorn horn. I mean, I really want to do that, and I don't know why. But I don't.

"We've got like five hundred likes on the last one," Brooklyn says to Emma. "I'll post 'Ask That Boy' tonight."

"Perfect," Emma replies, then turns to me. "You're following the dance account, right?"

I shrug. "You've seen my phone."

Emma looks at Brooklyn. "Jewel needs a new phone. Bad."

"Quel dommage," Brooklyn says, opening her Instagram and showing me a pic of the phrase "Ask Her Now" surrounded by what looks like stardust. *"Regardes."*

Emma groans. "Cut it out with the French already."

"You just don't like that we can talk behind your back," Brooklyn teases.

"Very funny . . . or however you say it in French." Emma gets up, actually annoyed, but surprisingly, Brooklyn grins at me.

"Come on everybody," Emma calls out to the room. "We've got to get these posters up."

Armed with glittery posters and huge rolls of masking tape, all twelve of us fan out down the halls and plaster Under the Sea dance posters everywhere.

Emma heads upstairs, which is where I was planning on going anyway, loaded with poster boards. The lunchroom is strangely empty and quiet. "Let's start here," Emma says.

I double-tape the backs of the posters, then hand them to her to hang on the wall. It's a good system, though it's easy to get ahead of her because she's very particular about placing them perfectly.

As I wait for her to catch up with me, my eyes wander. This is where Emma and I once ate lunch together. This is where the accident with Noah happened. This is where Carmen tried to comfort me every day after Emma left, before Nicholas and Mystic arrived.

"Do you remember Carmen?" I ask her.

Emma looks down at me, from up on her chair. "Your unicorn?"

"Yeah."

"Whatever happened to her?"

"I don't know," I say thoughtfully. It's not like I haven't been wondering the same thing.

"Guess you outgrew her then," she says, pressing a poster to the wall. "Finally."

"What?"

"I mean, you couldn't believe in her forever."

"Wait," I say, taking a step toward her. "'Believe in' her? You saw Carmen, too."

"We were kids," she says, grabbing another board from my hands. "Who doesn't want to believe in unicorns?"

"Yeah, but Carmen wasn't an imaginary friend. She wasn't a make-believe unicorn."

Emma looks at me, frowning. "Do you still see her?"

"Not lately, but—"

She shrugs. "If you don't see her anymore, she's probably not real."

I step back, feeling like the wind has been knocked out of me. "So you really didn't believe she was there? All that time? Why didn't you say something?"

"I don't know. Maybe I didn't want to upset you." Emma points her finger to the center of her forehead.

"What's that supposed to mean?"

"Nothing," Emma says. "Just, that thing with Noah was . . . intense."

What is she saying? I stare at her, dumbfounded. "You were scared of me?"

Emma returns to the poster she's hanging. "No. I didn't mean it like that. It's just . . . whatever, it's better now, right? You have to admit that."

"Yeah," I say, but it comes out tight.

Breezily, she changes the subject and starts telling me about the DJ they've hired for the dance. But I'm hardly listening. I can't believe she couldn't see Carmen. She always said she could. I try to gloss over it in my head, but I feel genuinely betrayed to learn that she was only pretending.

When the posters are hung, Emma texts her mom to pick us up, and we head toward the stairway.

"We've got so much more to do this week," Emma says. "There's the presales, and the decorations for the gym, and we have to get more volunteers to bake for the refreshment table, and . . ."

As we enter the stairwell, she's still talking, but the more she talks, the less I hear. Her mouth is moving, but somehow it's hard to make out what she's saying, and my forehead hurts—a sharp, intense pain, like an icicle pressing from the front of my head to the back of my neck. My fingers reach up to where my horn used to be and I suddenly find it hard to breathe.

"What's wrong?" Emma asks, but she sounds so distant—like I'm underwater again. "J," she repeats, sounding even farther away.

"I don't know," I tell her. I can barely see. Everything is quiet, and black singes the edges of my sight, like I'm looking through binoculars. I try to hold on to the rail. Then I don't see her anymore. I don't see anything.

Except the black. I hover there, only hearing my lonely breath, until . . . the black unspools and all of it changes.

Esmeralda

Slowly, I step up onto the sidewalk. The wooden sidewalk.

Before me is a pair of swinging doors. Over the doors is a sign that reads THE WATERING HOLE.

The Watering Hole? That's the saloon in *Highwaymen*.

A woman bursts through the swinging doors—a woman in a long green dress with black trim—and I gasp.

It can't be.

Transfixed, I watch Esmeralda survey the town. Her hands find her hips as her eyes fall on a scruffy dog hurrying nervously down the street. When she looks to see what the dog's running from—

A dust cloud rises in the distance. Something's happening out there.

"Wesley." Esmeralda and I say his name at the same time, and slowly, she turns to me.

Her eyes register my blue jeans and green sneakers with the pink laces before landing on my face. "You're not from around here, are you?"

I shake my head.

She turns back to the far-off disturbance, using her hand as a visor against the blazing sun. "How do you know Wesley?"

"That's sort of hard to explain," I say. I'm talking to Esmeralda! What? "I've never met him in person. I just know about him."

"You telling the truth?" she challenges. "People who know about Wesley usually work for Wesley."

I guess I shouldn't tell her how much I know about Wesley, then. Like that sometimes he beats his dog, Joe, with his tightly wound lasso, that he has a younger sister named Mary who walks with a cane, that he carries a crumpled-up four-leaf clover in his breast pocket, that his mission in life is to destroy every magical creature in and around Hot Springs, New Mexico.

There's a cry from the sky, and I look up to see an enormous bird flying above us. Wide purple wings.

Snakelike neck. Crest of feathers on its head. The phoenix screeches and soars past, disappearing over Holcomb's General Store.

"Was that—?"

"Marv," Esmeralda answers before I can finish. I was going to say that. I knew it was Marv. "What are those on your feet?"

"Sneakers," I tell her, and now she looks at me like I'm speaking another language.

A gunshot echoes from somewhere near the dust cloud. Bootsteps approach, and the saloon doors part to reveal Beaumont Monroe, sheriff of Hot Springs. He looks me over, then tips his charcoal cowboy hat. "Ma'am," he says, and joins Esmeralda, gazing at the dust cloud.

"Wesley is stirring up trouble again," she says.

"Yep," answers Beaumont, in his simple, laconic way.

"Is that Rock Canyon?" I ask these two people I know so well. They turn to me, puzzled.

Beaumont takes a step toward me and holds up his right hand, just like he did in the hospital back in Los Angeles. "Truth," he says, then opens his other palm. "Or consequences."

"Consequences" comes out of my mouth, just like I said in the dream, or what I thought was a dream.

And suddenly I'm afraid. Something doesn't feel right. This was what happened the last time I saw Carmen—I mean, really saw her. I only thought I glimpsed her at the gazebo, and I'm trusting my perception less and less. And now it all feels too long ago. What if something's actually wrong? "Where's Carmen?" I ask them, feeling a dread I can't quite explain.

Beaumont and Esmeralda stare at me oddly, like they don't understand me.

"What'd you say?" Esmeralda asks.

"Carmen!" I say, feeling the panic rise inside. "Have you seen Carmen?"

"Jewel."

Esmeralda cocks her head, looking perplexed.

A hand touches my shoulder.

"Carmen?" Esmeralda asks.

"Yes, Carmen!"

"Jewel?" The voice is more insistent. The hand is shaking my shoulder.

My eyes jolt open.

And Emma is standing on the stair below, looking at me. It's her hand on my shoulder. "What happened?" she asks.

"I don't know," I say, trying to catch my breath. What *did* just happen? I can still feel the desert sun of Hot Springs on my face.

"Are you okay?" Emma asks.

I pull my hand away from my forehead. It doesn't hurt anymore. But something else does. My heart is full-blown aching as I stare into Emma's eyes. What am I supposed to tell her? If she doesn't believe me about Carmen, she sure won't believe me about this.

"J?" she says, staring at me strangely.

Pulling it together, I nod briskly. "Sorry," I say. "Yeah. I'm okay." Though inside, I absolutely know that I'm not.

* * *

If that happened in front of anybody else, they'd make me tell my mom so she could drive me to the hospital. At the very least, we'd be calling Dr. Stein.

But it happened in front of Emma, and it turns out that Emma is easily redirected toward whatever is most important in her own mind. I didn't remember that about her.

By the time her mom picks us up, I've convinced her that little blackouts are side effects of the surgery and that they don't happen often. Soon, they shouldn't happen at all. She doesn't press the point.

When we get home, Emma asks if I want to come over, but I tell her I should probably go rest, so we head to our respective apartments. Actually, I just want to be alone because I can't get these thoughts out of my head. Why was I asking Beaumont and Esmeralda about Carmen? *How* was I asking Beaumont and Esmeralda anything? What *was* that?

I pass Soccer Sam kicking the ball around, and look up to see Grandma sitting on the top step outside our apartment door. When I reach her, I ask, "Are you waiting for me?"

"It's a nice day." She lifts her face up to the sky. "Thought I'd watch Sam play with that soccer ball I hear all the time." Then she adds, "Don't you have a phone?"

"Yeah, why?"

"You weren't on the bus. You didn't call me."

"Oh my gosh, I forgot. I'm sorry."

"Where were you?" she asks, squinting up at me.

"I was working on mermaids for the dance. I'm on the dance committee."

"The dance committee, huh?" Grandma says, and I sit down beside her. "That something with Emma?"

"Yeah. It's her committee. I didn't mean to worry you." I feel bad. How could I forget to tell her?

Sam's soccer ball bounces several beats before she asks, "Is everything okay with you?"

I look at her. "Why do you ask?"

"Grandmotherly feeling."

How does she always know *everything*? *No, I'm not okay* would be the truthful answer. I mean, what just happened to me was insane. I still feel a little light-headed, and I'm definitely confused. But how to explain it? I don't even know what it was. And I don't want to worry her, at least until I sort it out for myself first. But it felt so real. And now I'm worried about Carmen.

Grandma elbows me gently.

I'm not sure what to say so I confess the other thing that's been on my mind. "It's just weird being normal."

"How do you mean?"

I haven't said this out loud yet, so I search for the words. "You know when you want something so bad and you get it, and you think it's going to make you completely different?"

"I think so."

"Well, I don't feel as different as I thought I would. I mean, I look different, but . . .

"You don't feel so different inside."

"Yeah, something like that."

She pats me on the leg. "I think that's called being human. We can move around all the pieces, try to change them, try to control them, but at the end, we're still just who we are."

"Why didn't you ever tell me that?"

Grandma grins. "'Cause it's the kind of thing you have to learn for yourself."

I guess she's right. If anyone had told me that removing my horn wouldn't completely change me, I wouldn't have believed them.

"Just remember," Grandma says. "I love you normal, weird, and in between."

Good thing, I think as I look into the sky. Because I have the odd suspicion that I might be less normal now than I've ever been before.

Highwaymen Things

"Are you okay?" Mom says, sounding suspiciously like Grandma. We all overslept, and she's driving me to school.

"Yeah," I tell her, even though my forehead hurts, and I had a horrible dream last night. Carmen was falling and I couldn't save her. It was so terrifying. And so real.

"I talked to Dr. Stein yesterday."

"You did?" I ask, wondering if he knows what's going on with me. "Why?"

"He's been checking in. He wants to know how you're doing."

"What did you tell him?"

"Well, that the bad dreams have continued, but other than that—"

"I'm not having bad dreams," I say, because I'm not, except for last night.

"Sweetie, you've been having lots of them. Ever since you've been back."

I turn to her, baffled. "What are you talking about?"

"You share a room with your grandma, remember?" She looks at me. "And you're not exactly a quiet dreamer."

I suddenly feel exposed. They know something I didn't know about myself. "Why didn't you tell me?"

"I thought you knew and just weren't talking to us about it." Big drops of rain hit the windshield and Mom puts on the wipers. "What are you dreaming about?"

"I don't know," I say, but I do know. I must be dreaming about Carmen.

At school, I hurry past the main office and spot the clock that says I have about two minutes to get to homeroom. I sprint upstairs, past where I had my vision—vision, dream, encounter, whatever—about *Highwaymen* yesterday, and around the corner, passing dance poster after dance poster.

Suddenly, a locker slams shut in front of me, and a boy swings around.

BAM! His books go flying. I hit the floor. And so does he.

Dazed, I look up and see Noah.

"You okay?" I ask.

He pulls himself up. "Yeah, you?"

Kids avoid us like we're victims of a crime scene as we scramble to pick up everything, dodging feet, legs, and continuous motion. "Here," I say, and hand him his algebra book and a bunch of papers.

"Thanks." He takes them awkwardly. "Sorry about that."

"We've got to stop meeting like this," I say, but the joke doesn't land, so I add, "It's me, Jewel."

"Yeah, I know. I recognized you even without your . . ." He stares at my invisible horn, and my hand touches the bangs over my forehead before I can stop myself. "Did it hurt?" Noah asks.

I grab for my backpack, mostly just to do something with my hands. "You mean getting my horn taken off?"

"Yeah," he says.

"Not during. They knocked me out for that. But after, it did. It hurt a lot."

"That's what I thought," he says, but his eyes wander past me. Great, even as a former unicorn, I'm boring.

"Where—" he starts, and then the bell for homeroom rings.

"I've got to go," I say. "Talk to you later, Noah."

"Yeah, talk to you later, Jewel."

By PE my head feels better, and even though my life is going absolutely bonkers haywire, I feel good about my unexpected progress with Noah. Mystic and I are walking around the track, staying in an outer lane to avoid the runners.

"Can I tell you something?" I ask her.

"Yeah, of course," she says.

"It's just . . ." I stop, not knowing how to put it into words.

"Is this about a boy?" Mystic asks hopefully.

I shake my head. "Not about a boy."

"Then what?"

"It's weird."

Mystic laughs. "Oh, no, it's weird. I don't know if I can handle that."

I grab her arm. "No, I mean it."

"Okay," she says. "Go for it. The weirder the better."

I take a breath and say, "There's this thing that happened to me and I can't explain it." Then I just rip the Band-Aid. "I'm seeing things in my head like they're real."

"Like what things?"

I chuckle because I know how ridiculous this is going to sound. "*Highwaymen* things."

"*Highwaymen* things?" she says slowly, like I'm a child.

"Yeah," I say slowly back.

"You mean like that comic book you and Nick like?" Her brow furrows. "What does that even mean, 'seeing *Highwaymen* things'?"

"It happened yesterday, and it might have happened before, in the hospital, where I kind of blacked out—"

"Whoa," she says, concerned. "Are you all right?"

"Yeah, I'm fine, but . . . I was there, Mystic. In the graphic novel—I mean, the comic book. In the Old West. With Esmeralda and Beaumont."

"Esmeralda and Beaumont?"

"The people from *Highwaymen*! The characters were people who were real. Really real, and Old West-y."

"Like a movie?"

"No! Like this! I was there, in Hot Springs, talking to them just like I'm talking to you."

"Oh." Mystic bites the edge of her thumbnail, thinking.

"You think I'm weird," I finally say.

She turns to me. "I *know* you're weird. But that's separate from this. When did it happen yesterday?"

"After school." I omit the part about being with Emma because Mystic wouldn't like that.

"Should you maybe see a doctor?"

"I don't know," I say, getting quiet inside. Because I *don't* know. Like, should I call Dr. Stein and tell him I met my heroes in their make-believe town and I'm afraid my unicorn's in danger? Uh-huh, sure.

"Who else knows?" she asks.

"Only you."

Mystic smiles. I can tell that makes her feel special. "Have you ever thought this might happen to everybody who gets their unicorn horn taken off?"

"Ha. Ha. Ha."

That's when I see Emma and Brooklyn walking the wrong way on the track, coming toward us. As they get closer, I see that Emma is looking at me. They stop in front of us.

"Can you do a walk-and-talk?" she says, ignoring Mystic altogether. "We have dance deets to work out."

Mystic looks at me, so confused.

"I'm on the dance committee," I tell her quickly, then to Emma: "Um . . . sure. Is that okay, Myst?"

"Is that okay?" Mystic says, her feelings clearly hurt. "Yeah, I guess."

"See you at lunch," I tell her because I don't know what else to say. And then I start walking with Emma and Brooklyn in the opposite direction.

* * *

"So uncool," Nicholas says at lunch, after Mystic tells him what I did.

"I know. I know." I look at Mystic pleadingly. "I was going to tell you. It's just that it all happened so fast, and I thought it might be fun."

"Fun to not tell me you're hanging out with Emma again?" Mystic asks.

"No, not that! Fun to be on the dance committee."

"Which Emma asked you to join?"

"Yeah, but—"

Mystic shakes her head. "Emma is bad news."

"Okay, fine. If you want the truth, that's what I thought you'd say. It's kind of why I didn't tell you." I pause and add, "Remember, you didn't tell me everything lately either," referring to the Brooklyn essay situation.

"Which I apologized for like a million times!" Mystic says and looks over at the popular table. "So, just to recap— Emma dumped you, and Brooklyn stole your spot in the French competition. Now you want to be BFFs with them? You sure you don't want to rethink this?"

"It's just for the dance. They think I'm good at drawing. I like doing the posters."

Mystic's eyes shift to the walls in the cafeteria. "Did you do these?"

"Some of them."

Nicholas looks up. "Which ones?" he asks in a way that makes me not want to answer. "Come on! The giant clams or the hilarious mermaids?"

"The hilarious mermaids."

He grins.

"Shut up, Nicholas," I say. "They're supposed to be like that."

"I didn't say anything!"

Mystic eyes go wide. "Do you have a date to the dance?"

"No! Of course not. I'm on refreshment duty," I say, then brighten. "Why don't you guys come?"

"To the *dance*?" Nicholas asks dubiously.

"Yes, to the dance. Why can't we do stuff like dances? Dances are fun."

"How would you know?" Mystic asks.

"I'm guessing?" I say hopefully.

"I'm out," says Nicholas.

I turn to Mystic. "What about you?"

She looks at the nerd table. "I feel sorry for him," Mystic says.

"You mean Ethan?" I look at the nerd table, too, where Ethan is sitting next to Noah.

"You think he's going anyway?"

"Oh, not this again," says Nicholas.

Mystic doesn't even argue back. She's still looking, moon-eyed, at Ethan.

"Come to the dance," I ask her again.

"Maybe," she says, and looks back at me. "Just . . . don't lie to me anymore, okay?"

I'm about to say that I didn't lie to her because technically, I didn't, but instead I just say, "Okay. I won't."

Mermaids and Mermen

My breath comes out in clouds of fog as I wait for the bus. It's unusually cold, yet my freezing hand is wrapped around my phone, even though there's not much to look at because of my messed-up app situation.

I think about texting Nicholas, but for some reason, I open my photos instead and see the picture that Mystic took of me after she cut my bangs. I look so happy and normal. I flip back through other photos: a view of the sky outside the plane window on the way home, outside the Garbo with George after he gave me the Dodgers cap, on Hollywood Boulevard with Grandma standing over Barbara Stanwyck's star. Then . . .

Oh, wow. I'd almost forgotten about that. The selfie I took the night before the surgery in the hospital. There's me, my horn still on my head, wearing Mystic's Eiffel Tower hornlet. I stare at that Jewel with the horn.

There's a poke in the middle of my back, and I turn to see Emma. "Morning," she says, smiling at me.

"Hey," I say, surprised to see her. Emma's mom usually drives her to school.

"It's freezing out here." Emma shivers, folding her arms across her chest. Now that we're actually hanging out again, it's so clear how different we are. She's wearing cool furry boots and a puffy coat I haven't seen before, and I'm still jamming myself into my navy blue jacket we bought at the beginning of middle school.

"Guess what I got last night?"

"What?" I ask.

"My dress for the dance!" she says excitedly. "I thought I'd never find it, but Mom took me to look one last time, and omigod, J, it's gorgeous."

"Oh . . . that's great," I say, but I feel like a cold bucket of water just got dumped on my head.

"What's wrong?" she asks.

"I don't have a dress. I didn't even think about it until now. Do you really think I need one if I'm just at the refreshment stand?" As I say this, I kick myself for being stupid. Did I think I'd wear jeans and a T-shirt to a dance? Even the refreshment girl is supposed to be dressed up. Even I know that.

Emma frowns. "The dance is like three days away. And I thought *I* was cutting it close . . ."

"We definitely can't afford a brand-new dress right now," I say, starting to panic. "Or even something from Tina's Treasures. What am I going to do, Em?"

Her face lightens. "Don't worry. Come over after school. You can wear something of mine."

"Really," I say, filling with relief.

"Course," Emma says, and smiles. "I got you, J. We'll do dance committee, then you'll come over. You can stay for dinner, too."

"Sounds great," I say. Because it does. It sounds terrific.

When we get on the bus, I text Grandma so she'll know what I'm doing. I don't want to worry her again.

We ride to school together, and a satisfied smile blooms on my face. For the moment all my other cares fade away. My mind-bending trip to Hot Springs, my worry about Carmen, my disappointment about the French competition . . . in this instant, they all somehow pale against Emma being my friend again.

That afternoon at dance committee, I start working on the life-size cutouts of a mermaid and a merman. They have holes where the faces should be so it can be our photo booth. I'm painting the mermaid's tail when I spot Brooklyn striding quickly into the gym.

"Where have you been? You're, like, *really* late," I overhear Emma saying.

"I had to go by French," Brooklyn says, dropping her backpack on the bleachers by the Swimming with the Fishes display.

Of course she did. She's prepping with Monsieur Oliver for the competition. It's okay, I tell myself, unable to ignore the sharp dart of envy that just exploded in my chest.

I try to concentrate on my mermaid. I take my time, meticulously dabbing yellow highlights along the blue and green scales.

"Need some help?"

I turn and see Brooklyn standing over me. "Uh . . . sure . . . I guess."

Brooklyn plops down beside me. "Man, you make the coolest mermaids."

"Thanks," I say. "I'm just doing the painting. Courtney made the cutouts."

Brooklyn looks over at Courtney, who's putting the finishing touches on the Under the Sea mural. "She's such a talent, gosh." She picks up a paintbrush. "How can I help?"

"Um . . ." Brooklyn is the last person I want to be doing this with, but there's a lot to be done. "Can you use that blue on the merman's scales?"

"Sure." She dips her brush in the aqua-colored paint. We work silently for a minute until she stops and looks at me. "Hey listen. I wanted to ask you something."

"Yeah," I say, feeling suspicious as I keep painting.

"I just talked to Monsieur Oliver."

Rub it in, why don't you.

"And . . . we want you to do it."

Huh? I turn to her. "Do what?"

"The essay competition. I asked him if it would be okay. It's just, your essay was so good, and your French is so much better than mine. And let's face it. You were his first choice."

"I don't understand," I say, confused.

"I know I should have said something sooner. I mean, I should have. But I really wanted to go. I guess I was trying to tell myself you didn't want to do it. But I saw how you looked when you found out it was me. You want it, right?"

I nod slowly, stunned. Speechless.

"I get selfish about things sometimes," Brooklyn continues. "My dad calls it my fatal flaw. But Jewel, you're like, *really* good at French. I mean, we all know that you're in a totally different league than the rest of us. You deserve to be there more than me. So what do you say?"

"Really?" The emotion of it all seeps into my pores.

Brooklyn smiles. "Really."

"Are you sure?" I actually start laughing, it's all so unexpected. Maybe I misjudged Brooklyn. "I've been so jealous," I say, surprisingly uncensored.

"Of me?" Brooklyn says, like that's unbelievable.

"Yeah," I nod, relieved, flushed.

"I had to face facts. Monsieur Oliver actually helped me face them, if truth be told. He thinks you're awesome."

Monsieur Oliver thinks I'm awesome? "But wait!" I suddenly blurt out. "My essay is about having a horn. I don't have a horn anymore."

"Well . . . you could rewrite it about what it's like to be a girl *without* a horn."

That's what Monsieur Oliver told me. I guess he's rubbing off on her. And then it hits me. "The competition's Saturday!"

"I know! But I can help you get ready. Monsieur Oliver said we can get together during lunch for the next couple of days." I must still look stunned because she adds, "It'll be okay. You've got this. And everybody is going. We'll all cheer you on."

I feel overwhelmed and excited at the same time.

"Don't worry. You'll be fine," she says. *"Pas de problème."*

"Right," I say, cracking a grin. Not a problem at all.

* * *

Emma's closet has more clothes than they should be able to afford. When I ask about it, she tells me that her dad sends her "outfit" money. Outfit money? *Geez!* Where's my long-lost dad with *my* outfit money?

I try a white minidress and stare at my reflection in the full-length mirror on her door.

"I don't think that's quite right," Emma says, and goes back to her closet. Carefully, I take off the dress and lay it on her bed.

"How about this one?" She pulls out a light blue one. It's beautiful and goes all the way to the floor.

"Isn't that too fancy?"

"For the eighth-grade dance?"

"No, for me."

"Go on. Try it on," she says, handing it to me. "I have a feeling about it."

I pull the dress over my head and let it slip over my body. As I smooth out the front and straighten the shoulders, Emma's face lights up. "Oooh. Look at you!"

"Is it good?" I ask, hopeful and doubtful at the same time.

"See for yourself," she says, and points to the mirror.

I look at my reflection and think, *Oh.*

It fits.

It really fits.

I look so grown up.

I look so—

"Perfect!" Emma cries, breaking out into a little dance.

I turn around, gazing at myself from all angles. "Are you sure I can borrow it?"

"Of course!"

I brush my bangs over my forehead. If you didn't know me before, you'd have no idea I'd had a horn there.

Emma sits on the bed and her expression changes. "What were you and Brooklyn talking about at dance committee?"

"Oh, didn't she tell you?" I say happily. "She wants me to do the French competition in her place!"

"She does?" Emma says. This is clearly news to her.

"It was really nice of her. I've been thinking maybe I got the wrong impression of Brooklyn." I stop myself before I say too much. I don't want Emma to pass along anything mean.

"Are you going to do it?"

"I think so. I mean, I was Monsieur Oliver's first pick. But when I left . . . anyway, Brooklyn is being cool," I say. "The only thing is that it's Saturday."

"The day after the dance!" Emma shrieks. "You sure you'll be ready?"

"I have no idea how I can be ready."

"Don't worry. I'm sure you can do it all," she says, and I gaze into the mirror and feel like maybe I *can* do it all. "'Cause things are changing for you, J."

"What do you mean?"

"Uh . . . you're going to the dance. You're doing the essay competition. You don't have a horn." She meets my gaze, and there's a pause in the air before she says, "So what's the deal with you and Mystic, anyway? And that guy you hang out with?

"Nicholas?"

"Yeah, him."

"What do you mean, what's the deal? They're my friends."

Emma crosses her arms. "Well, don't take this the wrong way, but they're not really . . . you know . . . I mean, look at you. You don't belong at the freak table anymore."

My eyes catch my reflection again. She's right. I don't look like a freak anymore. I, Jewel Conrad, the queen of the freaks, am now—

"A popular girl," Emma says, almost proudly. "That's what you look like now."

"I was just thinking I looked normal."

"J. You're way past normal. Haven't you noticed people looking at you?"

"Sure, but that's because, you know, I got my horn taken off."

"At first. But now they're looking at you because you're hot."

"Hot?" My eyes dart back to the mirror. Okay, maybe I look good in the dress, but *hot*? Is she kidding?

"I knew it right away. As soon as you got back from LA. Everybody is going to know it when they see you at the dance, though," she says. "Nobody could see the real you with your horn, but now . . ."

That's what Mrs. Whatley said on my first day back. That now she could see the real me. I look at my reflection and wonder, *Is this what the real me looks like?* I can't tell anymore.

Back at home, I stay up late rewriting my French essay. Something still isn't right about it, and I can't figure out what. I stare out my window, trying to find the right words, and catch myself searching for Carmen. *Where is she?* The ache in my heart for her that was once only a pinprick has morphed into the size of baseball, and it won't go away. It's funny that I've never felt this about my dad. But my dad never watched out for me, or did any of those things that a parent is supposed to do. Carmen did that.

Closing the blinds, I clutch my chest and tell myself I can't think about her right now. I've got my dress for the dance. Mom's taking off work for the French competition. And somehow I'll figure out my essay. Aching heart or not, the next two days are mine.

Faster. Faster. Faster.

It's Friday morning, the day of the dance, and I'm in the locker room dressing down for PE with Mystic.

I woke up with a fierce headache and my heart was aching even worse. But that's not all. Something inside me wasn't right. Isn't right. Or maybe not just inside me, but everywhere. I don't know if it's about Carmen, or the thing that happened on the stairs with Emma, but whatever it is, it feels wrong.

As if she can feel what's going on inside me, Mystic asks, "How's your head?"

"It's okay," I say, shrugging.

"Any new *Highwaymen* stuff going on?"

"No." I knock on my skull. "All clear in there," I say, even though that's not true. It's like something is pushing on me from the inside. I'm trying to pretend it's not there, but it is.

Taking a breath, I calm myself down. *Just be cool, okay,* I say to whatever's going on. *Be cool until Sunday.*

"You okay?" Mystic asks me.

"Sure," I say, and close my locker door.

As we head up the stairs to the gym, late as usual, Mystic pinches my elbow. "Oh, and guess what? I convinced Nicholas to come to the dance with me."

My mouth falls open. "No!"

"Yep."

"Wait, is Ethan going, too?"

"Who cares?" she says. "JK. I hope so."

"Way to be bold, Myst," I tell her, and I mean it.

In the gym, the whole class is already assembled on the bleachers. We slip in and sit in the front row. Everything looks amazing, even in regular light, all decorated for tonight.

Coach T. eyes the gym like it's a pal that's betrayed him. "Because of all this," he says, gesturing toward my very own mermaid and merman cutouts, "the gym is unsuitable for our purposes today. So we're heading to the track, people."

There are groans, and someone calls out, "Coach!" from the stands. It's Emma, holding up her hand, trying to get his attention.

"Oh, yes, I almost forgot," Coach T. says, wearily. "It's

come to my attention that an item has disappeared from the locker room. *Again.*"

"It's my necklace." Emma says, her voice crisp. "And it didn't disappear. It was stolen."

As the chatter rises, Coach T. holds up his hands. "Quiet!" he yells. "Okay, as you just heard, it's Ms. Winslow's necklace that's missing now. Ms. Chambers had a similar experience with a bracelet a while back. Which showed up. Correct?" Brooklyn gives him a shallow nod. "So. Maybe this necklace will show up, too. People, if this keeps happening, don't make me have to send in Mrs. Whatley to stand guard while you change."

I turn to Mystic, who looks like she's struggling not to seem concerned.

"Now let's hit the track," Coach T. says, blowing his whistle.

As people peel off the bleachers, Emma shouts, "That's it, Coach?"

He gives her an unenthusiastic thumbs-up and says, "Time to run."

Emma rolls her eyes as she and Brooklyn head down the bleachers. When they get to us, Emma looks at me for a beat too long before moving past.

I stand up, but Mystic pulls me back. "What did that mean?"

"I don't know."

"Crap, does she think I stole her necklace?" she whispers.

"I don't know," I say again, trying to figure it out. Was Emma's look accusing or regular? It's been so long since she might have overheard us in the locker room, and she's never said a single word about it. But if so, could she be thinking that a bracelet thief could also be a necklace thief?

"What are you thinking?" Mystic asks, the wheels in her mind clearly turning alongside mine.

"Nothing," I lie, rubbing my temple, trying to calm my aching head.

"You're thinking what I'm thinking." Mystic gestures toward the stairs where Emma's gone. "Go find out."

"You want me to ask her?"

"I mean, she's your friend again, right?" Mystic says, bristly. "Might as well make use of it."

"You don't have to say it like that. I'm just helping out with the dance committee."

"If that's what you call it."

I sigh. "Come on, Myst."

Her eyes are sincere even if her tone is blustery. "Please."

"Okay, yeah," I say, acquiescing. "Of course I'll go."

I hurry across the gym, past Coach T. and down the stairs with the rest of the class, probably surprising him by actually running for once. By the time I catch up with Brooklyn and Emma, we're coming out of the double doors into the gloomy day.

"Hey," I say, pulling up beside them.

"Hey, J. You ready for tonight?"

"I don't know. I've never been to a dance before."

Brooklyn giggles, and I look over at her. "What's so funny?"

"I've never been to a dance either."

"You haven't?" It's hard to believe Brooklyn, of all people, is new to this just like me.

"Brook's parents are weird about stuff like that," Emma says.

"They wouldn't let me go to a dance until I'm a teenager, and since I just turned thirteen—" Emma and Brooklyn high-five. "It's dance time!"

"Who are you going with?" I ask.

"Oh, nobody," Brooklyn says. "Are you kidding? I still have the same parents. I can't go on a date yet. I'm just going."

"Can you believe that?" Emma says, shaking her head.

As we step onto the track, I clear my throat and ask as casually as possible, "Hey, so when did you lose your necklace, Emma?"

"I didn't lose it. It was stolen. Yesterday."

"How do you know it was stolen?"

"Come on, J." Her eyes meet mine. Knowingly? "And I was going to wear it to the dance tonight."

"Maybe Coach is right. It might show up."

"You mean like Brooklyn's bracelet?" Emma asks pointedly. "It's just *weird* how stuff gets taken from that locker room. Huh. Do you have any idea who might want to steal jewelry?"

I start to answer, but quickly stop myself as a thought burrows in that wasn't there a second before. Could it be possible that Mystic *did* steal Emma's necklace? I mean, she promised me she wouldn't steal again, but I know she's not thrilled about me being friends with Emma. Could she be jealous enough to have done this?

"J?"

"No, of course not. I have no idea who would take your necklace."

"Okay," Emma says. "Whatever you say."

I continue walking with them, because I don't want to seem like I'm reporting back to Mystic. When I look over to see her, walking by herself on the other side of the track, though, I feel bad. But for the first time today, my headache is almost gone. I can finally breathe.

It sounds mean, but for a few minutes, I pretend that Mystic's not there. Because truthfully, it's fun talking with Emma and Brooklyn. I like joking and laughing about the dance. And the way people look at us when we pass makes me feel like I belong here.

* * *

In the cafeteria, while in line to get a sandwich to take to Monsieur Oliver's room, I see Mystic sitting at our regular table with Nicholas. I need to go talk to her about the necklace.

By the time I got back to the locker room with Emma and Brooklyn, she'd already gone. The thing is . . . I *really* don't want to confront her about this. So I'm kind of happy to head to French for our second essay practice. My essay is mostly rewritten, but Monsieur Oliver and Brooklyn offered some suggestions for changes that I'm going to practice with them today. Brooklyn was there yesterday and was actually helpful, teaching me how to stand and look confident onstage.

"Hi."

Noah gets in line behind me.

"Hey," I say back.

"I hear you're on the dance committee."

"Yeah. You have me to thank for all those mermaids haunting the halls."

"Cool," he says, and looks down.

"Are you going?" I blurt out, and he looks up.

"Ethan wants to go so, yeah, I think we're going."

"Well, I'll see you there, then, I guess. I'm working the refreshment table."

"I love refreshments," he says, and grins.

Um, what is happening? I add this to my list of confusing things. A boy who should be afraid of me just made a dorky joke with me.

As I'm heading out of the cafeteria, I give Mystic and Nicholas a quick wave, but of course she leaps up.

"Where have you been?" Mystic asks.

"I've got to go to Monsieur Oliver's class."

"But what happened?" she whispers, pulling me over to sit beside her. Nicholas is across from us drawing a gorgon, with dragon heads dangling from long scaly necks instead of snakes for hair.

Without looking up, he says, "Don't mind me. I'm not listening."

Mystic seems to believe him, or she doesn't care. She looks at me urgently. "What did she say?"

"Nothing."

"Really?"

"She asked me if I knew anything about it, and I said I didn't. Case closed."

Mystic takes a breath. "Okay. I just don't want any trouble." She glances at Emma in the lunch line.

I hesitate, because I don't want to say this but I have to

ask. Leaning toward her, I whisper, "Is there a reason why there would be trouble?"

Mystic's eyes flick immediately down, and something about the way she looks back up at me tells me everything I need to know.

Oh, Mystic.

"What do you mean?" she asks.

I could get into it. I could make her give Emma back the necklace before the dance. Or . . . maybe this can wait until Sunday, too.

"Nothing," I say, shaking my head, feeling like I'm not sure who she is anymore. "Never mind." Mystic looks at me quizzically though so I pretend to brighten. "Oh, I almost forgot to tell you. Ethan's coming to the dance!"

Mystic's eyes dart to the nerd table. "How do you know?"

"Noah just told me. So, yay!" I say, holding up my fists in celebration.

"Yay," Nicholas mimics from across the table.

"I knew you were listening," I say.

He sighs at Mystic. "So I guess there's no way I'm getting out of this."

"Just call us a regular dance committee." Mystic grins. "We're all going to this thing!"

"I can't wait," Nicholas deadpans, then goes back to his gorgon.

* * *

I run through my essay in front of Monsieur Oliver and Brooklyn about five times. Monsieur Oliver sits behind his desk while Brooklyn is planted in a chair in the front row.

"You feeling ready?" Monsieur Oliver asks me when we're done.

"I think so," I say. Honestly, I know that this essay isn't as good as my original one. It's missing something. But Monsieur Oliver and Brooklyn insist it's ready.

"You're doing really great," Brooklyn says, and I feel like she means it.

I may not be as good as her in front of people, but I do feel more confident than before. Maybe I *can* do this. I've been wondering something, though. "Do you think people will think I'm making it up?" I ask them.

Brooklyn looks surprised for a second, then starts laughing.

I'm smiling, too, but my question is serious. "I mean, my essay is about being a girl who used to have a horn. Who's going to believe I actually had a horn on my head? It's kind of unusual."

Monsieur Oliver grins. *"C'est rare, sans doute."*

"They might have heard about you," Brooklyn adds.

"Not in a bad way. It's just there aren't, I mean, there weren't many people like you."

I feel a pang in my forehead and it makes me think of Carmen. Brooklyn has no idea the scope of who I really am.

"Don't look so worried," says Monsieur Oliver. "It will be okay. All you have to do is speak your truth."

If he only knew how complicated my truth is right now— Emma being my friend again, Mystic stealing her necklace, and Carmen being gone for so long.

"We'll be there to support you," Monsieur Oliver says. "I'm driving us in the wrestling van."

"The wrestling van?" Brooklyn says, scrunching her nose. "Doesn't that stink?"

"We'll find out together," he says, winking. "So don't have too much fun *ce soir*, girls. We've got a big afternoon ahead of us. We'll pull out tomorrow at noon sharp."

The rest of the day speeds by like someone's chasing it. French class, science class. I try to avoid the image of Mystic's face when I asked her about the necklace, and instead focus on the night ahead. My first dance ever. And the French competition tomorrow. Another first.

My headache's back though. And that unsettled feeling I woke up with has shadowed me through the day. Maybe it's because I'm aware of it now, but I swear it's getting worse. Could it just be nerves?

I'm at my locker at the end of the day when it all starts again. Without any warning, everything goes bonkers ballistic, and my forehead feels like fire. The unspooling black reappears like night has fallen in one instant, and swoops me up like I'm prey. Clutching the metal door, I lean into my locker, and . . .

I'm flying.

Tearing away on horseback.

Arms wrapped around a waist.

A blue shirt and a charcoal hat.

Beaumont's shirt. Beaumont's hat.

Hooves beating like a drum.

Esmeralda galloping beside.

Faster. Faster. Faster.

Tears blowing across my temples.

"Should I be scared?" I ask her.

"You should always be scared," she says.

* * *

I blink sharply as the light from the hallway reenters my eyes. Nicholas is standing beside me, looking concerned. "Are you okay?" he asks.

I shake my head, bringing myself back, and mumble, "Yeah."

"You sure? You made a weird sound."

"No. I was just talking to myself. Nothing to see here."

Nicholas looks at me oddly, and why shouldn't he? That was probably the weirdest thing yet, different than before. It was quick—flashes, coming so fast and so real. I wipe the side of my face and feel real tears there. I can't not notice that my hands are shaking.

"I've, um, got to catch the bus. See you tonight," I say, and take off without looking back.

The Dance

"Oh my gosh," Mom exclaims, clapping her hands together in uncharacteristic delight. I just walked out of my bedroom in Emma's blue dress.

"You look beautiful, Jewel," Grandma says.

"Hold on," Mom says and runs to her bedroom.

If I were a normal girl, I'd be out of my mind excited right now. But after what happened at my locker, I'm seriously on edge. I mean, none of this is *normal*.

"Hey, it's your big night," Grandma says. "You should be smiling."

I plaster a fake smile on my face and say, "This better?"

Grandma's not dumb. She knows something's up. But before she digs deeper, Mom rushes back in holding a little handbag. "Here, here. You need something to put your things in."

I take the bag, a little silver thing with a metal strap. "Like what things?"

"Mints, gum, money."

"Do I have any of those things?" I ask her.

Mom grins. "I guess not." Then she looks at my feet. "What's happening down there?"

I pull up the dress, revealing my green sneakers with the pink laces.

She and Grandma actually gasp. "You can't wear those!"

"Why not? Nobody's going to see them. And I need to be comfortable. I'm working the refreshment table."

"We should have thought about that," Grandma says, as they both stare at my shoes.

My footwear choice is about more than my lack of access to nice shoes. After what happened today, I'm barely steady on my feet. I'm hollow like I haven't eaten all day, even though we just ate dinner. I have a feeling I'm getting sick, but I refuse to acknowledge that till after the competition tomorrow.

"There's no way I'm wearing heels," I tell them.

"As long as they don't show," Mom concedes, and grabs her phone. "Let's take a picture."

Of course, it's not just one picture; it's like twenty—of Mom and me, of Grandma and me, and then of me by myself. "Can we be done?" I finally ask.

Mom comes over and hugs me. When she pulls away, she wipes her face.

"What's wrong?" I ask.

Grandma puts her arm around her. "It'll be okay, Angie. They grow up on you. Nothing you can do about it."

"Okay," says Mom, sniffing. "It's your first dance. Have fun. You only have one eighth-grade dance."

"I will. I promise."

Mom wraps her sweater around herself tightly as she walks outside with me. We stand on the stairs waiting for Emma and her mom to come out.

"Things are changing so fast for you," she says, shaking her head. "I hope you know you can talk to me about anything."

Okay, I'll bite. "Do you ever feel like you're seeing something but it's far away from where you actually are?" I ask cautiously.

"Kind of like a daydream, you mean?"

"Kind of. But bigger."

"I don't know," she says. "Maybe?" We look at each other, a question in her eyes. "What is it, honey?"

I know she means I should come to her about boys, and

friends, and competitions. Not about wacko haywire visions and missing guardian unicorns. Still, maybe I should tell her. Because what's happening to me can't possibly be okay.

But I want to go to the dance. I want to be in the essay competition. If I tell Mom now, she'll call Dr. Stein, and then what? Will he make me go to the hospital? Will they cart me off to the loony bin? Once grown-ups know about this, things are bound to change. And not in a good way.

All I need is twenty-four hours. Then I'll come clean.

* * *

When Emma and I get to school, she tells me to take off my coat before we walk into the gym. My headache has flared up again, but I try to ignore it.

"Why?" I ask.

"Just do it."

We throw our coats on chairs and walk through the ocean-colored doors.

The gym is not dance-magical yet. The lights are on as volunteers and dance committee members perform the final setup duties—that's one of the "perks" of being on dance committee. Still, as we enter, everybody looks at us.

"See, I told you," Emma whispers. "You look good."

"They're staring at you," I whisper back, because Emma looks amazing. She's wearing an emerald-green dress with black heels, and she actually went to a salon to have her hair done.

As she goes to talk to the DJ, I hurry to the refreshment table, where Brooklyn is setting up all the baked goods. In jeans.

"Sorry we're late."

"You came with Emma," Brooklyn says. "Of course you're late. You look good."

"Hey, I wanted to come in jeans! But Emma said a dress was nonnegotiable."

Brooklyn grins. "Emma likes to make an entrance." She points toward a cooler behind the refreshment table. "Do you want to help with the waters?"

"Sure," I say, and start shoving bottles into ice. For a while, we work in silence. Then Brooklyn says, "So, I was wondering. Is it true that Mystic stole my bracelet?"

I freeze. "Where did you hear that?"

"Emma said she overheard you guys talking about it."

I feel so flustered, I don't know how to answer, and my headache isn't helping things. I thought this attack would come from Emma, not Brooklyn, and I don't feel prepared at all.

A sharp blast from a speaker makes us jump, and it feels like my head might split in two. I look over at the stage, where Emma is covering her ears and yelling at the DJ. Turning back to Brooklyn, I think about lying, but I can't. She's been too nice to me.

"Kind of," I sputter. "She just picked it up. She's really into making jewelry and buys a lot of stuff secondhand, so I think she saw it as more like an inspiration piece or something. That was all. She's not a thief. She promised me she would give it back, so I didn't say anything because I didn't want her to get in trouble. And she did give it back."

"I get that," Brooklyn says thoughtfully.

We stand there awkwardly, until I say, "You don't think she took Emma's necklace, do you?"

"Oh, I don't know," Brooklyn says, looking genuinely surprised. *Oh, man, why did I say that?* "Do you?"

"No," I say, shaking my head. "I really don't."

I can tell Brooklyn's deciding if she can take my word for it. Finally, she nods. I take a breath and Brooklyn smiles, both of us relieved. "Now that that's settled," she says, "let's have fun tonight. I'm going to get changed."

"Can I ask you something first?" I ask, and she turns back around. "Since we're being real."

"Sure."

"Why do you talk to me now? Because when I had a horn, you didn't." Wow, that was uncomfortable coming out, but I'm glad it did.

"I should have," Brooklyn says. "But you didn't seem really open to friends."

"I didn't?"

"Not really. The three of you guys seem to like keeping to yourselves. But I guess I was wrong, huh?" Brooklyn says, and I hear regret in her voice. "I'm sorry about that, Jewel."

This girl keeps surprising me. "It's okay. Thanks for saying that."

She smiles again. "And think, we could have been practicing French together all this time!"

"*Quel dommage,*" I say, and smile back. She leaves to get changed and I wonder if other people felt that way when I had my horn. Was I so afraid that kids would make fun of me that I built my own moat to keep them away? I know I wanted friends, but it even took me a long time to warm up to Nicholas and Mystic.

I finish setting up the refreshment table, then check out the photo booth area. I stick my head through the hole in my mermaid's head to see how it feels, and the photographer, who's still setting up, snaps a picture of me. Grandma will love it.

"Attention. Attention, you guys," Emma calls out from

behind the mic at the DJ table. All us workers look her way. "Check this out," she says, and the lights go down. For a moment, it's completely dark. Then blue, white, and yellow lights flood the gym, making it look like an otherworldly ocean. Everyone oohs and aahs as hanging silver streamers, dangling fish, and wave-painted balloons come alive in our illuminated aquarium. It's an Under the Sea extravaganza!

Emma practically skips over to me. "Look how amazing!" she croons, stars literally in her eyes.

"It's beautiful, Em," I say in awe, and together, we gaze at the twinkling lights. This reminds me of how I felt when we were younger, watching fireworks together. If my head felt better, this moment would be perfect.

"It's going to be the best eighth-grade dance ever," she says dreamily.

I want to ask her about telling Brooklyn about the necklace, but it's too jarring an idea to hold in this epic moment. "You did great," I say instead, putting another thing on hold until later.

In thirty minutes, eighth graders start pouring in, and it's not long before the gym is packed with bodies. Courtney, who drew the mural, is selling refreshments with me, still wearing her jeans. I don't think she's much up for dancing. The music blares, and it pulses between my ears, not in a good way. But soon we're selling so many drinks, candies, and cookies that I get distracted from what's going on inside my head. Courtney and I get a rhythm going together, and it's almost fun.

She's making a joke about how every guy is buying only brownies, nothing else, when I hear someone yell "Jewel!" over the music.

Looking over, I see Mystic and Nicholas standing at the edge of the refreshment table. "Hey," I say, going over to them. Mystic is wearing a black dress, big surprise, and perfect eyeliner. Nicholas's T-shirt has a tuxedo design on it. "You guys look great," I tell them.

Mystic smiles. "Thanks. How's it going so far?"

"So busy. We've run out of brownies."

"Then I'm outta here," Nicholas teases.

Mystic takes him by the arm. "No, you're not. We're going to dance."

Nicholas groans. "Look, I'm dancing!" He fake tap-dances over to the plate of cookies and snags one, pretending to strut backward toward the door.

"Look," I loud-whisper, grabbing Mystic's arm. Noah and Ethan are coming through the entrance. Noah is wearing jeans and a nice shirt, but Ethan is dressed in a suit and bow tie.

"Is that guy for real?" Nicholas says, through a cookie.

"Leave him alone," Mystic says. "He looks nice."

I lean toward her. "Maybe he'll ask you to dance." She shrugs hopefully, and I hold out my hand toward Nicholas. "It's a dollar."

"Even for me?" he says, all innocent.

"Especially for you," I say, and grin.

Another song starts, this one more fast and furious, and everybody screams so loud, I squint trying to block the sound.

"Let's dance!" Nicholas yells, and pulls Mystic onto the dance floor.

He's so weird.

From behind the refreshment table, I rub my temples and watch everyone bathed in ocean light, jumping, dancing, and having fun. Emma and Thomas Kelly are in the middle of the action, waving their arms in the air, bouncing to the beat. Brooklyn is dancing with Eduardo Alvarez from my homeroom. She looks super pretty in her calf-length pink dress, and at the edge of the dance floor, Ethan is watching them, probably trying to get up the nerve to ask her to dance.

This is what it's like to be normal. So why does my head feel like it's having its own Under the Sea dance?

"Could I have a water?" a voice calls out over the music. I turn to see Noah pointing to the drink cooler.

"Hey, sure," I say, and hand him a bottle. "It's a dollar, please, sir." I do a fake curtsy. *What am I doing?*

He hands me a dollar but doesn't walk away, just turns and watches everyone on the dance floor. His head bobs to the beat. Then he turns to me. "Who won Japan?"

"Huh?" The music is too loud. I can't hear him. "What?" I shout.

"You want to dance?" he shouts back.

!!! *What?* "Uh . . ." No one has asked me to dance before. I look over at Courtney to see if she can spare me, and she gives me a thumbs-up, clearly ahead of me about what's going on.

"Yeah," I say, nodding, and Noah nods back. I can feel my smile taking up approximately 75 percent of my face, and I have to admit, he looks pretty smiley, too.

On the dance floor, he turns to me and, awkwardly, we start dancing. The first thing I learn is that, wow, I don't really know how to dance. But luckily, he doesn't either. We burst out laughing and focus on trying to move like everybody else.

When the song ends, a slow one begins, and lots of kids give up. I'm about to go back to the refreshments when Noah says, "You wanna?"

The lights dim as I look at him. "Okay," I say unsteadily, and slowly, we move closer together. Noah puts his hands around my waist carefully, like I'm made of glass. And

I'm about as awkward placing my hands on his shoulders.

It is so weird, dancing with this boy I never thought would want to dance with me, or even talk to me! I officially admit to myself that it's also really nice. In fact, I hardly feel my headache anymore. Did I just need a boy to ask me to dance to make it disappear?

The thought of Carmen flashes through my brain. Not sure why, but there she is. I picture her watching me dancing with a boy! *Tomorrow, Carmen, I promise. In twenty-four hours you'll have my full attention. Just wait for me, okay?*

"You look really nice," Noah says, breaking me out of my Carmen spell. "And you're a good dancer."

"Thanks," I say, feeling my face go hot. "And no, I'm not."

"Well, you're better than me." Noah says, grinning.

We sway to the music, and move a little closer, my cheek not far from his. Some of the couples around us are so close they're practically one person.

"Can I ask you something?" Noah asks.

I pull back and look at him. "Sure."

"There's just something I don't understand." He hesitates. "And I thought—"

There's a sudden commotion from somewhere on the

dance floor, and we let go of each other to look. Someone's yelling in the middle of everything, and the couples around us pull apart, too, searching for the source.

"What's going on?" I ask Noah, and like everybody else, we move toward the sound.

The slow song keeps playing, but no one is dancing now. A circle is forming around whatever is happening.

As we get closer, the voices get louder. And I recognize one of them. Thomas Kelly. Figures.

But then another voice becomes clear to me. Loud and elevated. It's Emma.

What is she saying? I strain to hear. She's going on about something, and her voice is relentless. When I hear the word "necklace" come out of her mouth, I don't need to hear what comes next.

Leaving Noah behind, I push through the throng of bodies and get to the front. When I see who is inside the circle, it all becomes clear.

Emma and Thomas are on one side. Mystic is on the other.

"You're a thief, you've always been a thief, and now everybody knows," Emma says, shouting at Mystic. "I know you took my necklace!"

I look around. Where's Nicholas? Why is he letting this happen?

"I did not!" Mystic says, her eyes wild.

"You stole Brooklyn's bracelet," Emma taunts. "I heard you, remember? You're a thief, Mystic Jenkins. Admit it!"

Mystic looks like a cornered animal. "Leave me alone," she says, looking around desperately until her eyes find me. Silently, Mystic is asking for help, but I just stand there, frozen. I should run in and defend her, but I can't. I don't. Ethan appears beside me, and briefly, Mystic's eyes shift to him.

Thomas Kelly throws up his arms and starts a chant: *"Thief. Thief. Thief. Thief."* Some other kids join in.

Frantically, Mystic searches for a way out. She's completely surrounded, but she doesn't let that stop her. She pushes through bodies and heads for the door.

The chant follows her. *"Thief. Thief . . ."*

"Mystic!" I yell, but she can't hear me, so I rush through the pack of people and collide with Noah. Of course.

"What's happening?" he asks.

"Mystic. I've got to find Mystic," I tell him, and take off toward the door.

Outside the gym, the bright lights of the hallway startle my eyes. Nobody's at the reception table. Any teacher or chaperone-like person has been magnetized to the disturbance inside.

A fast song starts in the gym, its muted beat pulsing through the door. "Mystic!" I call out, but she doesn't answer. *Girls' bathroom,* I think, and head toward the closest one.

Rushing down the hall, I burst through the bathroom door, and there she is. Standing in front of a sink. When she sees me, she wipes her eyes and disappears into a stall.

"Mystic, what happened?"

Her voice is high-pitched. "You saw what happened! Your *friend's* a real . . ." She pauses, sounding like she's catching her breath. "It's like she's been planning to humiliate me in front of everyone. It was horrible."

"I'm sorry. Come out. It's going to be—"

"It's *not* going to be okay!" she yells. "Did you see everybody looking at me? And that jerk Thomas Kelly . . . and Ethan was there. He saw everything, and he didn't even . . ." she drops off.

"Where was Nicholas?"

"I thought if I was alone, Ethan might ask me to dance. He wanted to get out of there anyway." Then she says, "Emma said you told her I took Brooklyn's bracelet."

My mouth falls open. I don't know what to say.

"You didn't, right?" Mystic calls to me. "I mean, I know you guys *were* best friends. I've seen the way you've looked at her. But you didn't tell her *that*, right?"

I hesitate. "She heard us in the locker room that day, re-member? She knew, Myst. I don't know what she was doing back there but she'll calm down."

The stall door slams open. Mystic stands there staring at me, eyeliner running down her cheeks. "You're defending her? You saw what she did. You saw that! Are you actually defending her?"

"Myst, listen—"

"Girls like her," Mystic hisses, "have hurt me my whole life. Yeah, I'm weird, tall Mystic who doesn't fit in. And it's okay once you learn not to try anymore. But it hurts when you're a kid and they treat you like garbage. I don't blame you for getting your horn taken off. If I could be different, or like, if I could be normal, I would. But I can't. And I promised myself a long time ago to be done with girls like her. Because I would never let any of them hurt me ever again."

I take a step back. I've never seen Mystic like this before.

"And then came you. I trusted you," she says bitterly. "But it's happening to you, too. Ever since you got your horn taken off. You know it, and I know it. I just can't be there while you become one of them."

"I'm not becoming one of them," I say, feeling sick inside, because part of me knows she's right. And my head is pounding again, making it hard for me to think.

She shakes her head sharply, her face miserable but fierce. "I know how this goes. You'll forget about me. By high school, you won't even remember I exist. It's fine. I'm just preparing myself."

"Mystic. Come on. That's ridiculous. You're my best friend."

She looks into the mirror and uses a paper towel to wipe the errant eyeliner from her cheek.

"Listen," I tell her. "You could give me the necklace! I'll say I found it in the locker room. Nobody has to know anything else. And then it'll be over. Emma will have her necklace back, and everything will go back to normal."

"Wow." She turns to me. "*Really*?" I can't read her tone. I haven't heard her pronounce anything in quite this way before.

"Yeah, really! It'll be like it never happened."

But Mystic's actually cackling.

"What's funny?" I ask.

"You think I took the necklace."

"I'm not judging you," I tell her honestly. "I know you love working on your creations and getting inspiration from all kinds of pieces. I get it, really and truly. We can figure out a way to get you inspiration without stealing. I'm not judging you, promise."

"Then I'm judging you." Mystic stares down at me. The missing eyeliner from one of her eyes makes her appear lopsided. "Because I DIDN'T DO IT!"

Her eyes bore into mine, and I suddenly understand. I step back, gulping on my stupid assumptions and wincing at the stabbing pulse in my head. I was wrong. I was completely—

"Yes, you did."

I didn't say that. I turn and see Emma standing inside the bathroom door. Brooklyn slides in behind her.

Mystic looks at me. "Thanks a lot, Jewel."

"I didn't know they were coming. I promise."

Emma steps forward. "Give me back my necklace, Mystic."

"I don't *have* your necklace."

"You stole Brooklyn's bracelet!" Emma accuses. "I heard you in the locker room talking to Jewel about it. What, do you think I'm stupid?"

Mystic looks at Brooklyn. "I'm really sorry about that. I shouldn't have taken it."

Brooklyn nods. "It's okay. I got it back."

"My necklace," Emma demands, and holds out her hand.

"I don't have it." Mystic stares at her straight on. "And even if I was a thief, do you really think I'd steal your crappy jewelry?"

I can tell that Emma is taken aback by that. It goes eerily silent, and then Mystic's eyes land on me. She looks at me for a full ten seconds. She's waiting for me to say something. But I'm frozen. You'd think without a horn, I'd be able to find my voice, but look at me, I'm still voiceless. I feel Emma's eyes on me, and I still can't speak.

"Right," Mystic says, "I guess we know what this means." She stares at me for one final beat, then pushes past Emma and Brooklyn like they're paper dolls and bolts out the door.

I look to Brooklyn, but she doesn't say anything. She stands loyally by her friend's side. So much for trusting Brooklyn. And then I think, *What have I done?*

I rush past Emma and Brooklyn and sprint down the empty hallway. "Mystic!" I call out. But she's not there. Turning the corner, I slam into Nicholas.

"What did you do?" he says angrily.

"Where is she?"

"Out there." He points to the double doors that lead outside.

"Where did you go?" I yell.

"I got bored and went to the art room. What happened?" he asks as Emma and Brooklyn appear.

"Aren't you coming back to the dance, J?" Emma says. When I don't answer, Emma stops, opening her hands like a question. "Whose side are you on, anyway?"

"Uh—I just . . ." I still can't come up with an answer. What is wrong with me? What am I afraid of? Not being popular? I mean, am I even actually friends with Emma again?

Emma shrugs and says, "Whatever," and she and Brooklyn disappear back into the gym.

I look at Nicholas.

"Wow," he says. "Whose side *are* you on?"

"Nobody's," I say, and look down at the floor.

"Really? Because from what Mystic's told me, this is about Emma and how you used to be best friends and how she abandoned you after the Noah thing when you started damaging her reputation. And now you've not only abandoned Mystic, but you're choosing the side of the exact person who's making her life miserable. And I don't think Mystic ever did anything bad to you."

"She didn't," I say, feeling everything closing in on me.

"You know, Jewel with a horn would never act like this. She was nice."

"Nicholas, come on—"

"No, you're not her anymore. You're not nice. You're not cool," he says. "In fact, maybe you should leave Mystic alone." This sentence, he says like it's final. Then he storms away, slamming through the doors and going outside.

A rush of air escapes my lips. What just happened?

I catch my reflection in the trophy case glass. At the girl without the horn. At the girl wearing Emma's dress. At the girl who did not stand up for her friend. And I wonder who that girl is.

"Nicholas!" I cry, and take off after him. As I push open the door, I get slapped by the cold night air. Wrapping my hands around my bare arms, I lurch forward, calling for them, but Mystic and Nicholas seem to have disappeared.

Alone, I stand there staring into the night. The streetlights shine into the parking lot, full of cars, no people to be seen. "Mystic," I say helplessly. "Where are you?"

Putting my hands to my face, I feel my bare forehead. I feel the shame crawling up my throat. I feel . . . I feel . . .

I feel *it*.

A sudden wave crests over me, bursting through my forehead, splitting it in half. It's happening. *Not now!*

My knees hit the cold pavement, and the faint beat of music disappears.

Then so do I.

Not the Only One

My hair whips me in the face. The wind is more intense than anything I've ever felt. I've never gone this fast without a seat belt or a helmet.

The drum of hooves beats a path across the desert floor. From the back of a saddle, I'm looking ahead over Beaumont's shoulder. My arms tighten around him, so close I can almost feel his beating heart. This is no dream. Beaumont is flesh and blood. Beside us is Esmeralda, riding Sheba, reins in one hand, flaming hair dancing behind her.

I hardly have a second to grasp my bearings before Beaumont calls out, "Whoa," and we slow down so fast I have to hold on even tighter so I don't fly off the saddle.

My eyes meet Esmeralda's and she says, "Best to go on carefully from here."

Looking behind, I spot the town of Hot Springs in the far distance. To the west is Tabletop Mesa. I know where we are. We're heading to Rock Canyon.

It's strangely quiet, and it occurs to me that we're sitting ducks out in the open. Wesley is good at hiding behind boulders with guns a-blazing. I take a breath and try to remember that I'm riding with the experts. I've seen them rescue centaurs and jackalopes. I've watched them fight off legions of fire-breathing drakes and capture lost and angry harpies. They know what they're doing. Me, on the other hand . . .

"Should I be scared?" I ask.

"You should always be scared," Esmeralda says.

She's said this to me before, in the vision yesterday, at my locker. Why is she saying it again?

Marv the phoenix swoops down so close that I can feel the breeze from his wings.

"Why does Wesley kill the magical creatures?" I ask. I've always felt like that's not been totally explained in *Highwaymen*, and if anyone can answer this, it's Esmeralda.

"He thinks they're an abomination," she says. "Demons

from hell. He's on a mission from God to destroy each and every one of them. At least, that's what he says."

"You don't believe him?"

"No. He's a pirate. Magical creatures release their magic when they die. The more he kills, the more magical he becomes."

I knew he sold off parts of magical creatures as trophies to the highest bidder. But this is even darker than that. "Is that true?"

"Sure is," says Beaumont.

"All those magical artifacts he wears hold the magic," Esmeralda says. "The necklace of claws and fangs around his neck binds the magic to him."

"Wow," I whisper. I knew he wore these things around his neck, but to get their magic? How did I not know that?

I hear a whinny in the distance, and this is no regular cry. It's the suffering call of an injured animal. For the first time ever, I see fear on Esmeralda's face, and that terrifies me.

"I'll meet you there," Esmeralda says, and squeezes her legs into Sheba. Sheba takes off at a gallop, her wings spreading from her sides. As they soar away, Beaumont coaxes our horse forward.

When we reach the edge of Rock Canyon, I gasp. I thought I knew what to expect, but I was wrong. Rock Canyon is a massive gaping hole in the earth surrounded by walls of multicolored prehistoric rock. At its center stand two tall, skinny rock figures that rise from the earth like twin Jenga towers. I've seen the illustrations. But seeing them for real is like the difference between black-and-white and color.

At the bottom of the canyon, we see a tiny Esmeralda dismount, then send Sheba back into the sky. Within moments, the flying horse lands beside us.

"I'll keep watch," says Beaumont. "Off you go."

He helps me down before I can object. As my sneakers hit the ground, I realize I'm still wearing Emma's dress. Sheba whinnies and stomps her hoof impatiently.

"Seriously?" I ask, staring up at Beaumont.

"Chet's late as usual, and Esmeralda needs help down there. I've got to keep watch. If Wesley's on his way, I'll keep him from you two for as long as I can hold him off."

"But I've never flown before."

"Oh, not to worry." He's grinning through gritted teeth. "Sheba does the flying part."

Ha. Ha. Ha.

Turning, I hike up my dress and awkwardly lift my foot into the stirrup. Grabbing the saddle horn, I pull myself onto Sheba's back.

Sheba takes off in a gallop, then wheels back around toward Rock Canyon—and I think I might die. She's going so fast and heading for a huge gaping hole in the ground. I watch her wings spread as we reach the canyon's edge, and . . .

We fly.

The wind beats against my face as Sheba's enormous wings pump through the air. She soars higher, in a long, elegant circle over the canyon. I'm scared to look down, but I can't help myself. It's unbelievable. Rock Canyon is so beautiful. I gaze all around me, amazed by the endless vista. This is nothing like being on a plane. This is nothing like being on Earth. THIS IS FLYING.

Cautiously, I take one hand off the saddle horn and let the wind rush through my fingers. As if it has a mind of its own, my other hand follows. I spread my arms wide. Free. Stretching upward, I feel my fingers touch the sky.

When Sheba starts to dive, though, I grab for her mane. My stomach leaps directly into my chest and I hold on tight. Careening toward the skinny rock figures, it's like

I'm on a roller coaster without any tracks. When Sheba's feet hit the canyon floor and I'm safely on solid ground, I can finally breathe again.

"Chet's still not here?" Esmeralda asks as Sheba stops beside her.

I shake my head, not able to speak, having just landed in the most miraculous faraway place of all.

Sheba folds her wings, letting me slip out of the saddle.

"All right, then," Esmeralda says briskly. "You'll have to do." Esmeralda disappears behind the tallest rock tower, and I scurry after her. I round the corner—and gasp.

Carmen.

She's lying on the ground. Her head flailing. Her legs thrashing.

"No!" I scream. "Carmen!" Shocked, I rush toward her, not believing what I'm seeing.

Her horn is gone. Someone cut off Carmen's horn!

"Jewel."

I look at Esmeralda, who is kneeling next to my unicorn. But it wasn't her voice that said my name.

A pulsing sound echoes, like someone clanged me on the head with a gong, and Rock Canyon disintegrates into a mass of black dots. I am alone in the void. No Beaumont. No Esmeralda. No—

Startled, I open my eyes, blinking over and over again, gasping for breath.

"Jewel." I look up to see Noah crouching beside me. "Are you all right?" he asks.

I wipe the tears from my eyes. I can't talk. My teeth are chattering.

"What's wrong?" Noah puts a hand on my hunched shoulder. "What happened?"

"I saw her," I say, panicked. "She was lying there. Dying." I look over at him. "Her horn was gone."

Noah doesn't flinch. He just says, "Are you talking about the unicorn?"

That snaps me back real quick. "You know about Carmen?"

"If Carmen is the name of that unicorn who used to follow you around everywhere, then yeah, I know about Carmen."

Dumbfounded, I stare at him. I put my hands on my cheeks to keep him from hearing my vibrating teeth.

"You're freezing," Noah says. "Let's get inside."

As he helps me up, I notice that Emma's dress is torn where my knees hit the pavement. How am I going to explain *that*? We walk silently back into building and sit down on a bench in the hall as the music still pumps away in the gym. Unbelievably, the dance goes on. I can't think straight, and the fact that Noah's hand is still on my elbow doesn't help.

"How do you know about Carmen?"

"Are you sure you're okay?" he asks.

"Just tell me," I plead, and our eyes lock together for a long moment before he nods.

"Okay," Noah says, "after you gored me with *your* horn, I started seeing this unicorn with *its* horn. At school, in town, even in the grocery store. I mean basically, whenever I saw the unicorn, you were always close by. So I figured I was losing my mind or that Unicorn Girl actually had a unicorn."

He pauses, then goes on. "I didn't say anything to anybody for a long time because the one time I pointed to the unicorn and asked Ethan if he saw him, Ethan thought I was kidding. He didn't see anything. So I kept him to myself after that."

"She's a her."

"Huh?"

"Carmen is a her, not a him," I say. "Why didn't you ask *me* about it?"

He points to my forehead. "You might remember there was an incident . . ."

"I'm so sorry, Noah."

"I know. I'm sorry, too. My mom got way too freaked out. She overreacts sometimes. She made me promise to keep my distance, which I wouldn't have really cared about except she made it official with the school and everything. I didn't mean to be a jerk."

I kind of understand. Seeing unicorns can be weird. Dealing with moms can be weirder.

"So, this unicorn, Carmen, she's real?" Noah asks. "I'm not crazy?"

"She's real," I say, exhaling. Someone finally knows what only I have known all along! He pulls up his shirt, revealing a puckered red scar on his stomach. "Noah!"

"No, listen. It was only after your horn did this that I could see your unicorn. So I've always figured—if I wasn't crazy—that there's got to be a connection."

"You really think so?" I was starting to think the same thing.

"If there's a unicorn, then there's got to be magic, right?" he says excitedly. "I mean, unicorns are magic. *Right?* Everybody knows that. So I figure that when your horn skewered me, some of that magic might have, you know, rubbed off. *Must* have rubbed off. I don't see any other explanation. Do you?"

"No other explanation," I murmur. I can't get over the fact that there's been no one in my whole life who could talk with me like this before. I thought Emma could, but that was a lie. This is real. "Hey, this might be a weird question, but—have you seen her since my surgery?"

"That's what I've been wanting to ask you." Noah looks at me intently. "The last time I saw her was in the hall after Ethan took your stuffed unicorn. Which I caught by mistake, by the way."

"Ethan took my unicorn?" I ask, confused. "Thomas Kelly took my unicorn."

Noah shakes his head. "Nope. It does sound like a Thomas Kelly thing. But it was Ethan."

"But why? Ethan's nice."

"Usually. But he got dumb over the Brooklyn stuff. So when Emma asked him to get the unicorn from your back-pack—"

"Emma? Why would she—"

"She said she'd put in a good word to Brooklyn for him. Which never happened." Noah looks down. "I told him he was aiming too high."

"I can't believe she would do that," I say. "But why were you in detention that day? Why not Ethan, if he was the thief?"

"Well, I covered for him. I was caught red-handed, at least from Whatley's perspective. It was easier to just keep him off the hook. He's had a rough year."

My mind is racing. There's so much to take in, so I focus on the most important thing. "Okay. Pause on all of that and help me figure this out. Carmen disappeared after I got my horn taken off. And just now I had a vision of her dying at the bottom of Rock Canyon."

"What's Rock Canyon?"

"Um. A fictional place in this graphic novel series I'm obsessed with." My eyes start watering again. "Long story. Forget that detail for a second. What if it's somehow my fault? I cut off my horn. And Nicholas always said . . ." My words trail off into thoughts I haven't let myself admit for the past couple of weeks.

"So how do we get to this Rock Canyon place?"

What a question. "I have no idea." I stare at Noah, shaking my head. "It's not even real."

I sink my face into my palms. Carmen, my Carmen, is lying at the bottom of Rock Canyon, suffering. But how? How could my unicorn be in some graphic novel's fictional Western town that existed over a hundred years ago? It doesn't make sense.

I want to convince myself that it wasn't her, that it was some other magical creature. But I can't. I know my unicorn. I know it was Carmen. And I have no idea how to save her.

Noah waits with me until Mom picks me up. When she sees the holes in the dress and my bloody knees, I tell her

I fell and that I don't feel good. When we get home, I go straight to bed.

What am I going to do! I've been worried about Emma being my friend and Mystic stealing a necklace, while Carmen is dying. CARMEN IS DYING!

She's out there, lying on the ground with her horn completely gone. She needs me. The image of the bloody stump where her horn used to be overwhelms my mind.

Finally, I let Nicholas's pronouncement come into focus: *A unicorn cannot live without its horn.*

I thought that was about me. But what if it's about her?

The Necklace

I wake up consumed with dread. Everything feels as real now as it did last night, and I don't know what to do.

When I walk out of the bedroom, Grandma is making coffee. "You feeling any better?" she asks.

I shake my head. "What time is it?"

"A little before eight. Maybe you should go back to bed."

"Is Mom asleep?"

"She went to work early so she can get back in time to go to your competition."

The essay competition. I'd completely forgotten about it! How can I read my essay in front of all those people now? I can't, not with Carmen out there somewhere.

"How was the dance?" Grandma asks, startling me back.

"It was okay," I tell her. "The gym looked really good."

"I bet you and Mystic danced the roof off."

I wish.

And then I realize—I've been so freaked out about Carmen that I haven't even thought about what happened to Mystic. I picture her face in the girls' bathroom like it was a bad dream, and remember how horrible Emma was. How could she have done that? Mystic didn't steal Emma's necklace. I know that now. I was dumb, but Emma was mean.

And even worse, I didn't stick up for my friend. By not saying anything, I let Emma think what she did was okay with me. It wasn't. Somehow I have to make things right.

I look at Grandma. "I've got to go to Emma's."

"This early?"

"Um . . . yeah." I hold up my phone knowing that Grandma isn't going to check my story. "She just texted me. I want to apologize about the dress."

"Whatever happened to teenagers sleeping late?" Grandma takes a sip of coffee and shrugs. "Go on, then."

I kiss Grandma on the cheek, then grab Emma's dress. As I walk through the parking lot, I don't even know what I'm doing. I don't have a plan. I just have to know why. Emma can't be as horrible as I remember. There must be some explanation.

It takes three sets of increasingly frantic knocks before Emma's mom answers the door, dressed in a robe with her head a mess.

"Hey Jewel," she says, surprised to see me. "Whew, it's cold out there! Come in!"

"I hope I didn't wake you. I just really need to see Emma."

Emma's mom gives me a side eye. "You're braver than I am." I give her a quick smile, then squeeze past her.

Quietly, I slip into Emma's room and almost step on the emerald dress she wore last night, which is crumpled on the floor.

"Emma," I say softly.

Sleepily, Emma opens her eyes, then jolts up, startled. "Jewel! What are you doing here?"

"I need to talk." I stand there, holding her dress.

"Now? Can't this wait?" She rubs her eyes. "What happened to my dress?"

"I fell and ruined it. I'm sorry. I'll pay for it."

"That's what you woke me up for?" Emma leans back against her pillow. "Don't worry about it. I'm done with that dress anyway."

"Okay," I say. Still, I place the dress on a chair. "But it's not why I'm here."

She looks at me, puzzled. "Then why are you here? What time is it?"

Clasping my hands together, I take on a serious pose. "What you did to Mystic was not cool. And I need you to know that."

"That's why you woke me up? To stick up for your friend the thief?"

"She's not a thief. I know she took Brooklyn's bracelet, but she gave it back. If she says she didn't take your necklace, she didn't. It's not who she is. I know her."

"Okay," Emma says, and yawns. "I don't really care anyway."

I stare at Emma, confused. Why isn't she fighting me on this? What's going on?

"Can I go back to sleep now?" she asks, yawning again.

"Sure," I say, because I don't know what else to say. She's being so casual about it all. Am I somehow overreacting? That's when I notice something hanging around her neck. "Hey, is that—You found it!"

Emma cups her palm over the teardrop pendant. "Oh yeah, omigod! You won't believe it! It fell through a hole in the lining of my purse. I had no idea. It was a miracle that I found it. But it was there the whole time!"

"What?" I say, finding it suddenly hard to breathe.

"How awesome is that? I got my necklace back." She's actually smiling about it.

"Emma! It was in your own purse?"

"I didn't know it was there. It wasn't like I hid it on purpose."

"Yeah, but what about Mystic? Everybody thinks she took it!"

"I mean, she does have a history," Emma says. "Relax. In a week, nobody'll even remember it happened."

I can't believe this. "Everybody will remember! That was like the most memorable event of the dance!"

"It's not like she's anybody *important*," Emma says. "And you needed a push. I was trying to help you out."

I step back. "What do you mean, a push?"

"To see that Mystic wasn't good for you anymore. That you needed to cut the cord. You can't be friends with Mystic *and* be popular."

Wow. How did she become like this? And why couldn't I see it until now?

"Did you ask Ethan to take my stuffed unicorn?" When Noah said it, I didn't want to believe him, but now . . .

Emma looks surprised by the question. But guilty, too.

"The stuffed unicorn. That you gave me. The one you got Ethan to steal from my backpack. Because, why? You didn't want people to remember that you used to have one, too?

Instead of answering, she looks down at her phone.

"I can't believe I've been such an idiot," I whisper.

Emma eyes snap up defiantly. "You're not being cool, J."

"No, I hope not," I say, and turn, leaving her bedroom.

Emma follows, and as I walk out the apartment door, she shouts, "If you leave like this, I don't know if we can still be friends."

I turn around. "Really? And if I choose you, what else do I get?" My voice is bitter, but that's how I feel.

"Don't be an idiot. Look at how your life has changed," Emma says, "You want to throw all of that away?"

A fire builds inside me, even though it's cold outside. "You didn't change my life. I did! I'm the one who figured out how to get my horn taken off. And I'm the one who got chosen for the French competition. Not because I'm popular—but because I'm good." I pause, searching for my old best friend, who is clearly no longer there. "I just wanted to be friends with you again, Emma. That's all. What happened to you?"

Her mouth tightens and her eyes go hard. "I made a choice, okay? I was there the day you almost killed Noah. Remember? I was right beside you. It was a freak show. You said it yourself."

I did say it.

"So what was I supposed to do? I just couldn't sit at the freak table with you anymore. Because I wasn't a freak." Her eyes soften. "Just like you're not anymore. This is our chance. I missed you, J. I actually really did. It just couldn't work before. But now—we can start all over. We're going to be in high school next year, and I mean . . . you look good without your horn. When I first saw Brooklyn, I knew she was going to be popular. And I had that same feeling when you came back from LA. That you were going to be that girl. That we could be those girls together."

"Because you thought I would be popular?"

"I thought you *could* be popular. You're pretty enough. Now that your horn's gone, you're not hiding that anymore. You can be like me."

"But I don't want to be like you," I tell her, realizing the truth of it as I say it. "And my horn wasn't hiding anything. My horn was *part* of me."

I feel a sudden pulse on my forehead, right where my horn used to be. It vibrates soft and steady, like a tiny heartbeat.

"What's wrong?" Emma asks, staring at me.

"Nothing," I say. "Not anymore."

When I get down to the parking lot, my stuffed unicorn arcs through the air and lands on the asphalt. Turning, I meet Emma's eyes one last time before she closes the door. For a moment, I stare after her, even though she's gone, and I know I have chosen. *"Au revoir, mon amie,"* I whisper softly, and pick up my unicorn.

As I rub the unicorn's pink fur against my cheek, the pulse in my head grows more insistent. It repeats over and over like it's trying to send me a message.

I don't know what to do. Carmen is out there and I don't know how to save her. I don't know how to get to Rock Canyon. I have no idea . . . *Nicholas! I need Nicholas!* But I know he won't answer my texts.

I rush toward Sam who's kicking his soccer ball against the building, already at this wicked early hour, and cut between him and his ball.

"Hey!" he exclaims.

"I need a favor."

He picks up his ball and tucks it under his arm. "Shoot."

That cocky nine-year-old might just have my life in his hands. So I pull back my shoulders and ask him straight-out. "Can I borrow your bike?"

Longitudes and Latitudes

It's miles to town and Sam's bike is too small for me, but I make it work. I'm out of breath when I pull up in front of Nicholas's house. There are no cars in the driveway. What if they're not home?

I knock on the door and keep knocking, and eventually a bleary-looking Nicholas opens it. When he sees it's me, he closes it again.

"Nicholas!" I'm banging on the door now. "Please, I have to talk to you!"

Nothing. "PLEASE! COME BACK!" I knock some more. Nothing. Sighing, I realize there's no other way.

"Nicholas, there's a unicorn!" I yell through the door. "A real unicorn! And she needs our help!"

Three, two, one. The door opens. "Don't mess with me," he says.

"I'm not messing with you. I promise," I say desperately.

"You've got like a minute."

"Okay," I say, holding up my palms. I can do this in a minute, right? "First, I'm an idiot. I was wrong about everything. I was a terrible friend and you can be mean to me all you want tomorrow. But today, I really need you."

Nicholas crosses his arms. "Talk about the unicorn."

"The unicorn," I say, and exhale. "The unicorn is named Carmen."

He rolls his eyes.

"No, really! She's been with me my whole life. She's like my guardian unicorn or something."

"Ha, ha," Nicholas says, looking around. "And where is this magical unicorn now?"

"She's not here. And you can't see her. I'm the only one who can see her. Well, somebody else can see her, too, but listen—"

"Bye." Nicholas goes to shut the door.

"Wait!" I tell him, scrambling. How can I convince him? What can I say? I look into his eyes and it suddenly comes to me. "Remember when your books just fell off the hood of your mom's car that day and nobody touched them? Or when you'd put something on your desk, and look away, and then it'd be somewhere across the room?" I pause, trying to remember more, then exclaim, "Or that time outside of detention when you felt like someone was blowing on your hair?"

He frowns. I know he remembers that!

"You were straight-up being played with."

"By an invisible unicorn?"

I throw up my hands, victoriously. "Whose name is Carmen!"

Nicholas's face goes into overload. "Dude, are you serious?"

"Totally. Cross my heart. I would not lie about this."

"And you didn't tell me?!"

"I couldn't. I didn't want you to think I was crazy."

His eyes go wide. "*Me?* You thought I'd think you were crazy? Have you met me? This is like my wildest fantasy coming true. Well, I guess in my wildest fantasy I'd be able to see her, too. And maybe ride her. And—does she fly?" He starts looking up in the air. "So where is she?" he asks. "Is she here? Is she here now?" He stares behind me, squinting as if it would help him see something invisible.

"No, she's not here. That's the problem."

And then I tell him everything—about Carmen disappearing after I got my horn removed, about the strange visions I've been having. He stares at me without expression through most of it—until I mention Hot Springs and seeing Carmen at the bottom of Rock Canyon with her horn cut off.

His jaw drops and his eyes go wide. "Oh, crap," he says.

* * *

In his room—where he led me, running up the stairs without another word—he hands me *Highwaymen*. It's the latest issue, one I haven't seen yet. Sheba's on the cover, flying with Esmeralda on her back.

"We don't have time for this," I tell him. "Weren't you listening—"

"Page seven," he says. "Panel three."

Rapidly, I flip through to page seven and stop. No, I don't stop. I freeze.

"If I wasn't so mad at you, I'd have told you last night," Nicholas says.

I hardly hear him. I'm staring at page seven, panel three. At the latest magical creature to show up in Hot Springs. For a moment, I can't speak. All my worlds are colliding.

"It's a unicorn," Nicholas says. "A unicorn finally showed up in Hot Springs."

"Not *a* unicorn," I say. "*My* unicorn. This is her. This is Carmen."

I look into his eyes, and there's no doubt in them at all. Nicholas believes me.

"Well, at least that makes sense of the coordinates," he says, and points to the big map on the wall. "Thirty-four-point-fifty-six degrees north, eighty-three-point-ninety-eight degrees west."

I stare at the new red flag on his map and feel no surprise at all. Because the latest global address is *our* global address. Our town.

"What does this *mean*?" Nicholas asks, his thoughts going into hyperdrive. I can see it on his face. "The unicorn . . . your unicorn . . . went through a portal in our town?!" He turns back to the map. "But where? The portal could be anywhere."

I put my hand over my eyes. I can see it just like it was yesterday. I was six years old. There was a boulder. And a trail covered in vines that descended into the earth.

"What?" he asks. "What do you know?"

"I think I know where the portal is."

* * *

Nicholas's parents took off early to go hiking in the mountains, so there's no one to drive us back to my apartment. We have to take bikes. So Nicholas is on his and I'm on Sam's.

When we finally pull up to the apartment parking lot, I'm shocked to see Mystic waiting on the stairs. Nicholas texted her before we left his house, but I didn't think there was any way she'd come.

"What did you say to her?" I ask Nicholas as we approach.

"That she needed to be here," he says solemnly.

Oh, man. What do I say? My eyes meet Mystic's as we roll in and stop.

"I'm so sorry," I start. "I was a jerk . . . *and* an idiot. You were right about everything, Myst. I promise to make it up to you every day in high school, and for the rest of our lives if I have to."

Mystic mulls this over, then glances at Emma's apartment. "What about her?"

I groan and shake my head. "She found it in her purse."

"No way!"

"I went over there this morning and told her she was wrong about you and that what she did was not okay." Then I say the important part. "What *I* did was not okay. I was so dumb. I believed the wrong person because I thought she was the right person. But she's not, and I've learned my lesson. I'm done with her. I chose you. I *choose* you. Will you please forgive me?"

Mystic is inscrutable. I don't have any idea what she's thinking. Her eyeliner makes her look so grown-up and serious. "You really hurt me."

"I know I did. And I'm sorry."

I stand there feeling like I'm waiting for a jury to read the verdict at my trial. I know I'm guilty, but I'm hoping for a second chance.

"Okay," Mystic finally says. "It's going to take me a while to get over being mad at you. Just so you know that."

"Yeah, be mad at me as long as you want. Just be my friend again." Mystic nods. Relieved, I give her a hug, and she lets me. She even hugs me back.

"Are we done now?" Nicholas says impatiently. "Because, you know. Unicorn."

"What?" Mystic says, looking at him like he's finally gone to another planet.

"Unicorn," Nicholas says emphatically, then looks toward the entrance of the parking lot where Noah and Ethan are riding up on their bikes. They skid to a halt in front of us.

I texted Noah, too. After all, if we're trying to find someone, it might be helpful to have more than one of us who can see her.

"Phew. I thought you might have left already," Noah says, out of breath. "We didn't have a rope. But Ethan's dad did." Noah steps off his bike and looks at me. "So now what?"

"Give me a minute. I'll be right back." I lean Sam's bike against the railing and run upstairs. Quietly, I unlock my apartment door and step inside. The TV is on, but Grandma is asleep on the couch. Perfect. I tiptoe into our bedroom, grab the box from my closet, and stuff it into my backpack.

The clock on the bedside table says 9:45. The wrestling van for the French competition leaves at noon. Maybe I can find Carmen and get back for the competition. I mean, Carmen's what's important, but she would want me to do both. And what if somehow she's okay and could even come with me? My chest swells hopefully at the thought of reading my essay in front of all those people—with Carmen by my side.

I slip out of the apartment and hurry down the stairs. My friends are all looking up at me. Nicholas has the new issue of *Highwaymen* in his hands. I hold out my backpack and he slides it inside.

"There's one more thing I have to tell you before we go," I say to Nicholas. "Full disclosure."

"What?" he asks.

I look at Noah. "He can see Carmen, too."

Nicholas turns to Noah, stupefied. "You can see the unicorn?"

"Yeah," Noah says. "We think it happened because of the . . . incident . . . you know. Some kind of magical transfer. That kind of thing."

"This is so unfair," Nicholas says.

Mystic and Ethan are looking at us very strangely.

"Oh, yeah," I say to them. "Long story short, there's a

unicorn that only me and Noah can see. And she's kind of my magical creature. But she's in trouble."

To give them credit, they take it in, look at me gravely, and nod in unison. "So what are we here to do exactly?" asks Mystic.

I look them over, my odd set of friends, and say with complete sincerity, "We save her. That's what. We have to save the unicorn."

Truth or Consequences

After crossing the street, I find the path that leads into the woods, and we start hiking. Nicholas and Noah walk behind me. Mystic and Ethan, rope slung over his shoulder, bring up the rear.

"I've set the coordinates on my GPS," Nicholas says, looking at his phone. "But it's not going to be totally exact. Not enough digits. Do you know how to get there?"

"She knows," Noah tells him. "She and the unicorn are magically connected."

Are we? Noah speaks with such confidence, it makes me feel like it's true. But honestly, I don't know how to get there. It was more than half my lifetime ago when I rode Carmen through these woods to where the boulder sat by the stream, and where the trail disappeared under a canopy of vines. I remember this trail though. All I know to do is follow it.

"How long have you been having these visions or whatever of Hot Springs?" asks Nicholas.

"Since after the surgery," Mystic says from behind.

"You told Mystic and not me!"

"Maybe because I knew you'd act like this." I turn and look at him.

"Act like what? I'm acting perfectly normal. So wait, when did you start seeing the unicorn?"

"Carmen," Noah and I say at the same time.

"Okay, Carmen," Nicholas says. "How long have you been seeing her?"

"Forever," I say.

"Sixth grade for me," adds Noah. "After Jewel's horn . . ." He points to his stomach.

"But like how much do you see her," Nicholas asks. "Once a month, once a—"

"Every day," I say. "I mean, everywhere I go, she goes." I can tell it's a lot for him to take in because he goes silent, until—

"EVERY DAY! Are you freaking kidding me? You saw a unicorn every day and didn't tell me about it?" He lets out an exaggerated sigh, then suddenly regroups.

"Wait, you said she knocked over my books? Carmen was around me?"

I almost snort with laughter. "You're just getting that."

"Whenever I'd see her," Noah says, "she was usually with Jewel. And you were with Jewel a lot. So therefore, you were with Carmen a lot."

I can tell Nicholas head's about to pop off. He looks at Noah. "And you saw her this whole time? Why didn't *you* tell anybody?"

"He told me," Ethan says.

"Yeah, but you thought I was crazy," says Noah.

"So are you saying that if you had nicked me with your horn, I could've been seeing Carmen this whole time?" Nicholas asks.

"Hey!" Noah says. "*Way* more than a nick, Nick."

"Does any of this relate to you abandoning us for jerk-face Emma?"

I look back at Mystic. "No, that was all me."

She nods. "As I suspected."

We crunch over dead leaves and wind through a cluster of trees.

"Hey, isn't your French competition today?" Mystic asks.

"Yeah. We're supposed to leave at noon, but—"

"You can't miss that! If you're not there, you know who will be happy to take your place."

Of course. Brooklyn. I feel so confused about her right now. I mean, for the past week, she's actually been nice to me. I was starting to feel like we could be friends. But last night she just stood by while Emma was so mean to Mystic, which makes me think I can't trust her after all. She's definitely Team Emma, right? So, do I want her to take my place at the competition? *No!* I've come so far. I want to do it!

But Carmen comes first. She's more important than all the competitions in the world right now.

The trail narrows, and Noah slips in front of Nicholas as we walk single file.

"I have one question though," he says quietly. "If Carmen's so important, why were you always pushing her away? Every time I saw Carmen come near you, you tried to ignore her, or you pretended she wasn't there. Which made me think either she wasn't really there and I was totally bonkers, or that you were messing with that unicorn's head."

I stop and look at them. "You don't understand." Hearing it from someone else's perspective, I feel like a horrible person. "When you're so different for so long, you just . . . you *want* to push it away. When the thing happened with you, Noah, I blamed Carmen. I thought if I could get away from her, maybe my horn would go away, just disappear, and I'd be normal. I'd get to do things that regular people do. Like go places. Like do French competitions."

"But didn't you go to LA with a horn on your head?" Nicholas says.

"And Monsieur Oliver wanted you to compete in the competition *with* your horn," adds Mystic.

"You don't know what it's like. You should have seen me in LA before my horn came off. I can't—couldn't be seen like that. By all those strangers. Watching me like I was a fr—" I can't finish the sentence.

A sharp wind sets the pine trees in motion over our heads, and everyone goes quiet.

"You know, none of us has a horn, but I definitely don't feel normal either," Noah says. "I'm sure none of us does."

Nicholas's hands fly up. "That's what I've been trying to tell her!" He nods at Noah as if they just became friends.

"A horn is a little different, you guys."

"A horn is cool," Ethan says.

"Yeah, what Ethan said." And Noah smiles at me.

"Well, you're normal now," says Nicholas. "How's that going for you?"

"No, I'm not." I shake my head. "I thought I'd get rid of my horn and magically change inside. But I never did. Horn or no horn, I don't feel normal. I still feel like me."

I start moving again, and the freaks and nerds follow. For the first time, I feel my friends around me like a security blanket. I linger in the feeling as long as I can before raising my concern. "That magical connection you were talking about, Noah? I'm scared that's the problem."

"What do you mean?"

"If our horns *are* magically connected, and I cut mine off, what did I do to her?" I pause and nobody answers, so it spills out—my greatest fear. "What if I killed my unicorn?"

I look back at them, but of course no one has an answer. So, silently, we walk on, treading deeper into the woods. White clouds block the blue sky above the swaying pines. The trail is fainter now. In some places, it's hardly there at all. "What time is it?" I finally ask.

Noah says, "Ten-twenty." We've been walking for half an hour.

"I'm not getting reception out here," Nicholas says, staring at his phone. "Are you sure you know where we're going?"

"No!" I suddenly snap, seeing the trail go cold. "I *don't* know where we're going."

"Hey, calm down," Nicholas says soothingly. "We'll find it."

"But what if we don't? What if this is the wrong trail?" I look at him, panicking inside. "Nicholas, what are we doing? We're looking for some portal to some faraway place from a comic book—"

"It showed up with this global address," he says firmly.

"It's a *comic book*!" I yell. "It's not real! What if there are no portals? What if there are no global addresses?!" Nicholas stares at me, and I watch his confidence crack. If Nicholas isn't sure about this, we're lost. I put my hands to my horn-less face and want to cry. I took off my horn. My unicorn left me. And now I'm leading a mission to rescue her from some place I visited seven years ago. To find some portal. TO A COMIC BOOK!

"I'm an idiot," I say, and look at my friends. An uncomfortable quiet swells between us. For all these years, I thought people wouldn't believe me if I told them about Carmen, but what if I invented her as a way to deal with having a horn on my head?

Then again, Noah says he saw her, too, and I remember that night so clearly, when I was six and Carmen brought me out here, but how can I be sure that any of it was real? *What if it's not here? What if coming out here the first time was just a dream? What if we're at the wrong spot? What if—oh my gosh. I'm an idiot.*

"Hey, idiot," Mystic says.

"What?" I answer.

"Is it just me, or does anyone else hear that creek?"

My head spins around. We all get quiet again, and then . . . I hear it, too. The sound of running water. A stream.

"Where?" I call out.

"There." Ethan points to our right and we fan out through the trees.

I trip over a fallen tree limb but stumble on. All I can see are pine trees, pine straw, and pine cones. No water, no boulder.

"Here!" It's Nicholas's voice. Mystic shows up beside me and we hurry toward the sound. We burst into a clearing, and—

Nicholas is smiling. "Found it," he says.

I exhale as I see the boulder beside him. It's still large, but smaller than I remember, I guess because I'm bigger now. Beyond the boulder is the canopy of vines. I rush past Nicholas and gaze at the trail that descends steeply under that canopy. "It's that way," I say, pointing down the trail.

Nicholas steps beside me. We stand silently for a moment until he says, "This is the global address."

"This place is in *Highwaymen*?" Mystic asks, appearing at my other side.

"Kind of," I tell her. "It's the place that leads there. I hope. Carmen took me here when I was six. I wasn't completely sure it existed in real life."

"It's a portal," Nicholas says matter-of-factly.

"A portal?" Noah asks. "Like to another world?"

Nicholas nods. "Exactly."

Ethan lifts the coil of rope over his head and sets it on the boulder. "So why the rope?"

"Because I don't want to go completely alone."

"You're not going alone," Nicholas says.

"I have to," I say, and look into his eyes. "I can't explain it, Nicholas. I just know it's how it has to be." I expect him to argue with me, but for once, he doesn't.

I pull out the box from my backpack, and place it on the boulder. When I open it, Ethan asks, "Is that your horn?"

"Oh, wow," whispers Noah.

"Good idea," Nicholas says. "There's magic in that horn."

I'm struck by how unmagical it actually appears. Without me, it's just a horn. I lift it out of the box.

"Let's do this," Nicholas says. "Ethan, tie the rope around Jewel's waist so it can't get undone, okay?"

"Sure," Ethan says, ready for instructions. This is the plan that Nicholas and I came up with on the bike ride from his house. I'll walk down the trail, rope tied around my waist, and they won't let go.

Ethan wraps the rope around me and starts tying. "Is it long enough?" I ask.

"Longest one we got," Ethan says, looping the end into a complex knot. Of course—he's a fireman's son.

I take a deep breath and stare at the opening of the trail as Mystic comes up and squeezes my hand. *"Bonne chance,"* she says, and gives me a small smile. "It'll be all right."

I squeeze her hand back.

"Done." Ethan backs away, inspecting his handiwork. "There's no way you're slipping out of that."

"Everybody grab a spot on the rope," Nicholas says as Ethan spreads the rope out among us. Ethan takes the far end, then Mystic, Noah, Nicholas, and me. We all stand there for a second and nobody moves. It's Nicholas who finally speaks. "You ready?"

I nod, and the pulse on my forehead from this morning reappears. As I step under the branches and vines, the temperature drops. Am I imagining this? Or creating it? Either way, I'm filled with a quiet foreboding.

"I hope I'm right about this," I say nervously as I take another step.

And Nicholas answers, "You are."

My foot slips on the damp leaves beneath us, and Nicholas catches me by the arm. We take several careful steps together until we're almost at the bottom of the trail—

where it turns, and I can't see beyond. Where I'll have to go on alone.

"Hey Nicholas. I'm scared."

"I can still come with you."

"You can't," I whisper, and look back at him. "You have to stay right here."

He wraps his fingers more tightly around the rope and gives me a nod. "Then you can do this. When you pull on the rope, we'll pull you back."

"Promise?" I say, and force a grin.

"Promise," he says back.

Then slowly, I turn and ease myself down the trail, acutely aware of the rope that is tethering me to my friends. I know they won't let go. Holding on to my horn tightly, I walk around the bend.

I don't know what I was expecting. Some blinding light to appear, opening a portal to Carmen, who's hidden somewhere outside of Hot Springs, circa 1888? It all seems ridiculous. I'm still in the woods outside of our town, circa present day. It's just a regular trail, and I'm a regular girl with a rope tied around her waist who has her friends thinking that Hot Springs is an actual place. And that the magic in this horn is real.

Pushing these thoughts aside, I force myself to trudge on. I take step after step, until my foot suddenly sinks into the ground. Another step and my other foot becomes stuck. *Oh, crap*. Do I turn back now? Already?

And then: a whinny.

Carmen.

With everything I have, I wrench my feet from the sticky soup. Another step and my hands fall forward into what feels like wet concrete. I'm up to my elbows in it and sinking by the second.

"Carmen," I call out, and as I do, I sink down farther. But instead of encasing me, the quicksand begins to come apart. I'm slipping through it, as if the planet is giving way. There's nothing to hold on to, the vines above too far out of reach, so I keep sinking. I go completely under. And I'm drowning.

Until I fall through the bottom and land on—

—hard, dry dirt. The rope around my waist leads several feet above my head, where it disappears, quite literally, into thin air. It's there and then it's not.

Wiping the gunk from my face, I stand and gaze up at the two prehistoric teeth that I've seen so many times. The tall, skinny rock formations of Rock Canyon.

The pulse in my forehead is throbbing now. I circle the rock formation closest to me, and there they are. Esmeralda and Carmen, exactly as I last saw them: Carmen lying on the canyon floor and Esmeralda kneeling beside her. Carmen's head flails when she sees me. She can't get up.

Esmeralda stands. "It was Wesley," she says. "Wesley did this."

"I know," I tell her. Esmeralda looks at me like she's never seen me before. I'm either unrecognizable under the muck or she doesn't remember the visions.

Then she sees the unicorn horn in my hand.

Straightening, she pulls a knife from her belt. She must think it's Carmen's horn, and in a way, she's right. "Who are you?"

"I'm a friend."

"A friend who has a unicorn's horn?" she says suspiciously. "We save magical creatures in these parts."

"I'm here to do the saving. Just let me get to her." I move toward Carmen, but Esmeralda gets between us, stopping me. I pull back my bangs to reveal the scar on my forehead. "I know this is going to sound weird, but the horn is mine." I know all too well how stubborn Esmeralda is though. She won't be tricked by strangers, and she would rather die than let a magical creature be hurt.

Carmen groans and her head falls back to the ground. She's breathing heavy. Way too heavy. I have to do this—fast.

"Okay, listen. The unicorn is named Carmen. She's my unicorn. She belongs with me."

Unmoved, Esmeralda holds her ground. I have to gain her trust. But how?

"Truth or consequences." It slips out of my mouth and I don't know why. I chose consequences when Beaumont asked me before, and look where it got me.

Now I choose truth.

"I know about you," I tell her. "I know how you play the violin and how you write to your mother who lives in Boston every week. I know you keep a gun in a holster strapped to your thigh. That you cheat at cards and that you love Chet. I know how Chet was saved by his horse, Billy, when he was left for dead in the desert. I know how Beaumont loves to read but never tells anyone, and how he built his cabin in the woods but almost always stays in town because he loves you. I know about Marv and Sheba, and I know about Wesley, too. And I hate him as much as you do." Her face is giving way now. I pause, then say the last and most compelling truth I can think of.

"I come from the future and I'm here to help."

Okay, I stole that line from a movie, but from the look on her face, I think it worked.

A figure appears from around one of the rock formations. It's Beaumont.

"How do you know all that?" he asks me.

Before I can answer, there's a loud crackle behind me and

I turn around. The space in the air where the rope dead-ends is sparking with electricity.

"I don't think you have much time," Esmeralda says. She looks at Beaumont, and carefully back at me—and then she steps aside so I can get to Carmen.

Plowing past her, I fall on my knees in front of my unicorn. I stroke her head, but she doesn't rise to meet my touch. She's breathing so slowly now. I lean down and whisper, "I'm sorry, Carmen. I was so wrong. I didn't understand. I didn't mean to leave you." I'm crying now, hard, and I feel like I might never stop. "I need you, Carmen. Please don't die."

Carmen doesn't respond. Her beautiful horn is gone and here she lies dying, and I don't know how to do this. So I call upon whatever magic might be between us. I wrap my hands around my horn, with the blunt side down, and slowly, I raise it over my head.

I can feel Esmeralda's fierce eyes on me. The pulse from my forehead is now in my hands. I take one last look at Beaumont, who nods, urging me on. Then, with everything I have, I drive my horn down onto Carmen's head—into the space where her horn used to be.

And then I get the burst of light I was expecting before. It's blinding. It's intense. It blows me into oblivion.

Oblivion

Tall pines sway gently beneath the sky.

My forehead tingles.

"Jewel."

I open my eyes and look up to see Nicholas standing over me. "Are you okay?" he asks.

Propping up on my elbow, I look around hazily. I'm back at the boulder, and Mystic, Noah, and Ethan are nearby, struggling to their feet. They look as dazed and confused as I feel. The issue of *Highwaymen* that was in my backpack lies open beside me.

"Where is she?" I ask, craning my neck, searching for Carmen.

Nicholas looks around. "She's not here?"

I shake my head and look to Noah. "Do you see Carmen?"

"No," he says, coming toward me.

I sit up and glance down at myself. I'm a dirty-dog mess, and the rope is still tied around my waist.

Mystic approaches. "What was that?"

"What?" I ask.

"You didn't hear it? It was like the earth cracked open or something," Nicholas says.

"It blew us off our feet," says Mystic.

"I think it blew you back here," adds Nicholas.

"I didn't hear anything. I saw a light though. That was the last thing . . ."

Nicholas kneels down to my level and looks in my eyes. "What happened?"

How to explain? "Well, I got swallowed by some quicksand that spit me out at the bottom of Rock Canyon. And Esmeralda and Beaumont were there—"

"No way."

"They were," I say to Nicholas. "They're amazing."

"Then what?" Mystic asks.

"I gave Carmen my horn. Or really, I *put* it on her. Like . . ." I make the motion I made when I slammed my horn onto Carmen's forehead. "And everything went haywire. There was this blasting light, and it all disappeared. And then I was back." I look at my hands for the horn that is no longer there.

"How was she?" Noah asks.

"Bad. Really bad," I say, shaking my head, remembering the fear and distress in Carmen's eyes. "I don't even know if she knew I was there."

Noah pulls me up from the ground, but I'm wobbly on my feet. I was in Rock Canyon. I was with Carmen.

"So, what do we do now?" Ethan asks, like he really needs an answer. I look at my friends gathered around me and choose truth one more time. "I have no idea," I tell them.

The sound of the nearby stream fills the silence between us, but there's a new bond there, too. No one else would ever believe what just happened. We share this now. The five of us.

I grab my backpack from the boulder and feel a shock run through my veins when Mystic shouts, "It's almost twelve!"

"What?!" I say. How did all that time pass? What happened to the last hour?

"You've got the French competition!"

The French competition! After everything that just happened, how could I even think of—

"You have to do it," Mystic says.

But Mystic didn't see what I just saw. There's no way I

could do the French competition now. "I'll let Brooklyn," I say. "She can—"

"Jewels!" Mystic says sternly. "Monsieur Oliver didn't choose Brooklyn. He chose you!" She looks to the boys for support, then goes on. "People like us need to do stuff like this. If you don't do it, you're just saying that good things only happen to the Brooklyns and the Emmas of the world. Not to us."

They all stare at me, waiting for an answer.

"She'd want you to do it," Nicholas says.

"Yeah, she would," agrees Noah. "Carmen would want this."

Would she? I hope she would. But it's all coming too fast. I put my fingertips to my temples, trying to rub out the confusion inside. "The wrestling van leaves at noon. There's no time. We'll never make it."

"It's a well-known fact that it always takes less time going back," says Mystic.

"But can I *do* this?" I ask her. I'm so confused. I'm so sad. And I suddenly realize I'm exhausted, too.

Mystic grabs my arm, her eyes filled with purpose. "You can. Now come on."

Before I can say anything, Mystic takes off into the woods, and Ethan follows. I hesitate, looking at Nicholas.

"What are we waiting for?" he says, and runs after them.

Then Noah puts out his arm in an elaborate gesture and says, "Ladies first."

I want to laugh, he sounds so ridiculous. And I want to cry, too. But right now, there's nothing to do but run.

I take off, hearing Noah right behind me. Up ahead, I see Nicholas, then Ethan and Mystic. Noah and I hurry to catch up, and soon we're running single file along the narrow trail. Mystic leads the way, running faster than I've ever seen her go.

The sun blinks through the trees, making the woods appear dream-like. Nothing feels real to me. It wouldn't surprise me if we came upon Hansel and Gretel on the trail.

There's no time to process what just happened. With every step, I picture Carmen's face, her flailing head, her labored breath. Why didn't I figure it out earlier? I was caught up in stupid things and didn't put the pieces together in time. I will blame myself forever.

When we finally burst through the trees across from the apartments, we're all gasping for breath. Ethan's hands go to his knees, and Nicholas looks like he's about to pass out.

I could pass out, too, except Mom is standing at the top of our apartment stairs, staring at us. "Oh, man," I say, and everyone follows my gaze.

We hurry across the street, and Mom meets us in the parking lot, looking frantic.

"Where have you been?" she demands, looking me up and down. "And what happened to you?"

"It's a long story, Mrs. Conrad," Nicholas says, but that's all he says, because her eyes might as well be daggers.

"You're late for the competition! Mr. Oliver called like ten times. They had to leave without you!"

"Listen, Mom, I know you're not going to understand but something came up. A REALLY important something. It couldn't be avoided."

"More important than the French competition?" she says, staring at me in disbelief.

"More important," Mystic says, and the boys all nod in agreement.

Mom shakes her head. I know I've disappointed her. But there was nothing else I could do.

"Get in the car," Mom suddenly snaps. "We'll catch them."

I look down at my dirty clothes. "But I'm a mess!"

"I've got your clothes in the backseat," she says, glancing at her watch. "It's over an hour away. I don't know how we'll do it. But we'll try."

My eyes find Nicholas and Mystic. "Go!" they say at the same time.

"I'll call my dad!" Nicholas shouts. "We'll be right behind you."

I jump in the passenger seat with my backpack, and Mom guns it out of our parking lot like she's a race-car driver. Behind I see my friends cheering me on. Pumping their fists and everything.

I turn back around and try to breathe. Ready or not, I'm going to the French competition.

La Fille Licorne

I've never experienced Mom driving so fast before. As a rule, she's a law-abiding citizen, always under the speed limit. But today, I'm scared to death we're going to get pulled over.

While she speeds down the highway, I crawl into the backseat and peel off my earth-caked clothes, ducking down so passing cars can't see me.

"There's a hairbrush with the clothes in the plastic bag. And your essay cards," Mom says while I'm wiping my face with the clean inside of my dirty shirt. I grab the bag and pull out my green sweater and black jeans, pretty much what I wanted to wear. Even when she's mad at me, she's a mom first. I slip on the sweater and then have to contort myself to get the jeans on in the small backseat area.

After I brush my hair, I lean back and close my eyes. Images of the day flit across the screen of my mind. I can't believe it started with seeing Emma this morning—that feels like a lifetime ago. Then going to Nicholas's, trekking through the woods, and Carmen. I picture her lying at the bottom of Rock Canyon, her horn gone, her magic gone, and my heart aches. Why didn't it work? I truly believed it would. And the fact that it didn't makes me feel completely undone.

I stay in the backseat while Mom acts like my manic chauffeur in front. When we finally get off the expressway, she has me call out directions from her phone, and even in a seat belt, I have to hold on at every turn.

But she does it. In less than an hour after leaving our apartment, we pull in under the Alliance Scolaire Americaine banner at the entrance of the French high school where the competition is taking place.

The parking lot is already full, so Mom stops and looks back at me. "Go! I'll find a space."

But I freeze. I suddenly feel completely unprepared. I look out the window at the tower of stairs that leads up to the building. It's lined with sculptures—actual sculptures. It looks like a faraway place from my collage.

"What's wrong?" Mom asks.

"I don't know if I can do it."

Mom reaches back and grabs my hand. Her eyes lock onto mine. "Jewel, honey, of course you can do it."

"But what if I can't?" What's happening to me? I feel so scared. Any confidence I've ever had is draining out of me.

"Listen. When I was your age, I was really good at something, too. I was better than almost anyone. I just was," Mom says, a fire in her eyes. "That's how you are with your French. I don't know where you got it from or how you do it, but you're exceptional, baby. You are the best at this. I believe in my heart that you can do it."

Wow. It's a real Mom of the Year moment. I stare into her eyes, full of determination for me. "Now believe in yourself and get out of this car."

"Okay, okay," I say, and grab my backpack and essay cards. "Mom—thank you."

"Go, Jewel!" Mom says, and there's so much love in her eyes.

I get out of the car and look up at those stairs. There must be two hundred of them. At the top, the front of the building is lined with columns. I've never seen a school like this before—even on TV.

A boy and his dad rush past, breaking the spell, and I sprint up the stairs after them.

When I reach the top, I'm totally out of breath. The dad holds the main door open for me, though, and we all walk inside.

The entrance alone is like two stories tall. All around are fancy display cases filled with trophies and awards. And there's a massive fountain. No kidding. With actual running water.

"Jewel!"

I see Monsieur Oliver and Brooklyn coming my way. "You made it," he says.

"I'm sorry I'm late."

"I'm just glad you're here," he says, his smile as warm as ever. Monsieur Oliver has a natural way of diffusing stress, which is a good thing because my heart rate must be in the 300s about now.

"Me too," Brooklyn says. "I was scared I was going to have to take your place."

Yeah, right. I bet she couldn't wait to take my place.

"Let's get you signed in," Monsieur Oliver says, bringing me back to reality. He leads us through some tall double doors, and wow!

This is no gym-turned-auditorium like at our school. This is a theater, with permanent seats, chandeliers hanging from the ceiling, and a real stage. More than half of the seats are already filled with spectators waiting for the competition to begin.

"You're going to be up there," Monsieur Oliver says, pointing to the stage. My eyes must be popping out because he adds, "It's all right. We've got seats saved near the front. We'll all be rooting for you. You can look right down and see us."

Some other teacher-like person approaches speaking French to Monsieur Oliver, and they embrace like long-lost friends.

"He knows everybody here," Brooklyn says, pulling me by the arm. "Come on, I'll take you."

Brooklyn leads me down the aisle and out a side door, leaving Monsieur Oliver behind. As I follow her along a deserted hallway, I wonder, *Why am I doing this?* She's probably going to lock me in a closet somewhere, and I'll be trapped in the dark while she tells Monsieur Oliver how I got cold feet and wanted her to go on in my place. Then she'll read her essay perfectly, win the whole thing, and ascend to the state finals. While I'm still locked in a janitor's closet.

My mind is racing when she stops in front of a door and says, "Everybody's in here getting ready," and all I can think is *closet.*

But when a boy cuts between us and opens the door, which turns out to indeed be a room filled with kids, I chill the heck out and go to follow him.

"Wait," Brooklyn says from behind me, moving to the side of the door. "Can I talk to you a sec?" Here it comes.

"What's up?" I ask, feeling suspicious.

Her eyes drop to the floor. "I just wanted you to know," she says, then looks back up at me, "that what Emma did last night was not cool. I didn't say anything, and I know how that looked. I just didn't know what to do. I kind of froze. But you need to know I'm not okay with it." She pauses. "I'm sorry. I really hope you'll forgive me. And Mystic, too. I don't think she's a thief. Or weird."

"I appreciate that, but I think Mystic's the one who deserves an apology."

"She'll get one. On Monday. I promise."

As I look into her eyes, it's hard to stay mad, because I believe her. In fact, I understand her. Because if I'm honest, the same exact thing happened to me. But what I did was worse. The person I didn't stick up for was *my friend*.

"I don't know if you knew, but we moved here right before sixth grade. I didn't know anyone, and Emma was really nice to me," Brooklyn says. "But she's not nice to everyone, and I'm really not okay with that anymore."

She looks at me for a long beat, and I say, "You're right. I've been dumb about her, too. We were friends for a long time, and I guess I didn't want to see certain things."

"Me neither. I'm glad we talked. This feels better." She smiles. "You ready?"

I shake my head. "No!"

"Yes, you are. You've got this in the bag."

Now I smile. Weirdly, talking with Brooklyn like this has calmed me down. I wasn't wrong to think she is actually nice. In fact, we're a lot alike.

Brooklyn opens the door, and we walk into a room filled with a whole lot of French fries just like us, and Brooklyn shows me where to sign in. The teacher in charge calls for our attention. "It's time for all visitors to head to the theater. The competition is about to start."

Brooklyn gives me a thumbs-up and leaves me with all these other kids practicing their essays. I open my backpack and pull out the big cards that my essay is written on, and for a few minutes, I do the same. I can barely concentrate, but I mouth my words one last time, wishing I felt more confident about what I've written.

It gets so serious when we line up and walk solemnly down the hall. When we stop outside a door in another hallway, I ask the kid in front of me, "What's going on? I think I was late for instructions."

"That door leads to the stage. One by one, we go in and read our essay."

"We don't get to hear anybody else's?"

"Nope." I must look scared, because he says, "Don't worry. It's not so bad."

But I am worried. I look down the hall, past the line, searching for Carmen. Because that's what I always do when I feel alone: I look for my unicorn.

This morning is still catching up with me. I don't know why Carmen didn't come back. I was so sure she would. And what about my horn? It's all too much to think about, so I try to tamp it down. Just for the next hour. Then I can go back to figuring it out.

But the thought of never seeing her again presses hard against my chest. How am I supposed to do this without her? How am I supposed to do anything without her?

After what feels like seconds or years, it's the boy in front of me's turn. I keep reminding myself that Carmen would want me to do this.

Then a teacher opens the stage door and waves me in. As I step through, I see Monsieur Oliver waiting for me.

"Bonne chance, ma fille licorne." He puts his hand on my shoulder. "You can do it. I've always known you could do this."

On the stage, a man is talking to the audience in French, saying my school and age. Then he announces my name.

Monsieur Oliver gestures for me to move onto the stage, and he whispers, "You got this, Jewel."

Holding my essay cards between my fingers, I step out on the wooden stage to the microphone and place my cards on the lectern in front of me.

The auditorium is filled with hundreds of people staring at me. There's a loud whistle and I see Nicholas, his dad, Mystic, Noah, and Ethan waving from several rows back. It takes a moment to spot Mom—and Grandma! Nicholas must have brought her!—sitting with Brooklyn and some kids from French class near the front. It's all so random and intense, I feel like I might burst out in nervous laughter.

"*Bonjour,* Jewel Conrad," a voice booms from another microphone at the table below. The judges' table. There are five of them in all, and the woman at the center is the one who spoke. She's gotta be actually French or the actual Greta Garbo—by far the most elegant person I have ever seen in real life. She wears wine-red lipstick and her silver hair is pulled back in a tight twist. Her demeanor is serious but her eyes are kind.

"*Commencez, s'il vous plaît,*" she says to me.

I clear my throat and look down at my essay cards. This is the new essay, the one I revised with Monsieur Oliver and Brooklyn, about what it's like to be a girl without a horn anymore.

Slowly and in French, I start reading it to the audience, but it's hard to keep my place on the cards and look out at the audience at the same time, like we practiced.

"I used to have a horn on my head," I say. "Some people called it a unicorn horn. Some people called me the unicorn girl. It was hard when that was all they'd see. So when I had the chance to get my horn removed, I was happy, and relieved, and ready. And it worked. I was normal. My life was finally better. It made me . . ."

I break off, staring at the next word on the card. And I can't say it. Because now I know that taking my horn off did not make me "whole." The girl who journeyed to Rock Canyon and couldn't save her unicorn isn't whole. Now I think that maybe, when I took off my horn, I took away a piece of me.

I glance to the side of the stage, where Monsieur Oliver is nodding at me, encouragingly.

Then I see my mom in the audience, fists together, willing me forward—worried, but silently believing in me.

Come on, Jewel—say something!

It's not that I'm nervous now. It's just that what I'm saying isn't true. I wanted my horn off so badly that I never gave myself credit for who I was with it. My horn is gone and I am no different. Life is not better. In fact, since this morning, it's exponentially worse.

"Mademoiselle," the elegant judge says, staring up at me.

"Oui," I say softly.

"Voulez-vous continuer?"

I look down at my essay cards, but I can't read what I wrote. I might be breaking the rules and blowing my chances, but I put my essay aside. It's time to make it real.

I have to do this in French, so I take a second, get on my French brain, and speak into the microphone. "Actually, I don't know if it was a good idea to have my horn taken off. In fact, today, I think it was a mistake." My French stumbles, but I carry on. "I thought my horn was the problem. But it was me. I couldn't accept myself as I was. So I blamed somebody else. I blamed Carmen."

As I mention her name, Nicholas and Mystic and Noah perk up in their seats.

I clear my throat and survey the crowd, which is now looking uncomfortable. *Come on, Jewel. Think in French. You can do this.* Taking a breath, I lean into the microphone, trying to find my voice. "The first essay I wrote for this competition was about how terrible it was to have a horn. I hated my life. I thought I wanted different friends. And I blamed my unicorn."

The judges look confused, because unicorns aren't real, right? Good. Maybe at least I can knock them off their rockers a little.

"If I could do it again, I would have written this essay differently," I say. "Because as it turns out, maybe my horn wasn't so bad. Maybe I couldn't see how magical it was."

My mind goes blank as I search for the next words, and I look at my mom. *What else can I say?* This is supposed to be an essay, and I'm so short on material. I'm supposed to talk about something that's important to me.

Something that's important to me. As those words seep in, my whole body exhales. Because it's easy to talk about that.

"Carmen was my unicorn," I say, feeling a melancholy smile spread across my face. "For my whole life, she took care of me. Which made me the luckiest girl in the world."

I look out at the audience. As I tell them about my guardian unicorn, my voice rises and the words flow more easily. I recount the story of how Carmen took me to the boulder when I was six. I tell them how she loved to prank my best friend who didn't know she was there, and I throw a grin at Nicholas. I tell them about what happened with Noah and how badly I treated Carmen afterward and how very sorry I am now.

And I tell them how I would do anything to see her again.

"I don't know why my unicorn came to me, but she did," I say, emotion seizing my throat. "To protect me, to calm me, to make me laugh, but mostly to love me. Because with or without my horn," I say, taking in the faces before me,

"I am the unicorn girl—*la fille licorne*—and I want her to know I'm proud of that now."

That's it. That's what I needed to say. As I finish, the pulse in my head returns. Everyone is staring at me in a very strange way.

Clapping starts at the side of the stage and I know it's Monsieur Oliver. He always claps for me. But then it catches like the wind, and the whole auditorium erupts in applause.

I seek out Mom and Grandma, clapping furiously, along with Brooklyn and my other classmates. Farther back, Mystic, Nicholas, Noah, Ethan, and even Nicholas's dad are on their feet, whooping and cheering for me.

I feel a jolt in my forehead that anchors me to the spot, and I can't move. It's a throbbing like I've never felt before. Reaching up, I rub the spot with my fingers, trying to ease the pain. And that's when I feel it. Right in the middle of my forehead. A tiny, pointy knot.

Suddenly, the doors at the back of the theater burst open and a blazing light shines through. Not real light. But the otherworldly kind.

And Carmen steps through that light.

My face crumbles, tears welling in my eyes. Her horn is back. She is back.

As she whinnies loudly, my eyes find Noah, who is gazing at her, too. When he turns to me, his face is red and splotchy. It's all the confirmation I need.

I look back at my unicorn, and that feeling of home ripples through me.

"Carmen," I whisper—and just start bawling.

Six Months Later

The lights are warmer than I expected.

I'm sitting in a yellow chair facing three cameras and several light stands. A woman with clear green eyes sits across from me in another chair. Her name is Joy. She smiles at me, and says, "Let's begin."

We're in our school library, and she's interviewing me about what I've been through. When you win the state finals for the best French essay . . . *in the whole state* . . . people want to talk to you.

Especially when you do it with a horn on your head.

Yep, my horn is back. Technically, I guess it's a new horn, but whatever it is, it's there.

For the state finals, I had to piece together my impromptu essay from the regional contest. Luckily, there was video. It was so crazy—people thought my essay was some kind of abstract expressionist piece. The elegant judge proclaimed it *"Brillante!"* Can you imagine? I had to change some things for the state competition because by that time, my horn had almost grown completely back. But I did it. I stood in front of hundreds of people, horn and all, and it was amazing.

After what happened, lots of reporters called. It took time to convince my mom, but she finally agreed to this interview. It wasn't just about the money, it was about how I would be treated and how my story would be told. My mom insisted the money (from this, and the Alliance scholarship) go to a college fund for me. Plus, she opened a special savings account for us to add to every month for a trip to go see the Eiffel Tower together one day.

I look at her now, beyond the lights, standing next to Grandma, and Nicholas, Mystic, Ethan, Noah . . .

And Carmen.

Joy's first question is one I get asked a lot these days. "What's it like to have your horn back?"

"It's okay," I tell her. "I mean it was interesting to be normal for a while, but I'm not sure I could ever really be that."

"Interesting?" she asks.

"Normal is weird," I say, smiling. I'm wearing the hornlet with the dangling Eiffel Tower that Mystic made for me.

"I hear you had to miss school for a while when the horn grew back. How was that?"

"Pretty horrible. It really hurt. My friends—my best friends," I say, glancing at Nicholas and Mystic, "and my mom and grandma saw me through it, though. I'm lucky to have them."

But they weren't the only ones.

While my horn grew back, Carmen was with me the whole time. She helped me get well enough to make the state finals. She even stood on the stage with me while I read my essay.

I look past Joy to Carmen, who's standing next to Nicholas in all her glory.

"Are you going to try to have it removed again?" Joy asks.

"Nope." I don't even pause before answering. Mom offered to let me try again. She even talked to Dr. Stein about it. But I knew it wasn't right. "This is how I'm supposed to be," I say, and smile. "I know that now."

After the interview, I walk with my friends for ice cream at Cones on the Square. Ethan and Mystic are holding hands, something I'm still getting used to. Noah walks with

Carmen because that's what they do now. And I'm behind, with Nicholas.

He loves that my horn's back. Big surprise. After everything, I just hoped things would go back to the way they were with us, but things are actually better. Because now, we both like my horn.

Nicholas and Mystic are even cool that I hang out with Brooklyn sometimes. Mostly we practice French, but it turns out the popular girl and I have more in common than that—like, neither of us is friends with Emma anymore. And with Monsieur Oliver's help, we started an actual French club. Meetings are every Tuesday afternoon, and even Mystic comes.

As we stroll down the sidewalk, Nicholas says, "She's right in front of me, isn't she?" Meaning Carmen.

"Yep," I tell him.

"Can we just have an accident already?"

"For the thousandth time, I'm not going to gore you with my horn."

"Please!" he grin-begs and I play-push him off the sidewalk.

Nicholas may not have a horn, but he's different, too. I understand that now. You don't have to have a horn to feel different. Different starts on the inside, and on first glance, it might not be seen by anyone else.

Carmen whinnies and glances back at me. We do a lot of that since she's been home. Looking at each other. We don't let the other out of our sight for long. I may never know how we're connected, but we are. Maybe she turned me into a unicorn on some long-ago magical night, or maybe I was just made this way and she came to protect me as my unicorn guardian. Either way, we are connected by more than our horns, and I will never abandon her again.

We are connected by *Highwaymen*, too. I still don't know how Carmen ended up in Hot Springs, but I haven't had a single vision since she came back. Nicholas and I are still planning our road trip to find the portals that we've marked on his map. Now it feels more important than ever. Maybe we'll find more magical creatures like Carmen out there. And with Carmen by our side, maybe they'll want to find us, too.

What I do know is this: On some mystical plane, Esmeralda and Beaumont are real, Esmeralda is the most kick-butt person I'll ever meet, and there really is such a place as Truth or Consequences.

When we reach the pedestrian crosswalk and wait for the cars to stop, a little girl holding her mother's hand appears beside me. When she looks up and sees my horn, her eyes go wide, and she buzzes with excitement.

"Are you a unicorn?" she asks in her best fairy-princess voice.

I smile at her. I never used to know how to answer this question. But now I do.

"Yes," I tell her. "That's exactly what I am."

Acknowledgments

Without these three people, I don't know if you would be holding this book in your hands:

Jen Brehl, my friend, who picked me up when I was truly down and set me on my path again.

Kate McKean, my agent, who believed in Jewel and said yes at exactly the right time.

Taylor Norman, my editor, who loves unicorns, loves Jewel, and helped me make this book what I always wanted it to be.

Thanks to you beautiful, smart, amazing women, this book is finally here. And I am forever grateful.

And my heartfelt thanks to the team at Chronicle: Mariam Quraishi, designer. Claire Fletcher, managing editor. Debra DeFord-Minerva, copy editor. Marie Oishi, proofreader. Kevin Armstrong, production manager. And the marketing team: Andie Krawczyk, Mary Duke, Eva Zimmerman, Kaitlyn Spotts, Samantha Chambers, and Carrie Gao. Thank you for bringing my book to life in such a beautiful way.

To the late Guy Oliver, my French professor, who made me love the language, just like Jewel.

To all my kid-lit buddies, especially the gang at the Monday Morning Write-in, and the Los Feliz Book Group for all the laughs, encouragement, and support. Special thanks to Ann Whitford Paul, Cynthia Surrisi, and Sandy Schuckett for their wisdom and generosity along the way.

To my Kids Need Mentors collaborator, Alison Snow, fifth grade teacher at Creek View Elementary. I shared Jewel with your kids first, and I am so grateful for their (and your) enthusiastic response.

To Jewel's first adult readers, who helped me believe in her even harder: Kate McLaughlin, Lori Bertazzon, Jill Diamond, and my mom. I'm so grateful to you for being there through the process of this book.

To Dahlonega, Georgia: I don't say that Jewel's town is Dahlonega, but it is. I've chosen bits and pieces of my experience there through the decades and squashed it all together to make Jewel's town. Even though I don't live there anymore, it's my hometown, too, and I love it.

To my friends and family, for . . . you know . . . everything. You know who you are and I love you. To my parents, Guy and Anita Middleton, I'm forever grateful for your everlasting love and support.

And to the guy who reads everything first, Pete, to whom this book is dedicated. Thanks, moonpal.